W0238528

Torquere Press Novels

911 by Chris Owen • Amnesia by Sean Michael
An Agreement Among Gentlemen by Chris Owen
Bad Case of Loving You by Laney Cairo
Between Friends by Sean Michael
Bus Stories and Other Tales by Sean Michael
Bareback by Chris Owen • The Broken Road by Sean Michael
Caged by Sean Michael • The Call edited by Rob Knight
Catching a Second Wind by Sean Michael
Cowboy Up edited by Rob Knight
Deviations: Discipline by Chris Owen and Jodi Payne
Deviations: Domination by Chris Owen and Jodi Payne
Deviations: Submission by Chris Owen and Jodi Payne
Don't Ask, Don't Tell by Sean Michael • Faire Grounds by Willa Okati
Fireline by Tory Temple • Galleons & Gangplanks, editor Rob Knight
His Beautiful Samurai by Sedonia Guillone
Historical Obsessions by Julia Talbot • Hyacinth Club by BA Tortuga
In Bear Country by Kiernan Kelly
Jumping Into Things and Landing On Both Feet by Julia Talbot
Latigo by BA Tortuga • Living in Fast Forward by BA Tortuga
Locked and Loaded edited by SA Clements
Long Black Cadillac by BA Tortuga
The Long Road Home by BA Tortuga
Manners and Means by Julia Talbot • Music and Metal by Mike Shade
The Name of the Game by Willa Okati
Natural Disaster by Chris Owen
Need by Sean Michael • Off World 1 & 2 by Stephanie Vaughan
On Fire I & II by Drew Zachary • Old Town New by BA Tortuga
Out of the Closet by Sean Michael • Perfect by Julia Talbot
Perfect Ten: A Going for the Gold Novel by Sean Michael
Personal Best I: A Going for the Gold Novel by Sean Michael
Personal Best II: A Going for the Gold Novel by Sean Michael
Personal Leave by Sean Michael • A Private Hunger by Sean Michael
PsyCop: Partners by Jordon Castillo Price
Racing the Moon by BA Tortuga • Rain and Whiskey by BA Tortuga
Redemption's Ride by BA Tortuga
Riding Heartbreak Road by Kiernan Kelly
Secrets, Skin and Leather by Sean Michael
Shifting, Volumes I-III, edited by Rob Knight
Soul Mates: Bound by Blood by Jourdan Lane
Soul Mates: Deception and Soul Mates: Sacrifice by Jourdan Lane
Steam and Sunshine by BA Tortuga
Stress Relief by BA Tortuga • Taking a Leap by Julia Talbot
Tempering by Sean Michael • Three Day Passes by Sean Michael
Timeless Hunger by BA Tortuga
Tomb of the God King by Julia Talbot
Torqued Tales edited by SA Clements
Touching Evil by Rob Knight • Tripwire by Sean Michael
Tropical Depression by BA Tortuga
Under This Cowboy's Hat edited by Rob Knight
Where Flows the Water and Windbrothers by Sean Michael

This is a work of fiction. Names, characters, places, and incidents either are the product of the author's imagination or are used fictitiously. Any resemblance to actual events, locales, organizations, or persons, living or dead, is entirely coincidental and beyond the intent of either the author or the publisher.

Off World 2: Sanctuary
TOP SHELF
An imprint of Torquere Press Publishers
PO Box 2545
Round Rock, TX 78680

Cover illustration by James McPartlin
Published with permission
ISBN: 1-934166-115-0, 978-1-934166-115-X
www.torquerepress.com

First Torquere Press Printing: August 2007
Printed in the USA

Off World 2: Sanctuary

Stephanie Vaughan

Torquere Press Inc.
romance for the rest of us
www.torquerepress.com

Dedication: For Rufus -- the inspiration for Alex. And for Don -- the inspiration for all the rest. My love and admiration, always.--SV

Chapter 1

D'abu lifted his gaze over the rim of his mug to the man writhing onstage, another man's clenched fist inserted wrist-deep in his ass, and stifled a yawn.

It was latex night at *Durty Nelly's*, so everyone performing in any of the club's various rooms was dressed accordingly. Some costumes were flesh-toned and so paper-thin the performers appeared nude. Almost. Others were thicker, colored in shades improbably and eye-catchingly bright.

"Hey, baby. Buy a boy a drink?"

Ignoring the rush of heat in his groin, D'abu turned toward the voice behind the bar. "Alex." They both knew the drill. Nothing changed but the date on the calendar and the theme of the night's shows. "Go hustle the tourists and leave the working stiffs alone, would you? And while you're at it, tell your boss he needs to freshen up the act. That's the third fisting I've seen this week."

The bartender tossed him a cheeky grin, unaffected by his brusque tone of voice. "Not everyone's the connoisseur you are, Sandy. The tourists like it just fine."

Alex gazed pointedly around the room at the rapt faces of the crowd, to a man their gazes riveted on the latex-clad figures on the stage, before throwing a wink and a smile in D'abu's direction and moving off down the bar. Letting his own gaze dip briefly to the perfect view of a very fine backside, D'abu turned back to his mug and drained it.

He scrubbed one hand over his face and sighed. Alex was right. The tourists did like the show just fine. Just like Sandy had… the first eighty or so times he'd seen it. In his marine days, back on Earth -- half a lifetime ago it seemed now -- he'd had fantasies. Exotic, erotic fantasies, or so he'd thought.

As things turned out, though, his kinkiest, most forbidden fantasy would be lucky to make it as the evening's first warm-up act at *Durty Nelly's*.

D'abu tried his best to focus on the goings-on onstage and block out the picture in his mind's eye. But, as he was finding with increasing frequency, his body overruled his head. Rolling his head, as though to ease a stiff neck, Sandy let his gaze slide sideways and pick up the tall, slim figure behind the bar.

Like every other night, Alex was dressed entirely in black. Where the other bartenders and entertainment attendants dressed provocatively, some wearing so little that two handkerchiefs could have served as cover-ups, Alex was clothed from neck to foot. High-necked shirts with long, billowing sleeves covered his upper body, while loose pants that reached the floor bunched up around nondescript shoes and hid his long, elegant legs.

Nothing could disguise the grace of that walk, though; loose-limbed and fluid, like a dancer.

While D'abu gave cursory attention to the

action onstage -- fisting man having climaxed and now being lowered, chaise and all, through the floor as stage hands began moving in a new set of props -- the bulk of his mental energy was focused on appearing not to watch the goings-on behind the bar.

As D'abu not-watched, Alex leaned an elbow on the bar to talk to a customer, his cute little ass sticking out and causing problems for the other servers. Flirting and laughing non-stop, Alex worked the mark. Right on cue, never even realizing he was being worked, the customer ordered another Bomb Pop -- the glowing blue drink that would have kept *Nelly's* in business even without the sector's hottest sex shows.

Card swiped.

Five credits for the house.

Alex smiled and, ever so reluctantly, moved on.

As the night wore on, D'abu found his concentration wandering. A man couldn't watch the same ten or twelve acts over and over without becoming at least a little bit jaded. After all, there were only so many orifices on the human body and no matter how creative the players might be, after a while it all started to look the same. Props and costumes could only carry things so far and, eventually, it was pretty much assured that Man A was going to insert Part B into either Orifice C or D.

Abandoning his empty mug along with his coveted seat at the bar, D'abu worked his way toward the door and out into the lobby. Alex was too busy earning a living to notice if he left and he might as well see if any of the other rooms had anything more interesting going. What the hell.

He hadn't so much as poked his nose into any of the het shows in so long D'abu wasn't sure if he even remembered how the other half did it. So he wandered in and found an empty table toward the back.

Like most of *Nelly's*, the Bird Cage room was done in the style of a pre-Republic Old West saloon. The ownership didn't try to carry the theme as far as subjecting the clientele to outdoor plumbing or gaslight, but the floors had been manufactured to look like unfinished real wood and the general staff wore someone's cheesy take on saloon gear.

"Hi, honey. What can I get for you?"

Sandy looked up at the pretty, blonde waitress with curves to spare holding an electronic notepad and gazing down at him expectantly. High cheekbones, a fantastic head of almost white-gold hair that reached half-way down her back, and legs that stretched from here to the next sector would have made her memorable even without the skimpy costume and pneumatic breasts. She gave him a big smile and tilted her head a bit as she pretended to check him out.

Smiling back, D'abu glanced at the waitress' nametag and forced himself to take a slow visual inventory.

"Hi, Reesa. How about an Adrastean ale -- tap, not container -- please?"

"You bet. I'll be right back with that." Winking discreetly, Reesa turned on her heel, the practiced move flipping up the back of her short skirt and giving D'abu a great shot of bare butt cheeks neatly bisected by her T-strap underwear.

He did a quick dick-check, but it was just a

formality. No interest -- as usual. At least, lately. Folding his arms, D'abu leaned back in his chair and tried to pick up on the action on stage.

In keeping with the latex theme, the stage was decorated to look like… what? An old fashioned parlor, he supposed. D'abu thought the stuffed moose head on the wall was a bit much, but maybe he'd been away from home too long.

Nah.

Nelly's staff did their research and if they had a moose head on the wall, there had to be a good reason for it. The guy in the chair being serviced by the latex maid looked more Sherlock Holmes than Wild West gentleman to D'abu's eye, but maybe it was just him.

A second maid, a latex hood covering her face in addition to the same type of short, tight dress worn by the other maid, was bent over the man in the recliner and alternately forced a more than ample breast into his mouth before using both to block the man's breathing so long D'abu started to squirm.

Smothering? Old West latex, for that matter.

Whatever.

Shuddering, D'abu looked around for his drink. Ah, there was the waitress, threading her way toward his table.

A noisy gasp of indrawn breath pulled D'abu's attention back to the stage, but the man in the chair had barely drawn a full breath into his starved lungs when the maid holding his head yanked him back and down, into her monstrous cleavage.

"Here you go. Did you want to pay now or are you running a tab?" Traumatized, D'abu looked away from the stage and into Reesa's smiling face.

Absurdly grateful for the interruption, D'abu realized his relieved smile was being misinterpreted when the pretty blonde rested her elbows on the table and gave him a perfect view of her own bountiful breasts. "Or would you like me to come back later?"

"No! Thanks. I'm good. I mean-- Here." In a hurry to leave, D'abu shoved his currency card at her so hard he nearly bounced her off the table and onto her ass.

Grabbing the edge of the table for support, the poor girl picked herself up and regrouped as she swiped D'abu's card. He tried to tell himself that she was a professional and probably had a non-stop parade of horny men and women doing and saying God-only-knew-what to her all night long. He couldn't be anything special in her cavalcade of strange. Mustering a smile despite his boorish behavior, Reesa even managed one last lingering glance. "Call me if you change your mind. Okay?"

Another protracted gasp from the stage had D'abu up and moving. "Sure thing. Thanks, Reesa." D'abu tipped his ale in the pretty waitress' direction and fled. He couldn't get out of there fast enough. Seriously? Was that what boys and girls did together nowadays?

It wasn't as though he'd been sheltered. D'abu and the rest of his unit had served all over the northern continent. He'd been sexually active since he was fourteen. But a night at *Nelly's* was like living in dog years; worth a decade lived anywhere else.

Fleeing back to the safety of the Men Only room, a lifetime of habit had him surveying the room in a glance. He took in the four men on stage.

Ah, *Nelly's* clientele did love their double-penetration and it looked like cute little Justin was the happy recipient tonight.

Breathing easier already, D'abu finished up the visual sweep of the room, instinctively searching for Alex, finally catching sight of him behind the bar. It took D'abu a second to figure out why his gut was suddenly clenching tighter than a frog's sphincter, but it didn't take him long to put the clues together.

Alex's arms crossed protectively over his chest.

That was Joe Sotheran, part-owner of *Nelly's*, talking to Alex with his arm braced against the wall as he talked. Not exactly boxing Alex in -- just almost.

Both men had their eyes focused across the room at the tall, good-looking blond man leaning casually against a pillar. It was the smile on the stranger's face that had D'abu making a beeline for where Alex and his employer stood talking. It was the smile of a man who'd just found what he was looking for and had come a long way for the pleasure.

That and the blank, emotionless look in Alex's eyes as he stared back.

***

Oh, no.

No, no, no. Hell, no.

His boss' slightly nasal drone faded into the background as Alex's vision narrowed and he looked into the bluest pair of eyes he'd thought he'd never see again.

Prayed devoutly.

Hoped like hell he wouldn't.

Cried buckets over.

But the man was shoving away from the column and walking toward him, all rugged good looks and bad boy smirk. Alex had fallen for that wicked grin once upon a time, but never again, and just in time he found his voice.

"Nick. Long time, no fuck over."

"Aw, c'mon Alex." Silky blond hair falling boyishly over one eye, Nick Andrade's smile only broadened. "You're not still mad, are you?"

His boss was the last person Alex wanted witnessing this particular conversation, but there was no help for it now. Without taking his gaze from Nick, Alex could still sense Joe Sotheran settling in beside him and he knew better than to be even remotely fooled by the politely dispassionate stance.

"Mad? No, I'm not mad. Honestly, I barely remember it. But then again, that could just be from all the drugs they gave me."

The bastard had the nerve to wince and even look a little pained. "Oh, ouch. Would you believe me if I said I was sorry? I am. I swear I didn't know—"

A snort of disbelief erupted and Alex wouldn't have stopped it if he could. "Please. You saved yourself. That's all that mattered. So what brings you to Doradus?"

"Business, actually." The grin was back and Nick's gaze slid sideways and came to rest on Joe Sotheran. "Joe, can I talk about it yet?"

The knotted ball of nerves in Alex's stomach grew when he turned his head and took in his boss' answering smile. "Sure. Why not? Alex is one of the family."

One of the family? Dear God. Had the Borgias begun adopting?

"I'm here to learn the business. I'm coming on as a partner and eventually I'll be opening up a second location. As soon as my new partner and I decide on the best spot." Nick stepped around the corner of the bar, drawing closer. "I didn't know you were here, Alex, I swear. But now that I do," Nick touched Alex's arm, "I think it's great. Maybe we can fix things. Redo what we messed up last time. Get to know each other again, like we never could have back on Earth"

We? Alex's mouth gaped. "We messed up?"

Uncharacteristically oblivious, Joe clapped a hand on Alex's shoulder. "Nothing would make me happier, Alex. You need to get out more. Maybe even think about performing again. All this self-isolation isn't good for you."

Alex couldn't breathe. He couldn't catch his breath and the walls were suddenly claustrophobically close. His boss' hand lay hot and clammy on Alex's shoulder and the smell of sweating bodies was overwhelming.

Alex stumbled. Hadn't realized he was moving. He must have backed away, instinctively shying backward.

"Alex." Ducking sideways, Alex cast a startled glance at someone behind him calling his name. It was only Sandy, thank God. "You okay, buddy?"

"Sandy."

Three pairs of eyes were staring at him. They must think he'd lost his mind. "Crazy tweaker. Fried his brain on Pink Diamond and grain alcohol."

Nick and Joe were openly watching him and Sandy now and Alex tried to see Sandy through their eyes: tall, broad, thick. His hair was shaved short, tribal tattoos running down the side of his face to his neck and disappearing beneath his brightly patterned shirt. No amount of clothing could disguise the layers of muscle that rippled easily under the smooth, coppery-brown skin, though. Intimidating as hell to most people, Alex had always thought Sandy was gorgeous. Too bad the feeling wasn't mutual.

His bosses didn't know that, though, did they? Aiming for a warm, familiar tone, Alex smiled. "Hi, baby. I'm almost done -- just wrapping up here." Turning away, Alex ducked under his boss' arm and headed for freedom. "Nick, great seeing you again. Joe, Teddy's closing tonight and I'm off now. So, I'll see you tomorrow?"

The key to a good bluff was a bold appearance and not giving the mark time to think -- or yourself, sometimes. Steeling his nerve, Alex took one of Sandy's big hands in both of his, leaned up and brushed a brief kiss over Sandy's beautiful mouth. "Thanks for waiting, baby. You ready?"

Meeting Sandy's startled gaze with his own, Alex shoved down the panic still beating at his insides and willed Sandy to read his thoughts. *Please, just go with it. Get us out of here. Please*?

Alex could tell the moment Sandy made up his mind. A quick glance over Alex's head to where Nick and Joe stood, then another down at Alex. "No problem, babe. I'm always ready for you." Sandy dropped a kiss of his own on Alex's cheek as he freed his hand to loop an arm around Alex's shoulder. "Let's get out of here."

Concentrating on weaving their way through the crowded room and leading Sandy out the back through the employees' entrance helped to keep Alex's mind off the muscular arm that lay across his shoulders. He knew that, if only for appearances' sake, he ought to have his own arm wrapped around Sandy's waist, maybe even tucked into a back pocket. It was all he could do, though, to keep putting one foot in front of the other and not rip his body away from Sandy's touch.

The awful sensation of being able to feel his own blood pressure building was still with him, but the sensation of being a hair's breadth from hyperventilating faded as they got further away from his boss and his ex-lover.

Sandy pushed open the back door and Alex stumbled across the threshold and out into the dank air of night on a hollowed-out asteroid with a dodgy artificial atmo' generator. The door slammed shut behind them and Alex stopped, hunched over, bracing his hands on his knees and gulping air as fast as his body could take it in. Flinching when Sandy touched his back, Alex recognized the touch for what it was only after he'd instinctively shied away.

"You okay?" The concern in Sandy's voice would have reassured any normal human being, Alex realized. But he wasn't normal. Not any more.

"Yeah. I'm good. Thanks." He obviously wasn't, but Alex knew Sandy was too polite to call him on it. Now that he was away from immediate danger, his hands had begun to shake and only the fact that he had his elbows locked and his arms braced kept his wobbly knees from completely giving way.

Sandy circled around in front and peered into his face. "Really? I don't want to burst your bubble, tough guy, but you don't look so hot."

Straightening, Alex looked up into Sandy's impassive face, wondering what it would take to throw the big man a jolt the size of the one Alex had just received. "Sorry. Doing the best I can under the circumstances."

"I know you are. What do you say we get serious about getting out of here?" Sandy extended his hand as he turned and Alex eyed it warily. When Alex didn't take the proffered help, Sandy stuffed his hands in his pockets and shrugged. "No skin off my nose. I just figured if you really want people to think I'm your boyfriend, a little acting might be in order."

Sandy was right, of course.

"You're right. Sandy… thanks. I, um… I appreciate your help." Alex forced his legs to take the few steps to draw even with Sandy and fall into step alongside him when Sandy headed away from *Nelly's* and toward the business district. Most of the businesses near *Nelly's* closed early so, except for the lights and low throb of music, the occasional burst of laughter or appreciative 'oh' that penetrated the manufactured walls of Doradus' premier night spot, the evening was as quiet as the small town outpost it really was.

"I know." Sandy kept walking, but he moved an elbow away from his body as he flashed Alex a look, inviting him to take hold.

Alex looked at it. Looked at Sandy. Measuring. Weighing.

When he'd been a little kid, spiders had been

the thing that always terrified him most. There was something creepy about them, in a sneaky sort of way. They could bite, obviously. But something about the silent way they approached in order to attack bothered Alex. And then there was the whole cocooning their prey thing. The thought still gave him a little shudder, even though spiders hadn't yet made it to Doradus' artificial environment.

Once upon a time, spiders were the scariest thing Alex could think of. Not any more, though. Not since he'd been unlucky enough to spend some time as a guest of the New Republican government, at its most exclusive pleasure resort.

Alex stuffed down his dread and placed a hand on Sandy's arm.

Chapter 2

One hand linked cautiously through his shouldn't have felt so damned good, and it sure as hell shouldn't be turning Sandy on. The sensation was unmistakable, though, and Alex's hand resting lightly on his forearm might just as well have been reaching for his dick. Time to think about something else.

"Aren't you going to ask me what that was all about back there?"

D'abu didn't have to turn his head to know that the studiedly casual tone of voice was the result of an effort that was anything but casual. He hadn't watched over Alex almost nightly for nearly three months without picking up a few clues. "Not unless you want me to." He took a chance and made an attempt at catching Alex's gaze. "Feel like talking about it?"

Alex allowed it, maintaining eye contact for several seconds before bringing his gaze back down to the patch of ground a meter in front of his feet. His tone, when he finally spoke, was diffident. "Not really."

Letting one foot fall in front of another, D'abu kept walking and let the silence spin out.

It was a nice night out.

Just like every other night on Doradus.

Dodgy C02 converters aside, the place ran pretty well and you could generally count on evenings inside the hollowed-out asteroid being pleasant and mild, if a bit muggy. Just like the days, only slightly less bright. The artificial lights that lit up the hours designated as daytime kept the grass, shrubs, and trees planted on every available inch of ground green year-round. Years, of course, were simulated, too.

"I didn't expect that. Running into… someone from home. I probably should have, though."

The hesitation in Alex's voice was so subtle, D'abu might have missed it if he hadn't been so attuned to listening to Alex. Sandy'd logged enough hours on a barstool within earshot of Alex as he worked to be a pretty good judge.

"Old friend?"

Alex let out a breath. D'abu had deliberately kept the pace leisurely, so that long exhalation probably had more to do with blowing off stress than exertion. "Sort of. A long time ago. Back… before."

Back. Before.

This was new territory for D'abu. Most of the background info he'd picked up on Alex had come from Sarhaan and Kai. The events surrounding their meeting and the short time they'd all been together back on Earth made up about ninety-percent of what he knew about Alex. Man didn't talk much about the past.

"Back at *Earthly Delights*?"

Alex shook his head and the streetlight overhead momentarily caught the sheen of dark hair cut fashionably short and choppy, until they passed beyond its light and Alex's face was in shadow again. "Earlier, even. When I was a kid."

"So, like, what? A couple, three years ago?"

"No. Longer than that."

His attempt at a joke had fallen flat, but that was nothing new. D'abu had no idea what to say to that, so, like usual, he said nothing. He rolled his neck a bit when the stiffness there broke through his consciousness -- so intent on listening for what Alex might say next he only noticed it now. "You don't know?"

Alex gave another shake of his head, this time with a shrug thrown in. "Not really. I think… God, it can't be… ten years? No. That would make me... Too old."

The little laugh Alex threw in at the end rang phony in D'abu's ears. "Yeah, positively ancient." Alex's mouth quirked as he met D'abu's gaze. He didn't hold it for long, though. It looked like he started to say something, thought better of it and kept walking. "I've got a question for you, Alex."

Even pressed together, those full lips gave D'abu ideas. More usually pulled into a straight line and paired with one raised eyebrow, Alex could convey skepticism dryer than the surface of Mars. Quirking from beneath eyes sparkling with mischief and humor, D'abu had seen them seduce members of both sexes. Full and soft as they were, D'abu wondered what they would look like slightly parted and panting with desire -- but that was one thing he'd never seen.

"Hmm?"

"Where are we going?"

Alex halted, drawing back his hand from where it had rested on D'abu's arm, gazing down at it as though it had done something that made it no longer trustworthy. After a few moments, Alex shrugged. "I don't know. I don't care. Anywhere -- just not back to *Nelly's*."

"Okay. Not a lot open this time of night." It was true. Even on an artificial environment created inside a hollowed-out asteroid, a simulation of a diurnal world was created whenever possible. Humans didn't do well when their bodies' natural rhythms weren't respected. "The Pike. Or my place. That's about it."

A vehement shake of the head answered D'abu's opening salvo.

"Not the Pike. Too noisy. Too many people." Looking suddenly exhausted, Alex's weary gaze rose to meet D'abu's. "Could we go to your place?" Before D'abu could even open his mouth, though, Alex began backing away from the suggestion. "No, forget it. You're probably not interested. I can go find something to do. You probably want to get some sleep. I'll go find an empty entertainment pod."

"Don't worry about me. I'm sleeping at the office while the rest of the crew is off on their run. There's an entire apartment overhead, so don't worry. There's plenty of room."

"I couldn't. But you can walk me down to The Pike."

Turning, Alex continued on in the direction they'd been heading. D'abu had no intention of letting Alex follow through on his idea of spending the night in a rent-by-the-hour cubicle jammed with every form of real and simulated entertainment yet invented. Nobody had to tell him how easy it was to lose yourself in that world and

D'abu wasn't about to let Alex get lost, so he caught up before Alex could go a half-dozen steps.

"Okay. Follow me -- I know a short cut."

Puzzled look and all, Alex followed. When D'abu's short cut took them two streets over and one section down to put them squarely in front of the little storefront that comprised the offices and system headquarters for VSS, Inc. -- his place -- Alex frowned.

"VSS, Inc. That's you? Sandy…"

"Yeah. *Vigilant* Security Services -- we're a creative bunch. And don't get your knickers in a twist. It's no big deal. You need a place to stay tonight; I could use the company. Where's the harm?" Swiping his card key, D'abu pushed the front door open. "Besides, it's not like you haven't been here before."

As though held down by magnetic locks, Alex's feet didn't move. "Actually, I haven't."

"Get outta town. Are you serious?"

Trying unsuccessfully to contain his curiosity, Alex was taking in everything that could be seen from the doorway. "No. No one ever—"

"Well, come on in, then. You crane your neck any harder you're going to do yourself a damage."

Alex, it seemed, couldn't defend against a two-fronted assault: his own curiosity and D'abu's efforts. "You're sure?"

"Quit wasting my time and get in here. Want something to drink?" As though luring a wild creature, D'abu turned his back and walked away. Instinct told him Alex couldn't handle much in the way of pressure, so he stood back and gave the man some room to breathe.

The door slid closed with a whoosh and the

situational awareness D'abu had honed during his years in the marines confirmed that Alex had trusted him enough to enter.

"So this is where you work."

Alex's normally slinky smooth gait had a hitch in it as he moved toward the bank of computers along one wall. A long-fingered hand touched briefly on one of the pair of costly machines; a major expense of the business' start-up, but vital. Their fledgling security and transportation business was utterly dependent on up-to-date intel from a variety of sources.

"No, that's where Cal works. He's the hack boy genius, I'm just the grease monkey. Only my baby's out of town right now."

"Your baby?"

"The *Vigilant*. They're off on a run right now."

"Right, right. I knew that." Alex sat down in what was normally Cal's chair. Cal was the newest member of their crew and -- not coincidentally -- the CO's lover.

D'abu rummaged through the cooler for drinks. "Ale, water and… eesh, *bái jiu*. That must be Xuwicha's. Sorry, not much to choose from. Alex?"

Up and prowling the room again, Alex looked up, distracted. "Huh?"

"Water or ale's about it. You thirsty?"

"Water'd be great. Thanks."

Alex reached and D'abu tried not very successfully to hand off the container without touching, even just that minor physical contact sending a jolt of electricity up his arm. Unperturbed, Alex took the water and twisted the cap loose. Taking a sip, a small trickle escaped down Alex's chin and he swiped at it with the fingers of one hand.

"I'm such a class act. You can take the boy out of the brothel, but…"

"You are. And I mean that compared to regular folk, too, not just me and my ex-mil grunt friends."

"Thanks." Looking embarrassed, Alex darted his gaze around the room, bouncing off the office equipment, over to the computers. From there it banked off the cooler and landed on the tacky orange couch where it lingered a brief moment before leaping like a scalded cat back up to meet D'abu's.

Oh, really?

Something told Sandy he wasn't alone in entertaining an illicit idea or two about the uses that particular piece of furniture could be put to. Stashing that thought for later consideration, D'abu moved away, hoisting himself up onto the open desk space between computers.

"So. You want a pretend boyfriend to keep this Nick guy off your back. Is that it?" Folding his arms across his chest and slumping comfortably against the bulkhead, D'abu narrowed his gaze. "Just how far are you prepared to go to make this little charade stick?"

***

"How far do I need to go?" A blatant stall tactic, it was the best Alex could manage under the circumstances. His brain was still fried from trying to deal with seeing Nick and what it had taken to get away.

God, but Sandy looked good. So big and solid.

Anyone whose back Sandy was watching could rest easy, that was a given. Sandy wouldn't mess up and he wouldn't quit. If he gave his word something would happen, it would. Failure was not an option.

"I guess that depends on how big a threat this guy is. What's he likely to do?"

Big arms bulged with muscles where Sandy sat with his arms folded across his chest, and what a chest. Broad and deep. A picture of him resting his head on that chest popped into Alex's head and a slow curl of pleasure grew in him. For a few seconds, calm reassurance and something else wove themselves around Alex's gut. Until another memory replaced it. This one of arms gripping him and holding him down as he struggled -- fought until he was exhausted. And then those arms held him as the others did whatever they wanted to him.

"I don't know. He's capable of doing a lot." Thinking back to when they came for him, some vicious quirk of memory had kept those feelings alive, like it was yesterday, and the memories of the fear and pain and humiliation were as fresh as ever. They'd taken him away and Alex had been lost -- vanished down a rabbit hole of his own government's making. Nothing would ever be the same again and he had Nick to thank for it all. "He's capable of anything."

Sandy looked back at Alex, his chest rising and falling as he drew slow, regular breaths and just watched. Watched and thought.

"We should work on our story, then." Sandy sat up straighter, tucking his hands beneath his massive thighs. "I'm your fella. And you're mine. How long have we been seeing each other?"

"Just like that? You're going to help me?"

"Sure. Why not? You're a friend of Sarhaan's and Kai's. You and I know each other a little. Why wouldn't I?"

"Why would you? What's in it for you?"

Sandy only cocked his head a bit. "Does something have to be in it for me?"

"Mmm, let's see… you're human, aren't you? Then, yeah, something has to be in it for you. Why else would you do it?"

"Can't I just want to help someone out? Maybe I don't like this Nick guy. Maybe I think you're an okay person and you don't deserve to have some jerk from your past come and disrupt your nice, quiet life. Maybe I don't like good-looking, arrogant assholes who think life owes them something because they hit the genetic lottery. Maybe I just want to help."

Alex stared at Sandy. "Do you expect me to blow you? Is that it? Because I don't do that any more. I don't know what you've heard, but—"

"Relax, would you? I don't need your pity fuck, or blowjob, or whatever. I'm just saying I'll be your pretend boyfriend if it'll help keep Nick off your back. Unless you were just playing with me back at *Nelly's*. And even that's okay. I understand. Just tell me what your game is."

So calm. So steady. Sandy just watched him from the seat between computers, posture relaxed, legs swinging a little. "Are you for real? People don't just help people for no good reason. What do you get out of it?"

"It's not that big a deal, okay? I'm not offering you a kidney. All I'm saying is that I'll hang around. Hell, I'm there most nights, anyway. We can swap a little spit, feel each other up some, and just generally give people ideas. No big lifetime commitments here, and only as much as you can handle, all right?"

It almost sounded like something Alex could do. It sounded like a deal. God knew he'd give a kidney of his own to have someone stand up to Nick with him.

This wasn't even the first time Joe had suggested that Alex get out of the service side and into the performing side of the business. Joe knew about his past. Joe couldn't really understand, though, if he could still suggest anything like that.

God, it was tempting.

But could he do it? He hadn't touched anyone voluntarily since he'd escaped and made his way to Doradus. Except that wasn't exactly true any more, was it? He'd already touched his mouth to Sandy's tonight, put his hand on one of Sandy's arms twice and lived to tell the story. Maybe he could do this after all.

"Thanks. I appreciate your offer. But…" Alex kept his distance. Sandy seemed like a nice guy. Seemed. No one knew better than Alex that looks could be deceiving. "You know that I have a few… issues."

"I know you don't like to be touched. You seem big on personal boundaries -- yours, especially. I've never known you to show much skin."

Alex nodded. He knew how he must look to outsiders. To anyone who didn't know about his past, Alex realized he probably came off as more than just a little peculiar. Especially in a place as free and easy with its actions as *Nelly's*.

"Yeah." For the first time since he'd left, Alex

wanted to talk about the time he'd spent inside *Earthly Delights*, but the sudden lump in his throat wouldn't allow words past.

Oh, no. God, no.

The prickle of tears behind his eyes was as shocking as it was horrifying. Alex hadn't cried in years. Not since those first few months behind the high-security walls of the New Republic's most exclusive pleasure resort, as just one of its rentable pleasures. Turning his head away, Alex willed his emotions back under control. "I…" Words wouldn't come. "I, uh… I could use… I appreciate the help."

"Okay. You've got it, then. How about we talk more in the morning? I'm ready for bed. What about you?"

Those big, dark eyes were looking at him. What did they really want from him? Sandy was too good to be true and Alex had learned from long, bitter experience how things that seemed that way turned out. "What about me?"

"Ready to go to bed? To sleep -- just to sleep -- I promise."

Okay, so his impassive 'never give 'em a reaction to punish you for' face was obviously history.

"Where?" Besides the orange couch, there was nothing that looked even remotely like a bed. Although there was a staircase that presumably led to the second level Sandy had mentioned.

"Wherever you like. There's a bed upstairs. We can share it; or, if you want, we can flip for who gets the couch. I'll give you a hint, though -- it's nickname is the corkscrew. 'Cause that's what you need a spine like to get any sleep on it."

Maybe it was and maybe it wasn't. Either way, though, it didn't matter. "I'll take the couch. I'm a pretty restless sleeper. Trust me, you don't want to share a bed with me."

And maybe Sandy's measuring look held on a millisecond longer than usual, Alex couldn't tell.

"Whatever you say. The toilet's behind that door." Sandy gestured toward the only door visible besides the one they'd entered through, not counting the opening to the stairway. "Yell if you need anything."

Alex nodded and Sandy headed up the staircase to the second level. Rubbing one hand over his eyes, Alex thought back over what Sandy had said.

Could anyone really be as genuine and even, God help him, as kind as Sandy seemed to be? Was he being paranoid again? It was entirely possible. Better paranoid, though, than dead in a ditch somewhere with a head full of chemicals.

Sandy seemed like a good guy, like someone who might just possibly be trusted. He'd been coming into *Nelly's* for as long as Alex had been working there. Longer, even. Hardly ever took a room, though.

Alex lay down on the couch, facing the door, his back against the wall -- or as close to it as he could get, which happened to be the back of the couch. He tried to think back, if he'd ever seen Sandy take one of the themed rooms *Nelly's* provided -- for a small fee, of course -- for the comfort and convenience of its customers.

Twice. No, three times: once with Justin, once with Aaron, once with Pavel. A pretty eclectic sampling, now that he thought about it. Alex couldn't say why he was thinking about Sandy's choice of bed partners, he just folded one arm beneath his head for a pillow and settled in.

This section of buildings must be pretty solid, because once Sandy disappeared up the stairs, Alex didn't hear a thing. He couldn't tell if it was just his imagination or if maybe that low rumble was Sandy letting out a groan. What did Sandy have to groan about? Maybe Sandy was really tired. Or maybe he was thinking about that little bitch Aaron and touching himself.

It was none of Alex's business whether or not Sandy jacked off, much less who Sandy thought about while he was engaging in that particular exercise.

Alex closed his eyes and wondered what that would look like: Sandy touching himself.

Chapter 3

"How's the coffee? Black, extra sugar, right?"

"Actually, I've been easing off on the sugar lately. Or trying to, anyway." Finished stirring his coffee, Alex poked one of the beignets D'abu had had delivered along with the coffees, licking at the powdered sugar that came off on his finger. "What's this?"

"Beignet. They're Southern. I got hooked on 'em when we were stationed in Alaska."

"I'm sure that statement makes sense in some alternate universe somewhere."

Alex sipped at his coffee and eyed the pastry suspiciously. His hair stuck out in about two dozen different directions and his clothes were wrinkled from having been slept in. D'abu decided he must be pretty far gone if the only word that came to mind to describe Alex was "adorable."

"You're not much of a morning person, are you?"

"And here I thought I was hiding it so well." Alex looked up, something furtive hiding behind his misty blue eyes. "I'd kill for a smoke about now. You don't have any, do you? No. Forget I asked."

Looking away, Alex began fidgeting with his food, tearing the innocent pastry into a dozen small pieces, not eating any of them. That perfect, kissable mouth, its high cupid's bow drawing attention away from the full pink lower lip, beckoned.

D'abu disliked having to ask, knowing instinctively that Alex would hate talking about it; hate revealing what he would no doubt consider weakness. "Do you still get cravings?"

"Yeah. Once in a while. Not so much any more." Even with the amount of time that had passed, Alex was still paying the price for something that hadn't been in any way his fault.

"Eat," Sandy suggested.

Alex glanced up quickly, but just as quickly his gaze skittered away. "Later, maybe. Can we talk about… It's sick. I hate it."

"If it ever gets bad -- I know it's bad, but I mean really bad. If you're thinking about getting some and using again -- will you come to me first? I want to help."

"Sandy, I—" This time the pain was nakedly visible in Alex's eyes and the sheer depth of it took D'abu's breath away. "You don't have to help. I'm fine. Same goes for Nick and that situation. I know you're just trying to be a nice guy, but I'll be fine. Really."

D'abu reached out and captured one fidgety hand, grasping it lightly in his own. "I'm helping. It's a done deal, so let's talk about our plan. How long have you and I been seeing each other?"

Just holding Alex's hand had D'abu's blood flowing south. A few square inches of bare flesh touching and D'abu's cock began to stir. How would he ever manage to kiss Alex, take Alex in his arms, and not push things harder than Alex could stand, if just palm to palm contact was making him hard?

"You're not really going to go through with it, are you?" Alex's laugh was high and nervous and completely charming. A dimple on one cheek made a rare appearance and it was all D'abu could do not to wrap a hand around the back of Alex's head and pull him close for a slow, hungry kiss.

"You bet. How long have we been together? I say not long, or people would have noticed. Is our story going to be that we've been talking for a while now, but we only recently decided to take it further?"

What panic-crazed thoughts were going through the man's head? Alex was staring at their linked hands, his breath coming in short, choppy gasps. If Alex couldn't tolerate even holding hands -- and in private, at that -- what hope did they have of making anyone believe they were lovers?

"Give me a minute, okay?" Alex withdrew his fingers and D'abu's heart sank. Until Alex, not removing his hand completely, began to touch the pads of D'abu's fingers -- lightly, in the most tentative of gestures. "This is hard. Harder than I thought."

Not as hard as I am.

Their gazes met and D'abu tried to control his own breathing, even as he prayed that Alex couldn't read in his eyes what was going through his head.

He wanted Alex.

Bad.

"Take your time. I think maybe we ought to experiment a little bit, don't you? Just a little. Until we're comfortable around each other. It's got to be believable that we're seeing each other if you want your boss and his new partner to leave you alone."

He wasn't trying to actively manipulate Alex -- that would be unconscionable. The words had come out of his mouth, though; had taken on a life of their own, almost without his choosing, and D'abu had recognized the perfect truth of them. Part of him was reveling in the fact that Alex's request was playing so perfectly into his hands, even as another much bigger part of him squirmed with guilt.

Alex continued to stare at the points where skin touched skin, letting his fingers float delicately over D'abu's. Slowly, almost imperceptibly, Alex nodded his head. More slowly yet, Alex raised his gaze and those tantalizing lips shaped a single word. "Okay."

"I'm going to kiss you now, Alex. Are you ready?"

Alex nodded and, like in a dream, D'abu slowly leaned forward across the corner of the table that separated them. As the distance between them grew smaller, D'abu fought the urge leap on Alex, to take everything he wanted from that beautiful mouth. Alex moved closer by the tiniest of increments until they were centimeters apart, only to stop. D'abu flicked a quick glance aimed at catching Alex's gaze, but found it was fixed firmly on his own lips. Anticipation eating him alive, D'abu moved closer still, until all that separated them was a few microns of filtered, purified, manufactured air.

He touched his lips to Alex's and had to close his eyes against the rush of emotion engulfing him. The sensation of soft lips beneath his own fired off neurons in his brain that communicated instantaneously with his dick. God help him, if a kiss did this to him, if Alex ever touched his dick D'abu's heart would probably stop.

Pressing against Alex's mouth, gently, so gently, D'abu tilted his head a fraction and licked delicately into Alex's mouth. The taste of Alex was -- God -- incredible. Alex's shallow, panting breaths in D'abu's ear were like an igniter to a plasma charge and D'abu had to touch. Had to. He brought a hand up to feel the dozens of tiny bristles stubbling Alex's chin; knew in a momentary flash what it would be like to feel them rubbing against his face, his chest, his belly.

It all happened in a moment and only a few seconds of real time elapsed before Alex pulled back. Quick, heaving little breaths made Alex's chest rise and fall while his tongue flicked out daintily to catch the foreign taste on his lips.

"I don't know how to do this, Sandy. I don't know if I can." Alex ran that delicate, pink tongue around his lips again and D'abu was so hard he was afraid he might go off in his pants. "I'm sorry."

"Alex, honey, you have nothing to be sorry for. Nothing that happened to you was your fault." Alex's head jerked up at…what? His use of a pet name? D'abu could have kicked himself. Goddammit, he'd have to keep a stranglehold on his tongue before he let anything else slip out. "We'll get through it, one step at a time."

"Sandy, I know you're only trying to help, but… Respectfully, you don't know anything about it."

Fair enough.

"Maybe not. But I was a Marine in one of the Republic's toughest units for over a decade and I do know a little bit about having to do things I had no control over. I know what that can do to your head sometimes. So any time you feel like talking about it, I'll listen."

Alex stared introspectively at the table, chewing on his bottom lip as he thought about who-knew-what and D'abu wasn't about to be the one to point out that their hands were still linked. Instead, D'abu used the time to study Alex in the bright, simulated light of the morning. He didn't get the chance as often as he'd like.

Dark hair complemented naturally pale skin and those pink undertones probably meant that Alex would flush charmingly when embarrassed or aroused. A fleeting smile crossed Alex's face, allowing a glimpse of a mouthful of teeth before it was gone again. The prominent canines were hard to miss and the slight overlap of the two front teeth had D'abu wondering why, with the prevalence of cosmetic enhancements in this day and age, Alex had chosen to leave things natural. Or had the choice been his to make?

"Sandy?" Alex glanced up.

"Yeah?"

"Have you ever-- Oh, sorry." Noticing their entwined hands, Alex quickly pulled his back and, clasping both together, folded them self-consciously in his lap. "Have you ever done anything really bad? Something so terrible, that you felt like anything bad people might say about you later would be deserved? Something you could never forgive yourself for?"

Trying to figure out what Alex could possibly

be talking about in his own life kept the images at bay for a few moments, but inevitably they came. Usually they waited until he was asleep and his guard was down, but an invitation like Alex's trumped D'abu's defenses and memories of a dozen years of "peacekeeping" duties flooded his head. He shook his head to short-circuit the process, but a few snuck in anyway.

Shattered lives.

Dead children.

Women who wished they were.

Maybe Alex had a point. He couldn't talk about it to someone who hadn't been there.

"No. Just the usual."

* * *

"Alex, I needed a vodka tonic. This is gin. Could you fix it for me, please?"

Shit.

That was his third mistake already. He needed to focus. *Nelly's* was busy tonight, but there was nothing special about that. *Nelly's* was always busy. Doradus was the last speck of civilization in this sector of the asteroid belt and beyond it there was a whole lot of nothing. Last chance for gas, next five-hundred-fifty-million kilometers. Even if it hadn't been, *Nelly's* red-hot sex shows, made possible by the laissez faire non-New Republic laws that prevailed on Doradus, would have ensured its nightly packed house.

"Try explaining to them that it's not what they think they want -- it's what I know they need. Save us both a lot of time and aggravation." Alex's withering glare back wasn't an act. Normally the give-and-take banter between him and the servers was a big part of what he liked about the job. Tonight he just didn't have the patience for it, though, so he remade the drink and tried to find it in himself to apologize.

"What's up with you tonight? It wasn't my mistake. I even said 'please.'" One of *Nelly's* newest servers, Shae hadn't been on Doradus long. Cute, red-haired, and petite, like most people who made it this far from the heart of civilization, Shae had come looking for a less regulated version of the society he'd come from. Who could sympathize more than Alex with that particular sentiment?

"Sorry, Shae. No, you're right. Here." He handed over the fresh drink. "Tell your customer I made it a double -- on me."

"Thanks, Alex." Shae turned to go, then turned back. "Why don't you ask Joe to let you off early tonight? No offense, but you don't look so hot. Are you feeling all right?"

"I'm good. Just a little tired. Sorry about the drink, honey."

"That's okay. If there's anything I can do to help, let me know." One last long, meaningful look and, cute little ass swaying, Shae left to tend to his tables.

"Well, I see someone hasn't lost any of his old magic. You always did know how to charm a boy out of his pants." Smiling the quirky smile that had haunted Alex's dreams so long ago, Nick Andrade leaned on the bar; his bright blue shirt shimmered, bringing out the blue of his eyes. "Could I trouble you for a sparkling water, do you think?"

Refusing to rise to the bait -- and that's what

Nick's remark had been, although, for the life of him, Alex couldn't think why, Alex kept his expression neutral. "Sure thing, Nick. Here you go. On the house. Which would be you now, I guess."

"I guess it would be." Nick sipped his water and watched Alex over the rim of his glass. "I really am sorry about how things turned out, Alex. You know I never meant for—"

"You're not going to keep bringing that up every time we see each other, are you? Once upon a time an apology from you might have meant something to me, but that water's way under the bridge now, as far as I'm concerned."

"I guess."

Cutting limes into wedges to keep his hands busy, Alex looked up. "You guess what? That you will keep bringing it up? Please don't."

Gesturing for Alex to hand him one of the lime sections, Nick squeezed it into his drink before helping himself to a stir stick from Alex's bar supplies and stirring his drink. "Okay. I'll try. I feel bad about what happened the last time we saw each other."

"Yeah, nothing like being hauled away by a secret government security squad to kill the mood." Nick shot him a look full of appeal and, although Alex had never hit anyone before in his life, he really wanted to now. "Don't."

"Hey, bartender. How about a little service down at this end of the bar?"

Without turning his head, Alex held up a hand, acknowledging the call from down the bar. Ordinarily that sort of remark would only earn the customer an even longer wait for service, but tonight it suited Alex's needs to act on it.

"Excuse me, boss, but I've got customers to take care of."

***

Climbing the stairs later, up to his apartment, Alex was still kicking himself mentally over all the mistakes he'd made tonight. Wrong ingredients. Miscalculated proportions. Entire orders forgotten. While he wished for the dozenth time that he had Sandy to talk to, Alex couldn't decide if having Sandy to talk to would help or hurt, since it had been his preoccupation with the man that had been interfering with his ability to do his job efficiently.

Alex swiped his card and let himself into the apartment he'd called home for the past six months, snorting again at the irony of people leaving one place because of its intolerable strictures and then doing everything humanly possible to recreate it somewhere else.

Not exactly. Not perfectly, though, by any means. Thank God.

Peeling off his bartender's apron, Alex let it drop, not caring where it fell. He loosened the cuffs of his long-sleeved shirt next, before moving on to pop the fastening at his throat. Dropping down onto the nearest horizontal surface -- a moderately comfortable padded chair -- Alex propped his elbows on his knees and ran both hands through his hair.

What the hell was he going to do now?

His thoughts were a hopeless jumble -- a tangled knot of colliding ideas, feelings, and images. Lately, now that the drugs were mostly out of his system, he'd begun to be able to sort through things in something approaching a logical fashion; little things, like arranging his apartment how he liked or what clothes to buy. But he'd been advised that because of the amount of chemicals his brain had been fed, combined with the duration and how young he'd been when they started, he'd probably never be really normal again. Whatever that was.

Something like figuring out odds and probabilities, though… and big, intangible things, like was he still safe here? Could he manage that? Alex covered his face with his hands, cradling his head as he tried to think.

He'd made it out of that hell hole and off Earth successfully, working his way out past Mars and on into the asteroid belt on an ore freighter. While not something he'd recommend to the uninitiated, Alex would have done anything to get out of the gilded cage he'd spent the last portion of his life in. It was strictly by pure chance that he'd landed on Doradus.

Wanting only to be as far away from New Republican Earth, with its institutionalized hate laws and barely disguised caste system, as he could get, Alex had bribed his way on board first a freighter and then a smuggler's cruiser. They could have been going anywhere, he hadn't cared where, so long as it was far away.

He'd been such a mess mentally and physically it hadn't struck him as odd, or even particularly unusual, that he'd found people he knew when he got to Doradus. But Sarhaan, Kai, and Sandy had already been docked here with their "borrowed" military ship, fleeing Earth for some of the same reasons Alex had. Although he couldn't prove it, he had the feeling they'd helped him out some behind the scenes.

The life he'd begun to build here wasn't half bad. He had a job and his own little living space. Not much more than one room, with a reconstituter, a comm channel, and one entertainment channel. Still …

Alex leaned back and put his feet up.

He had the companionship of the other employees at *Nelly's*, that was something. His regular customers -- the ones who came for the socializing and to soak in as much human interaction as they could before they headed back to their source of livelihood in all its solitary splendor -- they craved the back and forth of the rituals of conversation as much as Alex had come to.

One thing he hadn't craved, though, was sex. He'd had a lifetime's worth back at *Earthly Delights*. Several lifetimes, in fact. If he never touched, or was touched by, another human being again for the rest of his life, that would be A-okay with him.

If that was true, though, why had he done both?

He'd let Sandy touch him. Just an arm around the shoulders, true, but still it was something he hadn't allowed anyone else to do since he'd landed on Doradus. He'd even touched back and it had been… tolerable.

And then there'd been the kiss.

His almost nightly conversations with Sandy had started out as purely business, on Alex's part, anyway. He'd worked Sandy just like any other gullible customer, smiling and doing his best to simulate flirtation to sell more drinks for the house. Alex didn't feel guilty. That was his job, after all --

and about the only thing his twisted background had left him qualified to do.

But somewhere along the line, what had begun as strictly professional had become personal and he'd started looking forward to the big man's presence. To looking into Sandy's brown eyes, the lines at the corners testimony to the man's sunny good nature. To the low rumble of Sandy's laughter as Sandy alternately teased and mocked him.

Sandy had never flirted back, though.

Not until last night, that is, and it had scared the hell out of Alex. Either Sandy was faking it, in which case he was dangerous because the act had been so utterly convincing, or he wasn't and Sandy wanted Alex.

Alex wasn't sure which was more frightening.

Chapter 4

"Hi, there. What can I get you tonight?" A cute redhead slapped a cocktail napkin down on D'abu's table since he was, for once, not sitting at the bar. Just enough of a costume to be decent, the boy managed to convey both worldliness and naïve enthusiasm, like he'd just discovered fucking and couldn't wait to make up for lost time.

Despite a gorgeous body, the combination left D'abu cold and it was no hardship to pretend he was already taken. Turning down the unspoken invitation in those pretty, brown eyes became an act of honor -- chivalry, even -- instead of a complete lack of interest. "Adrastean ale, please. Extra cold. Tap, not container?"

"You got it. My name's Shae. I'll be right back with that, so don't go away." The flirtatious smile combined with the sidelong glance confirmed D'abu's gut instinct that Shae had been angling for a little extra business. Did the house take a percentage of credits earned on after-hours activities? D'abu wondered.

"I'm not moving." When Shae didn't either, D'abu raised an eyebrow. "Looking forward to that ale, though. I'm pretty thirsty."

The boy didn't have enough experience to play off the fact he'd been caught staring. "Oh, um…

right. Be right back."

"I won't be." Starting to have a little fun at the server's expense, D'abu repeated himself. "Still not moving."

"Right. Okay. Be right back."

Shae swung by another table on his way back to the bar and following his progress gave D'abu the excuse he needed to swivel in his chair and gaze at the tall figure in black behind it. Alex had done something different with his hair tonight, something smooth yet fluffy that made D'abu's fingers itch to sift through it. He'd have to find a way to work that into the boyfriend act.

When the pint-sized waiter finally made it to the bar in the back, he leaned over and gestured Alex closer; Alex complied, laughing almost immediately in response to whatever it was Shae told him. D'abu loved -- absolutely loved -- the way Alex threw his head back and laughed. Full-bodied, seemingly so carefree. Was he the only one who could hear the pain it was hiding? It couldn't have been more obvious to D'abu, but then he'd put in more hours observing than most, probably.

Alex suddenly looked up and stared straight at D'abu. A smile spread slowly over his face, his eyes taking on a heavy-lidded, I'm-thinking-about-fucking-you look. Holding the look for several seconds, Alex finally nodded a little, dragging the full lower lip between his teeth before licking at his upper lip.

Jesus, Mary, and Joseph.

Now D'abu spread his legs a bit to accommodate the swelling in his pants -- in response to a look. One simple look and he was getting hard. Good God.

Sandy was half-way to rising out of his seat when another waiter tapped Alex's arm, pulling his attention away from D'abu. Sandy sat back down, covering his frustration by tugging at his pants and adjusting himself. If someone hadn't interrupted, he would have…

What? Pushed his way across the crowded nightclub and laid one on Alex? Grabbed the man with both hands and kissed him until they both gasped for air? Sandy still had a firm enough grip on reality to realize that it might spell trouble and that it didn't sound like a half-bad idea at all. He was supposed to be steadying himself, not picturing Alex's face between his own hands as he helped himself to one lingering kiss after another.

"Here you go." Shae was back with his drink and Sandy was reaching for his paycard when the waiter put a restraining hand on Sandy's arm. "Don't worry about it. Alex took care of it."

Glancing quickly in Alex's direction, but getting no clues from Alex, who was busily preparing drinks behind the bar, Sandy looked back to Shae. "What do you mean, Alex took care of it?"

A shrug. "He took care of it -- put it on his employee card. I didn't realize you two were together." The redhead was openly scanning Sandy's assets now.

"He… what? Goddamn it, he's not supposed to be doing that. I told him—." He hadn't really, but that wasn't the point. Sandy reached for his card again, this time giving Shae no choice but to take it. "Here."

"Uh, whatever. You two'll have to work that out on your own time. I don't know what you want me to do with this." He indicated the card Sandy had thrust at him. "The drink's already paid for."

Sandy only barely resisted telling the suddenly snippy waiter what he could do with the card. Smart-mouthed kid like him probably carried lube on him at all times, anyway. Pissed, but realizing he wasn't going to get any satisfaction out of harassing the help, Sandy glared as he grudgingly took his card back. "I'll straighten this out with Alex later."

"Okay. I'll, uh, see you around, I guess." Another sweep of that impudent glance over Sandy's body and the little waiter was gone.

Sitting back down, Sandy took a swig of his ale, still fuming. Goddamn… stupid… Alex. Sandy couldn't even form a decent sentence. It wasn't all bruised ego on his part. Sandy would have no problem with Alex buying him a drink… a dinner. Hell, a hundred dinners. If -- and this was a big 'if' -- Alex had the money.

Alex didn't have the money, though.

Sandy knew for a fact that when Alex had arrived on Doradus the only thing he'd had to call his own besides the clothes on his back was a raging drug addiction. Alex'd been too much of a mess at first to perform any kind of paying job and had survived by promising future labor to *Nelly's* co-owner and operator, Joe Sotheran. That the pile of debt Alex had run up wasn't double its size was due primarily to behind-the-scenes help from Sandy's teammates, Sarhaan and Kai. Later Sandy had helped out, too, although Sandy hadn't felt the need to inform anyone beyond Alex's boss of that little arrangement.

It was all well and good to lay down some cover fire to confuse the enemy, but they needed to be smart about it. Sandy wasn't about to let Alex jeopardize his future by throwing around credits he didn't have.

Two minutes later Sandy was standing at the bar, a stool miraculously becoming available at the precise moment he appeared. Alex was working the other end of the bar for the moment, but Sandy could wait, so he sat and nursed the ale Alex had paid for. When a half-hour had gone by and Alex still hadn't made his way anywhere close to where Sandy was sitting, it became harder and harder for Sandy to tell himself that Alex was just busy.

"Teddy. Hey, bud." Sandy signaled to Teddy, another bartender who frequently worked in tandem with Alex. "Could you tell Alex I need to talk to him when he's got a second?"

Word must be spreading because Teddy gave him a wink and an indulgent smile to go with his, "You bet," before he moved away to take care of an impatient customer waving a credit chip.

Good. The sooner word got around, the easier things would be for Alex.

Tonight's theme at *Nelly's* seemed to be "School Days," a nod to everyone's fantasy of what things could have been like if only they'd been more self-assured, had better hair, or been in with the in crowd. The three athletic young men on stage were putting the set's gymnastic equipment to good use, a pommel horse currently enduring a workout its inventor had probably never envisioned.

Sandy wondered briefly what Alex's school experience had been like. Relatively certain that Alex hadn't been one of the cool kids, Sandy had no trouble picturing him active in drama. One of those arty, 'Come on kids, let's put on a show!' types.

"Uh-oh. Am I in trouble?"

Alex must have snuck up while Sandy was immersed in his fantasy of an adolescent Alex. The tilt of his chin was cocky, but the shadow behind Alex's eyes took all the steam out of Sandy's argument. More than anything, Sandy wanted never to see that look in Alex's eyes again.

"Alex."

Hands braced on the bar, a towel dangled from one of Alex's hands -- long hands, surprisingly broad for someone as lanky as Alex.

"Sandy."

"I told you, I don't want you spending your money on me." Sandy spoke loud enough for an obviously eavesdropping Teddy to be able to hear.

"And I told you, I'll spend my money on you if I want to."

The music was still thumping, indolent and sexy; the low buzz of the crowd's chatter as they watched the stage show was full of the expectation of promises as yet unfulfilled. Why was it getting to Sandy tonight when he'd been a regular patron for so long he'd long since considered himself immune?

Must be the eyes.

Alex's smoldering blue eyes gazed down at him and they were having an effect on him. It couldn't be an accident. Alex had to know the power of those eyes.

"Alex, we agreed..."

"I don't remember agreeing to any such thing." Alex's beautiful face was somehow only inches away. Who had moved in on who? "If I promise not to do it again, can we kiss and make up? I hate it when you're mad at me." Alex's voice had gone as smoky as the room, and those lips… Sandy had a hundred Alex fantasies and every one began and ended with those full, provocative lips. Alex hooked two fingers in Sandy's shirt, tugging him closer. "Tell me you're not still mad at me," he coaxed.

As their lips met, Sandy's eyes drifted shut, his heart suddenly pounding. He couldn't believe Alex was kissing him. Alex had boundary issues -- big ones -- and Sandy had imagined that it might take weeks or even months before Alex would feel comfortable enough to initiate anything. But his mouth was warm and soft, his tongue silky smooth as it flirted briefly with Sandy's mouth.

The hand in Sandy's shirt relaxed a little, but otherwise stayed where it was, fingers curling into Sandy's chest. Trying to coax Alex further, Sandy opened his mouth a little, but Alex pulled away and Sandy groaned in protest. "Alex."

"I'll be off in a couple of hours. See you then?"

Prying his eyes open, Sandy leaned into Alex's hand as it stroked the side of his face. Pressing his face deeper into Alex's hand, Sandy caught site of Joe Sotheran and Nick Andrade, standing side by side, talking quietly as they watched the room.

"Sandy?"

"Sure. I'll see you then."

He hadn't even gotten to touch Alex's hair.

***

Alex and Teddy worked steadily, cleaning up the bar area, making sure the glasses were gathered up for the kitchen crew to wash and the liquor put away in locked cabinets. Even though parts of *Nelly's* were open continuously, the live floor shows for which it was famous, the bars, and wait staff were only scheduled during peak business hours. The rooms available for rent to anyone inspired by one of the shows were scheduled according to availability, pretty much any time of the artificial day or night. Anyone so moved but without a companion could, of course, be accommodated -- for an appropriate fee.

The host staff had cleared the room of the general public, so it was just Alex and Teddy cleaning up the bar area, while the waiters dumped the contents of their electronic pads into accounting's central computer. Alex had learned early on that waiters were paid according to a complex formula based on an hourly rate plus commission and tips. Hours and drinks sold were all logged in their notepads, but some customers still liked to tip with cash cards and those had to be counted out the old fashioned way.

"Here you go, Alex."

Busy wiping down the prep area, Alex looked up. Shae had divided up his tips, keeping the bulk for himself, dividing the rest between the bartenders and the kitchen staff. Alex took it, automatically doing the math in his head to split the money between himself and Teddy and the guys in the kitchen. "Thanks, Shae. See you tomorrow."

Teddy looked up from a squat as he stowed away the alcohol to throw in, "Have a good night, man."

"Alex?" Shae hadn't moved, still standing on

the room side of the bar.

"Yeah?"

"You seeing your fella tonight?" The tone was casual, but Alex knew more was coming.

"I think so. Why?"

"Would you do us all a favor and get fuckin' laid, man? Please? Between you messing up orders and your new guy being a general asshole, I'm not enjoying the experience. I mean, I'm all happy for your romance and whatever, but I've still got a living to make here."

Alex put out a hand to brace himself and looked down for a moment, speechless with amazement. He hadn't seen that one coming, not by a long shot. Too busy mooning over his 'new guy' and licking his lips for a little more of Sandy's taste, no doubt. He looked up.

"You—" obnoxious little shit, his subconscious helpfully supplied, but he couldn't say that. He had to work here, so Alex bit his tongue. Even if it was true that Sandy was his new lover, would that really be so bad? Wasn't he entitled to even a little happiness?

Joe Sotheran chose that moment to sweep into the room, his new little sidekick, Nick, in tow. "About finished up here, gentlemen?" Glancing from Shae to Alex and feeling the energy bristle, Joe brightened a bit. "Problem?"

"Not at all. We're almost done." Alex looked at Shae. "Aren't we?"

"I'm outta here." Shae took his tip money and left, nodding deferentially in his bosses' direction as he went.

Joe grinned briefly in Nick's direction and Alex wondered momentarily at the unspoken undercurrent between the two. He didn't have time to speculate, though.

"Alex, I'm glad I caught you. Can you spare a moment?" Joe stepped back, indicating Alex should follow him. "Teddy, would you mind finishing up, please? I need a word with Alex."

The corners of Teddy's mouth tightened a bit, but he nodded as Alex came out from behind the bar and left him to finish the rest of the clean up alone.

Joe led the way to a semi-private corner of the room, far enough to put them out of earshot of Teddy, with Nick casually bringing up the rear. Surveying the room with a self-satisfied air, Joe shoved his hands into his pants pockets, balancing lightly on the balls of his feet. "How are things going for you, Alex?"

Alex shifted, giving himself a bit more breathing room between him and his two bosses. "It's going all right. How's it going for you? Business okay?"

"Business is good." Joe nodded, considering. "Of course, there isn't a businessman alive who doesn't think it couldn't be better. Things could always be better."

"I guess." Alex had no idea where this was going, but it didn't feel right. Joe had never singled him out for a one-on-one conversation like this before. "Did you need to talk to me about something?"

"Well, since you ask, there is something you could do for me. For us." He glanced at Nick, to his left, that private smile making another appearance. "Alex, I'd like you to consider transferring to the talent department. What would you think about being a performer for *Durty Nelly's*?"

Alex looked from one to the other, incredulous. "A performer? No way. Absolutely no chance."

"No? Just like that? You don't want any time to think it over?"

"I don't need time, Mr. Sotheran. My answer is no. Absolutely not." Alex's stomach roiled at the mere idea. His arms folded protectively across his chest, one hand going to his throat, holding his collar closed.

Nick joined in as they double-teamed him. "You'd earn a lot more as a stage performer. Even more for private shows. Right, Joe? I noticed that you have some debts you're trying to pay down."

Alex swung his gaze to focus on Nick. Did they really think that that's all it would be to him -- another way to make a living?

"Are you saying I'm not paying it off fast enough?" Watching their faces closely, Alex tried to guess at their motivations. "I can work more shifts. Other rooms, even, if you need it."

Joe's brown eyes were full of regret. "I'm really pretty well set for bar staff right now, Alex. *Nelly's* has a certain reputation to maintain, it's true, but when it's all said and done, bartending's a helluva lot easier to teach someone than how to put on a top notch sex show. Wouldn't you agree?"

"I…" There was every chance that Alex was pissing away his only source of income, but not even the prospect of being homeless again could get him to agree. He wouldn't even consider it. "I'm sorry, Mr. Sotheran. I can't."

"Oh, well." Joe shrugged. "I guess if you can't, you can't. I had to try."

"Why?"

Looking at Nick again, Joe's expression grew even more neutral, if that was possible. "There have been certain… inquiries, on your behalf. You must know you're very popular with *Nelly's* clientele."

As a matter of fact, Alex didn't know any such thing. The conversation was getting weirder by the minute. "What kind of inquiries?"

Joe shrugged. "It has been communicated to me by," again the hesitation, "…certain parties that should you ever become available, your time and talents would be very much sought after."

Alex was stunned. So much so that his mouth actually fell open for an instant. "Certain parties? Like who?"

"Oh, I couldn't say, of course. Privacy concerns and all that; I'm sure you understand. Besides which, you're not interested." Visibly changing focus, Joe turned to Nick. "I think we're all done here. Care to go back and look at the numbers again? The basics are fairly simple, but learning some of the nuances takes a bit of practice."

"Sure. Sounds good." Nick smiled and clasped his hands behind his back as he and Joe wandered off, leaving Alex standing frozen, mind racing. Someone had seen him? Maybe even been watching him. But who? It was creepy. God, it was…

"Hey, Alex, you about done here? I saw the big boss leave and— Are you okay?" Sandy walked in, looking like a safe, peaceful island in the middle of a stormy sea.

"Huh? Oh, yeah, sure. Um, just let me…" Alex looked around, hastily trying to pull himself together.

Sandy came close, forcing Alex to look up to meet Sandy's gaze. "Are you sure you're okay?"

Alex tried to swallow. "Uh-huh."

"How about a kiss, then? I'm supposed to be your boyfriend, remember?"

"Oh, yeah. Right." He nodded.

"Okay, I'm going to kiss you. I should probably grab your ass a little, too. Okay?"

Sandy was standing closer now, his voice a soft rumble only Alex could hear and a tiny spark of heat began to burn low in Alex's groin. Still clutching his own shirt, Alex's field of vision was completely filled by Sandy now, big and dark and somehow reassuring instead of scary. "Yeah. That'd... all right."

"Good." Another half-step closer and the heat from Sandy's big body began to seep through Alex's clothes. A hand slipped in behind Alex's head, fingers weaving into his hair as Sandy lowered his head. Dark eyes, warm like melted chocolate, were so close Alex was mesmerized -- drawn irresistibly by their magnetic pull. "Close your eyes, dummy. Try to look like you're enjoying it."

Sandy's lips were so close they brushed Alex's as they murmured, his warm breath malty from the ale he'd been drinking. One big hand curved around Alex's butt, nearly spanning it, and Alex's heart, already beating hard, pounded harder. First licking gently at Alex's mouth, Sandy brushed a light, playful kiss over it next, took Alex's upper lip between his teeth and drew back, using only the lightest of pressure.

Sandy played.

Not harsh. Never demanding. Instead, almost carelessly, Sandy let his mouth tangle with Alex's, lips and teeth and tongue sampling Alex's as Alex stood disorientated.

The hand on Alex's ass swept in slow circles, as though committing the shape to memory in exquisite detail. Alex tried to keep some space between their bodies, but Sandy seemed to have other ideas and kept nudging Alex closer, the hard length of Sandy's cock pressing into Alex's belly.

"G'night, you two. Lights on or off?"

Alex pulled away, panting, trying to focus on Teddy, who stood expectantly next to the lighting control panel nearest the door. Looking from Teddy back to Sandy, Alex sucked in his breath at the look on Sandy's face.

Eyes slumberous. Breathing rapid. Tongue slipping out to taste his own wet lips.

Pure lust.

Panic fluttered in Alex's breast, until the sudden realization hit him: Sandy was acting. It was all for show -- for Teddy. As the fear receded, admiration took its place. Not only was Sandy an expert strategist, but he would do anything for a friend.

"Suit yourself. I'll see you tomorrow, Alex." Tired of waiting, Teddy shrugged and left.

As Alex called a 'See you' after Teddy, Sandy raised his head. "C'mon, baby, let's use your place. It's closer."

Chapter 5

Sandy was hard.

His balls ached.

His body was revved up and ready to go. Sandy wanted sex and he wanted it with the man whose fingers kept sliding out from under his as they climbed the stairs.

He wasn't going to get it, though -- and what's more, he knew it.

Still, Sandy kept reaching for Alex's hand every time it slipped out of his as Alex led the way to his room upstairs.

The fluid cut of Alex's pants pulled taut alternately over the round curves of his butt and the long length of his thighs as they climbed the stairs, giving Sandy an eye-level visual of what he'd just had his hand on. Sweet. He might be guilty of trying to create a not entirely truthful impression of himself as Alex's boyfriend, but one thing Sandy didn't have to fake was his sincere appreciation of that stunning backside.

Sandy'd known for a while that Alex rented a small efficiency apartment on the second floor of *Nelly's* and it looked like tonight he was finally going to see the inside of it. What Sandy hadn't counted on, though, was how getting his hands on Alex -- even for just the brief taste he'd had downstairs -- had gotten him more wound up than he'd figured. He might not be the brightest guy on the team, but even he could see that Alex was nowhere near ready for what Sandy'd been imagining. That didn't keep his body from clamoring, though. What he wouldn't give for this little exercise to be what they were pretending it was…

Stopping in front of a plain white door with a number four on it, Alex swiped his security card, his gaze catching Sandy's for an instant before he walked in and stood aside for Sandy to follow. As soon as they were both through, Sandy closed the door hard, falling back against it with his full weight. The door shuddered under Sandy's weight and Alex took a step back, watching Sandy with big, uncertain eyes.

"We couldn't wait to be alone and I'm kissing you hard," Sandy whispered. Closing his eyes, he groaned and moved against the door, making sure it vibrated beneath his weight.

"What are you—"

"Sssh!" Sandy cut Alex off, motioning him closer at the same time. Alex hesitated briefly before approaching. Using the toneless whisper that had been a combat necessity in his Marine days, Sandy spelled out what he had in mind. "Make a little noise. We're supposed to be having a good time in here."

Catching on, Alex relaxed a little and even smiled as he moved closer. Joining Sandy in leaning on the door, Alex grinned and let out a moan so realistic it nearly brought Sandy to his knees. "Oh, Sandy."

Oh, Sandy.

Oh, fuck -- he was in trouble.

Serious trouble.

He couldn't do this. Already close, already so hard he could drive titanium rivets with his dick, Sandy couldn't take Alex standing this close, moaning in his ear.

"Sandy. Oh, baby, do it. Do it to me, now. Please."

The breathy panting that followed had Sandy closing his eyes and banging his head on the door. He had just enough ironic detachment left to appreciate the fact that it worked for the act they were putting on; irony didn't do shit to distract Sandy from the tightness of his pants, though. Forcing his eyes open a crack, Sandy was just in time to see Alex raise an arm, almost as if he was going to—

Sandy blocked Alex's hand centimeters before it connected with his crotch.

"Don't."

Alex's grin faded. "Why not?"

Painfully aware of his situation, Sandy jerked his head in the direction of the room and away from the door. There wasn't much room to retreat into. Just a small table and chair set barely big enough to sip a cup of coffee at, a tiny hygiene area, a reconst' unit, and… a bed.

The bed was out.

Completely unsafe, uh-uh, no way.

"Sit there."

Giving Alex a little shove toward the bed, Sandy picked a spot on the floor a meter or so away and sat down.

"Sandy," Alex landed on the bed with a bounce and turned. "I can take care of it for you. It's no big deal."

Sandy tried not to glare; tried not to take it personally. But, damn it, it was personal.

"It should be a big deal, Alex. It's a big deal to me. It's my dick and I get to say who touches it -- and why. It's not a transaction and you don't get me off as a way to say thanks, got it?"

"But..." Confusion and hurt flickered over Alex's face. "But what if I wanted to?"

His dick and balls -- already lobbying hard that they had no problem being a transaction, in fact, it was okie dokie, A-OK with them -- surged at Alex's plaintive question.

"Wanted to why, though?"

Alex shrugged a shoulder. "I don't know. Because you've been nice. You're helping me out. It doesn't cost me anything and if it makes you happy, then that's okay."

Considering where they were, the kind of place Alex worked, and where Sandy had been spending most of his nights lately, this was going to sound a little odd. Sandy knew from experience that telling people what they ought to do was a waste of breath, but here he went anyway, trying. "Don't do it unless it makes you happy, too, Alex. It's too important."

Those big eyes stared at him. Sandy wanted to fall into them, pull Alex in around him and never climb out again. "But what if I just want to be nice? What if it's someone I like?"

"Alex." This was hard. Poor guy, he was so screwed up by what he'd been through. How to reach him without making him feel ignorant or like some kind of freak? "They took you so young. You didn't have a chance to work through any of this like a normal human being, did you?"

"Work through what? You need to get off -- I want to help you with it. What's so hard about that, except that you won't let me help?"

"Because sex should be more than that. It should be about two people who care about each other."

Something flickered behind Alex's eyes and his mouth took on a firmer line. "Like with you and Aaron, you mean? That must mean that you and Aaron really care about each other."

Crap. He hadn't thought anyone had noticed, least of all Alex. How to explain dabbling in sex with hired companions?

"That was... an experiment. An experiment that didn't work out."

"What, you didn't get off?" Alex was justifiably skeptical; *Nelly's* staff was nothing if not competent. Professional.

"Whether or not I got off isn't the point."

"It's not? Since when? Did you ask for your money back or not?"

"No. I didn't." Arms folded across his chest, gaze that wouldn't meet Sandy's... That might even be a quivering lip he saw, thrust out so bravely against the world. "That's not the right question though, Alex. The question should be, did I go back again? Did it buy me what I was looking for? The answers are 'no' and 'no.' I tried it and it didn't give me what I wanted."

"What did you want?"

Oh, shit. This was getting deep in a hurry and Sandy wasn't at all certain this was where he and Alex needed to go -- not at this juncture, anyway. Alex was plenty smart and Sandy should have known he wouldn't get away with simple statements or convenient half-truths.

"Emotional closeness. Affection. Love."

Alex's snort of derisive laughter wasn't flattering, but what did he expect? "Love? You're shopping in the seriously wrong store for that commodity, hon."

"Yeah, no shit." Sandy shook his head a little and glanced up at where Alex sat, gazing off at nothing. His eyes had a distant, unfocused look to them and Sandy wondered what he was seeing in his mind's eye. What was Alex's idea of love? Or did he even believe in it, considering what he'd done -- and what had been done to him? It was hard to imagine anyone looking at that quirky, unique, beautiful face and not immediately sensing the singular personality behind it. "No shit."

They sat, each lost in his own thoughts. At least, Sandy presumed Alex was thinking. Sandy was mostly just running his gaze over Alex's profile, with its straight, slightly upturned nose, strong jaw, and intelligent brow. And those lips. God. So full and pink. Now that he'd tasted them, Sandy only wanted more. He wanted to explore Alex's mouth, slip his tongue inside, nip and play and just…

Aw, man.

The hard-on that had been ebbing slightly was back. With a vengeance. The quiet was getting to Sandy. Knowing he and Alex were alone, with no prying eyes on them, free to do whatever they wanted, Sandy was hard again and fantasy after fantasy slipped into his mind. If he just kissed Alex a little, he could—

"Sandy, could I…?" Alex was turned back

toward him now, casting nervous looks at Sandy, around the room, and back to Sandy again. "Please. If you won't let me… do anything for you. How can I—?"

As if the furtive looks weren't enough, the gusty sigh of frustration that burst out of Alex would have been a big-ass clue. The atmosphere must be getting to Alex, too. How could it not? It was thick enough to reach out and touch. Sandy kept his voice deliberately calm. As a Marine sergeant, he'd worked with enough rookies to know somebody had to maintain calm.

"What, Alex?"

In agonies of…something, Alex shot him another tortured glance. "I need a favor, Sandy. How can I ask you when you've done so much already and you won't let me do anything for you?"

"Done? What have I done besides mooch drinks and cop a quick feel?"

"Just knowing you're in the picture is huge, don't you see? Joe's not going to really try anything with you around. I know it. Now that Nick's here and they're feeding off each other, it's going to be worse; except he won't push that hard if he thinks he might have to answer to you. See what I mean?"

"Alex, honey, what are you talking about?"

"Would you mind… could you sleep with me tonight?"

***

He'd gone too far.

Asked for too much.

The way Sandy was looking at him -- like he'd finally lost his mind -- was all Alex needed to know he'd pushed too hard. "Forget it. That's okay. I know you're busy."

He was babbling. But, God, what if he'd totally ruined things? What if Sandy decided not to help him? It wasn't impossible that Sandy might stop talking to him, period. Cut him off completely.

"It's the middle of the night, Alex. What am I supposed to be so busy doing?" A slow smile spread over Sandy's face. A wry smile, to be sure, but Alex would take anything.

"I don't know. Business-y stuff. Security stuff. Sending communications to your friends, maybe? Fucking cute go-go boys."

Sandy had the nerve to laugh at him. "Go-go boys?"

"Okay, Recreational Time Specialists, then. Whatever."

Openly laughing now, Sandy's eyes crinkled appealingly. "Say that again for me. That's too cute, the way you say it."

"Are you laughing at me? What a jerk. Forget it, then -- I don't need your help." Folding his arms, Alex looked away. Whatever. It was probably better this way, anyway. He'd learned to deal with things on his own a long time ago and the number one thing he'd learned was to never let his guard down. Never. Trust no one.

This really was better.

"Hey, hey. Calm yourself down. I was just having a little fun with you, Alex. As it happens I'm fresh out of go-go boys, so I'm free tonight. I can stay."

"Forget it. I don't need your help."

"Alex, come on. Lighten up, I was just playing. I'd like to stay."

Alex chanced a look. "Are you sure? You're not just goofing with me?"

"I'm not goofing with you. I'll stay."

Sandy's eyes were big and brown, his expression serious, but what did that quirk of his mouth mean? What if…? But Sandy had said he didn't expect anything in return. He'd said he was just doing it as a friend. Did friends sleep over to help out other friends? Alex didn't know. He was pretty sure he could still manage a handjob. He wouldn't have offered, otherwise. Anything more, though, was out of the question.

"Thanks. I appreciate it -- a lot." Alex stood. "You take the bed. It's probably smaller than you're used to, but—"

The truth was it was an efficiency apartment, and a rented one at that. There were more luxurious surroundings for the RaTS, both those who danced and performed in shows and those who couldn't dance or act to save their lives, but liked the straight fucking. The efficiencies were small and dorm-like -- strictly for accommodating new employees who weren't yet earning enough to move on to private quarters. Not that the rooms were exempt from all sexual activity; still, there was nothing luxurious about them.

"Thanks, but I'll take the floor." Sandy unfolded big, sturdy legs and pushed himself up to a standing position. "Mind if I take off my shirt?" Pausing as he reached for the bottom of the shirt, Alex realized Sandy was waiting for an answer.

Alex paused.

Swallowed.

"Sure. No problem. I'll just, um, change out of my work clothes. They stink by the end of the night; you probably noticed. I mean it, though, Sandy. You're taking the bed. I won't take no for an answer." When Sandy resumed pulling his shirt over his head, Alex grabbed his sleep clothes at the first glimpse of bare, tanned belly and fled to the bathroom.

Stalling as long as he could, Alex did his best to clean up. He took a quick shower, trying to distract himself from what Sandy must be doing by thinking of all the ways the hygiene units in the employee apartments weren't like the luxury models in the theme rooms.

Paying customers were paying major credits for a fantasy experience -- sometimes with a regular companion, other times with one of *Nelly's* highly skilled technicians -- so besides the basics, the rooms were filled with luxurious extras. Alex had been inside two: the Tahitian Room, filled with sand, palm trees that swayed in a realistic-feeling tropical breeze, and a fake moon that hung low in a balmy evening sky; and the Harem Room, where silk-covered walls, dozens of satin pillows littering the floor, hookahs, and fan-waving attendants completed the fantasy.

The lights in Alex's room were dimmed and it was quiet when he finally ran out of things to do and left the relative safety of the cleansing stall. Taking up most of the available floor space, Sandy lay flat on his back, his shirt wadded up and stuffed under his head as a pillow.

Alex wouldn't have believed it was possible, but Sandy with his shirt off was an even more impressive sight than just Sandy, period.

Kilometers of bare, cocoa-colored skin showed, with dark greenish-black tattoos in geometric shapes covering most of the exposed skin along one side of Sandy's body. Only having seen the bits extending up Sandy's neck previously and occasionally a small glimpse of the design covering the chest and pec, Alex had never imagined it was anywhere near that extensive. He couldn't distinguish much, but it looked dense, layered, almost like clothing in the room's poor lighting.

How far did it reach? Down the torso and leg, maybe?

"Come on, Alex. Maybe you can work half the night and party the rest, but some of us need a little shut-eye."

How could he possibly take the bed and leave Sandy to try to get comfortable on the floor? It was rude, bad hospitality, and no way to thank someone who was already putting himself out to help Alex.

"Sorry. But… Sandy, you agreed you'd take the bed."

"That's not the way I remember it. You offered -- I said no -- discussion over. If you really want, we can talk about it some more in the morning. Right now I'd like to get some sleep."

It didn't seem possible that Alex could feel Sandy's gaze on him in the dark, but he could. Felt the burn of it on his cheeks and face as he stood, looking ridiculous in his flannel pajama pants and threadbare t-shirt.

"Sandy—" Rolling away and onto one side, Sandy effectively ended their conversation.

So what was he supposed to do now? Sandy was huge -- he probably outweighed Alex by thirty kilos, if not more. There was no way Alex could make Sandy do anything.

He had to stick to his guns, though. He had to prove to Sandy that he meant what he said. Alex couldn't let the man get the idea that Sandy could just walk all over him. He'd worked hard to get this far and it seemed like every hurdle he made it over just brought five more into view.

"Okay, if that's the way you want to handle it." Alex grabbed his pillow from the head of the bed, pulled the blanket off next, and dropped them both on the floor beside Sandy. "Move over."

"You're not serious." Dark eyes glinting in the half-light, Sandy peered over his shoulder at Alex.

"I so am. If you can be a stubborn ass, so can I. Are you going to move over?" Alex couldn't tell if his bluff was working or not, but his stomach was tied in knots.

Sandy leaned back a little and just looked. "How long do you plan on keeping this up?"

"Until you agree to take the bed."

"Not while you sleep on the floor."

"Same here."

They stared at each other, Alex willing his eyes not to blink.

Sandy's gaze slipped over to the bed and then back to Alex. "We both can't sleep on that thing. It's maybe… what?… one-and-a-half by two meters? If that?"

"Then move over and give me some room here." Alex wasn't sure how much longer he could hold the glare. His eyeballs were drying out and his nose itched.

"You're tougher than you look, you know that? It would serve you right if I tossed you down on it and tied you there." For a moment, Alex couldn't speak. "Alex, I was kidding. Breathe, okay?"

He was okay again. He could breathe and blink and maybe even talk. Still he held back.

"Okay, okay, you win. I'll sleep on the bed. But you do, too, or the deal's off."

Chapter 6

Down.

Across.

Over.

Up again -- diagonally, this time. Back across. Down and over.

Designs traced slowly over Sandy's skin. Repeated endlessly, until he thought he was going to lose it.

Sandy'd already lost control of his body once. Asleep -- dreaming of Alex's kiss, of being completely naked, with Alex's hands on his body -- he'd slowly realized that was a real, live human touch on his back and not just some phantom conjured by his unfettered libido.

Not just any human touch, either. It was Alex, touching him, willingly. Tracing his tattoos.

He'd come in his pants.

Quiet as he'd been, though, Sandy didn't think Alex had noticed. Or if he had, it hadn't stopped Alex. He was still driving Sandy crazy with touches so light they were barely there. But, oh, were they there. Little shivers raced up Sandy's spine at random intervals, his scalp prickling with awareness. He fought a whole-body shudder of desire.

Alex was touching him.

Sandy called on his soldier's training to hold as still as he possibly could, while Alex drove him slowly out of his mind.

"Sandy. Sandy, are you awake?" A puff of warm breath ghosted over Sandy's back. A tentative touch of a hand passed lightly over his shoulder blade as Sandy lay on his side, turned away from Alex and facing the wall. "Sandy?" Warm, moist heat. Lips. A kiss, placed tenderly on his back.

"Yeah?" Sandy kept his voice low, afraid to break the spell.

"How long have you been awake?" The hand gently stroked the bumps and hollows of Sandy's neck and spine, moving down into the groove of his lower back.

Closing his eyes, Sandy focused on breathing in to a slow five count, then out again. Lust, combined with something even more powerful rolled over him. Afraid of losing control completely if he was to turn around and face Alex, Sandy held still. "A little while."

"Why didn't you say anything?"

"Like what?"

A soft lick flicked across Sandy's shoulder blade. Alex's tongue on his skin -- his bare skin. God!

"Like, 'Hey, who's that touching me?' Or maybe, 'Hey, who's that licking my back?'"

Sandy slowly -- slow as a glacier, slow as military pay -- raised his hand to where Alex's rested on his hip and very carefully placed it over Alex's. It was all he could do not to take Alex's hand in his and hold it to his ever-hopeful hard on, the mere thought of pushing into Alex's hand drawing an involuntary flex from Sandy's hips. "How about, 'Why is Alex licking me in the first place?' Huh?"

"Good question. I don't know. To see what you taste like? You taste pretty good, actually."

"Lot of people taste good, Alex. Why me? Why now?"

"Do they, really?" There was a brush of soft hair across Sandy's skin as Alex rested his head against Sandy's back.

"Sure. You don't think so?" Sandy dragged a suffering breath into his lungs. He wanted… Sandy wanted… everything. Anything. Anything Alex was offering.

"Not really. I mean, if you're high enough, you can tolerate just about anything -- I should know. But actually enjoy it? No way."

You can tolerate just about anything.

Sandy dropped his head, burying it in his arms. He had to get out of here. He was only human -- he could only stand so much torture. Every time Alex shifted so much as a millimeter, some body part of his came into contact with some part of Sandy. A foot. A knee. A calf.

Sandy wanted…he'd give a lot to be able to roll over and press Alex into the mattress, grinding their cocks together as they kissed, until the glorious friction took them both over the edge. Or to lie on his back and have Alex crawl over him, jack him, ride him -- anything. Touch him. God. He could even just lie back and watch Alex touch himself; he was so far gone that something so simple as that would do it for him.

Way to go, dumbass. Way to get your mind off your dick by thinking of all the things you'd like to do with it. "Alex, I need to use the head."

"The... oh, right. Gotcha." Alex scrambled off the bed, tangling his feet in the bedding and nearly falling on his face in his hurry to get out of Sandy's way. Jesus, what had they done to him inside that place? "You know where? Of course you do. Okay, I'll just... it's..."

"It's okay, Alex. I'm just using the head." With a hard on he could drive rivets with, although he saw no need to mention that fact. Not that there was much of a way to hide it, though, without so much as his shirt to hold in front of himself. Maybe he could pass it off as just an everyday morning erection. Sure, that could work. Sandy rolled off the bed, telling himself to act natural. He could sell this.

The harder Sandy tried to avoid Alex's eyes, though, the more the thought of them drew him. The way your balls itch the second you're hunkered down in a foxhole, or how the mere fact of being in a church made him want to swear. Sandy glanced briefly to where Alex stood, two meters away, gaze glued determinedly on the floor.

It was the subtle shift of weight from foot to foot that got to Sandy, even more than the single furtive glance up, before he resumed his thorough examination of the floor. Much as Sandy wanted to go to Alex and hold him -- even the vague idea of what might have conditioned that kind of behavior into someone as intelligent as Alex was like a fist to his gut -- Sandy knew he couldn't.

Which only pissed him off more, the frustration giving his voice an edge. "Alex, it's okay. Just give me a second?"

Biting his lip, Alex nodded.

Shit.

Sandy stepped into the tiny hygiene station, closing the flimsy accordion-style folding door with force born of intense frustration. Goddammit, this was looking more hopeless by the minute. What made him think he had what it took to fix problems the size of Alex's? Just because he was the fix-it king of the unit, the one everyone from Sarhaan on down looked to to come up with the solution for whatever was broken? Was his ego really that oversized that he'd taken one look at Alex and thought, 'Sure, you can do it?'

More like he'd passed the time after his friends left him behind by drinking too much and watching too many pretty boys getting off while he kept a not-so-casual eye on their old friend. It might have started out as a favor to Sarhaan and Kai, but it hadn't stayed that way for long. Alex and he had talked, traded insults and observations, and somehow become the unlikeliest of friends.

So when had, 'He's an okay guy' become 'He's so beautiful, I want him more than my next breath'?

As Sandy peeled off the pants he'd worn to the club the night before and the sticky briefs beneath, he mused on what had recently become his obsession: how to reach Alex without scaring the shit out of him and traumatizing him further. Figuring Alex's economy flat didn't come with many extras, Sandy decided to forgo a shower and instead found a washcloth.

Cleaning the partially dried semen from his body, the dampened material stroked the sensitized skin of his dick. As he rinsed out the cloth and wiped down his balls, Sandy tried telling himself he wasn't a pervert for enjoying the way it felt.

He was naked in Alex's room, with only a crappy folding curtain between the two of them. He'd slept in Alex's bed and woken to Alex's touch on his body. Holding the washcloth under the hot water outlet, squeezing out the excess before palming it with one hand and applying it to his aching cock, Sandy finished the clean up job. Still, he couldn't get away from the feeling that there was something disgusting and predatory about jerking off in the bathroom while Alex was just a few meters away, any more than he could keep from closing his eyes and imagining it was Alex's hand that stroked him as he came for the second time that morning.

Tossing the briefs in the waste bin for Alex to find was as unacceptable as the idea of putting them on again, so Sandy rolled them up and stuffed them in a pocket after donning his pants. He snorted at the realization that this was about as close as he got these days to being a commando, shoved the curtain aside, and stepped back into Alex's room.

Alex had moved to the bed, where he sat, staring at the floor while he kicked his legs restlessly. "Everything okay?"

"Yeah. Shouldn't it be?"

Looking up, then down at his feet again, Alex shrugged. "I don't know. You just, kind of took a while. I never heard you pee."

A flush of heat rolled up Sandy's neck and he hoped somehow his natural color hid the blush. "I borrowed some water and a washcloth and gave myself a once-over. I'll take care of it with Sotheran if I put you over your limit."

"No, it's okay. Of course it's okay. It's the least—"

"Would you shut up with the gratitude, already? I told you, it's no big deal, Alex."

"But it is a big deal. Don't you see?"

Sandy looked away and scratched an elbow. Those eyes would be the death of him yet. "Listen, what do you usually do for breakfast? If I'm your fella and I'm trying to show you any kind of a decent time, I'm probably taking you out. What do you like to eat?"

"Not much. Just coffee, usually."

Sighing, Sandy looked Alex up and down. "That's right. You're not much of a morning person. I forgot. Well, you could stand to put on a few kilos and, besides, we're giving folks a show. Get dressed and I'll take you to Grandma's."

***

"Can I get you folks anything else? Coffee? More French toast?"

"Nothing. We're fine, thanks." Alex hoped that would shut the guy up and get him out of there, but no. He just stared expectantly at Sandy, tonguing the stylus he used to take orders with like he wanted to give it fellatio.

"Alex, you sure? You didn't eat much." Sandy's arm rested along the top of the booth, millimeters from Alex's shoulders, sitting so close that when Alex turned to meet his gaze, the scents of coffee and the maple syrup he'd poured over his breakfast toast filled Alex's lungs.

"Are you kidding? I'm stuffed. Couldn't eat another bite." Letting his gaze fall from Sandy's eyes to Sandy's mouth, Alex smiled. He knew as long as Sandy was pretending to be with him, little waiter boy wouldn't get the time of day, but it didn't hurt to play it up a bit. So he dipped a finger into the puddle of syrup remaining on Sandy's plate and touched it to Sandy's lower lip. "Well, maybe one more mouthful."

Alex didn't need the indrawn breath in stereo to let him know he'd scored a direct hit. The way Sandy's eyes half-closed, even as his mouth opened to draw Alex's finger inside, would have been enough. The waiter's sharpened gaze as he watched with avid interest was obvious and Alex wondered for a moment who else might be watching. Letting Sandy hold his finger in place with suction alone, Alex paused briefly before drawing it out, running it back and forth over Sandy's lower lip. He gazed into Sandy's warm, chocolate eyes before turning to dismiss the waiter. "We'll call if we need you."

The waiter left and Sandy's groan drew him back as Sandy's arm curled closer around Alex's shoulder. Dropping his head as though to nuzzle Alex's neck, Sandy used the closeness to murmur in Alex's ear. "Whoa, babe. Save the big guns for the important battles, okay? I don't think my heart can take much more of what you were dishing out." Sandy took small nips at Alex's neck as he kissed and nibbled his way up. Alex arched his neck to give Sandy more room and closed his eyes, as though overcome with passion.

Except, he wasn't completely faking.

It really did feel good, the way Sandy used his lips and teeth and tongue. Shivers chased over Alex's skin, even as a small curl of warmth heated up in Alex's groin. So alien it was almost unknown, the tingling in his dick increased and he started to get hard.

Now it was Alex's turn to suck in his breath. He even groaned a little, so startled he reached out to steady himself, blindly grabbing Sandy's arm.

Clients always wanted to think they had great technique; that they were the one who could draw a genuine response from a pro; they must be something special if they made a whore groan. Just because no one wanted to think they'd been conned or that every response from the moment they stepped through the door was scripted, didn't mean they couldn't or that it wasn't. Just like no one lasted very long in the sex business if they couldn't fake the basics at least moderately well and Alex had survived for almost ten years.

"Alex." Sandy drew back, one big hand coming up to cradle Alex's face. Stroking a thumb over Alex's cheek, Sandy's voice dropped to a whisper. "Alex." And then Sandy kissed him, full on the mouth, kissed him with a tenderness that threatened to shatter him into a thousand tiny pieces.

Sandy's tongue, smooth and sleek, like nothing Alex had ever felt before, stroked gently into his mouth. Lips, firm but gentle, played with Alex's, drawing Alex's lip through them only to let it slide slowly back into place.

Glorious.

It was a wonder, how something so simple could feel so good, make Alex feel so cherished.

"Hey, D'abu. I thought that was you. Glad to see you finally getting some. Finally figured out which way you swing, I guess."

A little disoriented and a lot turned on, it took Alex a few seconds to realize the gravel-voiced commentary was aimed at them. Sandy pulled Alex closer, lifting his head to gaze with a cold-eyed stare that would make most men wet themselves. "Dave. Still hanging around, huh? You know, that's the problem with life on an asteroid -- taking out the trash is almost always more trouble than it's worth."

Alex recognized the man standing provocatively close to their table. Blond, not bad-looking, Alex'd seen him in *Nelly's* a few times; more often when Alex had first started than lately. With a gift for causing trouble and -- more importantly-- a lousy tipper, Alex hadn't missed his business. Hadn't even noticed his absence until now.

"Yeah, still hanging around, D'abu. Kinda like you, I guess. Where's the rest of your buddies? Off having fun and leaving you to take care of business? I guess some things never change."

"Dave, if I wasn't so comfortable right now I'd take you outside for a little private conversation. But I am." Sandy interrupted his monologue to brush a kiss over Alex's hair, his voice cold. Alex decided Dave must be dimmer than he looked to even think about yanking Sandy's chain. "I'm going to kiss my man here, and if you're not gone by the time I'm done, I promise you this'll be the last conversation you and I will ever have. Is that plain enough, even for a moron like you?"

The tension in Sandy's body telegraphed itself to Alex, his stomach beginning to knot up as the conversation escalated.

"Hey, hey, hey, now. Don't get your blood

pressure up there, big guy. I've got bigger fish than you to fry, don't worry. In fact -- how's this? -- I'll even make you an offer. You ever get tired of wasting your time playing grease monkey for Sarhaan, you let me know. I'll put you to work making enough credits to afford a rental with… uh, how shall I say it… a few less miles under the hood?"

Alex gasped. He didn't know what Dave's history was with Sandy, but Sandy and Sarhaan were like brothers.

"Dave, you'd better go now. We'll talk about this again later."

Smile fading rapidly, Dave shot Sandy a measuring look, "Looking forward to it, D'abu. See you around, barkeep." Tossing the sugar packet he'd been toying with in Alex's direction, he sauntered off.

Alex looked up at Sandy, the impassive expression on his face now overtaken by annoyance. "What an asshole. Sandy, how did you keep from slugging him? I wanted to hit him and I've never hit anyone in my life."

Sandy's gaze remained on the door, hard and flinty, following Dave's exit. Long moments passed and Alex wondered if Sandy had heard him. Thought about repeating the question and decided against it.

When the look in Sandy's eyes finally softened, he turned back to Alex. "How do I keep from hitting him? Practice. A lot of practice."

"How do you know him? What a dick."

"We were in the service together. Matter of fact, he was part of my unit for a long time up until a few months ago, when Sarhaan finally got fed up and tossed him out. Good move on Sarhaan's part."

"Good for Sarhaan. I wanted to kick his ass. The jerk called you a grease monkey."

Sandy was smiling at him, a hand in Alex's hair and stroking Alex's cheek again. "You wanted to kick his ass, huh? That's great. I'm glad to hear that."

"Don't patronize me." Alex's breath hitched as Sandy closed his eyes and kissed Alex on the forehead. Still worked up over that jerk who'd insulted his friends, Alex needed to burn off the nervous energy buzzing around inside him. But how was he supposed to do that when Sandy made his insides go all squishy? "And don't try to get around me with sex, either, because it won't work."

"Is that what I'm doing?" Sandy kissed Alex's neck again, opened his mouth and took gentle little bites along Alex's jaw line, until he'd worked his way around to Alex's mouth. "What do you figure I'm doing now?"

Sandy held him close, one arm around Alex's shoulder while the other slipped up his thigh, until it came to rest on his hip. Restrained, Alex should have been shutting down -- closing off his feelings until the unpleasant thing passed, the way he'd done so many times it had become not just second nature, but default response.

Alex was amazed to realize he didn't want to. Sandy smelled good and tasted better. For maybe the first time in Alex's life, a strong man's surrounding presence felt warm and sheltering instead of cold and frightening.

He trusted Sandy. Somewhat, anyway.

Besides, they were in a public place. A

restaurant. How out of hand could things get?

Sandy's kiss wasn't overpowering, it was just right. Slow and wet: just a little suction. His tongue was gentle and coaxing, not jammed down Alex's throat like a weapon. Alex let his head relax against the arm behind it, trusting Sandy to hold him and not let him fall, and soaked it all in.

It was nice. Alex couldn't remember a better kiss in his entire life.

Slipping his hand underneath Sandy's shirt, Alex sought skin, curling his fingers into Sandy's side when he found it. Sandy squirmed, twisting sideways.

Alex broke away. "What's the matter? Is it not okay to touch you?"

"No, it's okay. Touching is definitely good. You just caught me in a sensitive place." Sandy's nostrils flared with his heavy breathing, two furrowed lines bisecting his brow. Alex couldn't tell if Sandy was giving him the straight story or not.

"You are not ticklish. If you don't want me touching you there -- or anywhere -- just tell me. I don't have to." Alex looked around. There were no other occupied tables anywhere near them. "We can relax. There's no one watching."

"Alex, can I be totally honest with you? No bullshit -- just the real deal?"

Sandy looked absolutely dead-on serious. Already his breathing was slowing, but the intensity in his eyes said that Alex was the only person on his mind right now. Whatever it was Sandy had to say, it was going to be bad.

Alex squared his shoulders and nodded. "Absolutely. You can tell me anything, Sandy."

Sitting silently for a moment, when Sandy finally stirred it was to lift his hand. He ran the backs of two fingers down Alex's cheek, smiling a little despite the stubble Alex hadn't shaved off that morning abrading them. Stupid. He should have shaved.

"I should have—"

"Sssh. No, stop," when Alex tried to speak. "I like it. Even if they hadn't lasered me, I could let mine grow for a month and not get that much. It's nice. Sexy."

Alex looked at him suspiciously. Sandy hadn't been drinking. Had he been successfully hiding mental instability from Alex all this time?

"But what I was going to say was, no one has to be watching for me to want to kiss you. I like kissing you. No other reason that that. Just for me. Because I like it."

Looking into Sandy's deep brown eyes, Alex stared hard, trying to read what was in Sandy's heart. It would be just like him to try to ease Alex's guilt by taking more responsibility on his broad shoulders. Sandy was a good guy that way.

"Sandy. I don't know …"

"I mean it. Just for me. No other reason." Sandy lowered his head again, moving to within millimeters of Alex's mouth, only to stop. "Will you kiss me? Just you. Just me. No one else."

The next thing Alex knew, they were kissing. He didn't know who'd moved, but it was another sweet, serious kiss of amazing, unbelievable tenderness. Tongues and lips and heat, and Alex groaned. Sandy's hands cupped his face, and he hung on to Sandy's waist as the world spun around him.

"Oh, for God's sake, D'abu. I told you to keep an eye on him, not molest the man in a public restaurant."

Chapter 7

"I hope you know what you're doing, bro."

Sandy'd known it was coming. Had been expecting it, in fact.

While they walked the short distance between Grandma's Café and the team's storefront headquarters, Sandy and Sarhaan were comparing notes on both the trip to 10-Hygiea and Sandy's progress on drumming up new business. He didn't like having to put Alex aside, but the team was back and work would begin in earnest again.

"Don't I always? I'll probably need Naslund and maybe Sutton or Vilnius to help out with the life support system, but the rest of this should be no big deal." Sandy indicated his mini-comp, now loaded not only with his own list of regular maintenance and wish list of upgrades he'd like to implement, but the crew's bitch list of things they'd managed to break on the short trip just completed. "I've never been happy with the water system, but you know that. Money and time permitting, there's a new strain of Nitrobacter I'd like to try and see if I can get rid of some of the metallic taste. It'll mean stripping the whole system back to nothing, but I think the results'll be worth the effort."

The trip had been the longest in the brand-new

company's short history and Sandy, as acting chief engineer, really should have been on it. Inner ear infections bowed to no man, however, and the one that had plagued Sandy had been maddeningly tough to kick. Due possibly to the long periods in artificial gravity, no one was sure, what should have been a minor ailment had hung on with dogged tenaciousness. Since the art-grav on a ship the size of the *Vigilant* was even more suspect, and as Sandy rather liked being able to hear, he'd reluctantly agreed to stay behind.

"You're the expert on that one; I trust your judgment. But I wasn't talking about the ship and I think you know that. I'd like a sit-rep on the Alex situation. If you can spare the time."

Sandy looked at his friend, his nominal boss, and took in the body language: the hands clasped behind the back, the slightly raised eyebrow, the no-nonsense expression on that face. Sarhaan had been noticeably mellower since they'd landed on Doradus -- since settling into domestic bliss with Caleb. So mellow, in fact, that Sandy had gotten used to the more relaxed, 'run a clean shop and don't bother me with minutiae' leadership style Sarhaan had adopted since falling for Cal and all of his glorious blond cuteness.

On the outside Sarhaan might still be every inch the intimidating warrior, but knowing he had something to live for besides Honor, God, and Corps had changed him. Maybe it was knowing he had someone at home who cared whether he lived or died -- Caleb certainly filled that bill. In Caleb's eyes, Sarhaan hadn't hung just the moon, but the planets and every hunk of orbiting rock as far as the Kuiper Belt. For his part, Sarhaan looked at

Caleb with an expression that told anyone with eyes to see that he'd rip the beating heart out of any man's chest who thought he could come between them.

Sandy had worked and fought alongside Sarhaan for enough years to know he was fully capable of delivering on that threat.

It was the God's honest truth, though, that it got a little hard to take sometimes. Not that he begrudged Sarhaan happiness; not by any means. But Ess was his friend, his compatriot, his teammate since boot camp, and he'd gotten used to having Sarhaan's ear first. Taken it for granted, even. Caleb had done his best to fit in with the rest of the team -- not always easy as the only civilian on board -- and no one questioned that Caleb had Sarhaan's interests foremost in his mind any more. In fact, to the average bystander the intensity of the blaze between them could be a little blinding at times.

Sandy was starting to realize, though, just what a man might be willing to do to get something like that for himself and viewed his friend accordingly. "Alex is doing okay. He's got steady work, no enemies that I know of, and as far as I can tell he's not on anything."

"Good. That's good. So… mind telling me exactly what I saw going on back there?"

The businesslike pace of their walk slowed and Sandy's hands, jammed into his pants pockets, tensed. "Guess that depends on who's asking. My friend, or my CO?" Sandy took a deep breath and checked Sarhaan's reaction from the corner of his eye.

"A little of both." Sarhaan's hands, like usual,

were clasped behind his back, his hair hung past his shoulders in its customary mass of small braids. "I feel responsible for Alex, and I'm the one who asked you to keep an eye on him. Were you looking after business the best way you know how, or was that something a little more personal, maybe?

Little bubbles of resentment began floating up in Sandy. Who he chose to get involved with was nobody's business but his own. Sarhaan might be the nominal leader of their ragged little bunch, but it had been a lot of years since Sandy'd answered to anyone about his personal life. Stopping, Sandy stood still to meet Sarhaan's gaze.

Opening his mouth to tell Sarhaan to go fuck himself, Sandy thought better of it and closed it -- before he said something he couldn't take back. His friend knew him well enough to read the silence, though, and, for whatever reason, wasn't willing to let it go. "What? Why don't you tell me what's on your mind?"

Sandy stared. Words welled up in his throat, only to jam. A small part of him wouldn't mind some help on this one -- somebody to bounce ideas off of. But the other, larger part of him said this was too personal. Nobody else's damn business. "Nothing to talk about."

One of Sarhaan's eyebrows went up. "Really?"

"Nope."

"Odd, because I can think of any number of times you've protected a target, but I don't ever recall you having to swap spit with one before."

"Nothing to say." This had nothing to do with security, safety, or anything at all to do with the team. Sandy wasn't going to talk about it and he gazed steadily back at Sarhaan until the message sank in.

"D'abu! What's up, my man?" Kai Xuwicha, XO of the *Vigilant* and number two behind Sarhaan, slapped Sandy on the back. "Tell me good things about the business you brought in."

Sandy turned to Kai, keeping an eye on Sarhaan as he moved on. "Hey, Kai. I got a couple of things on the line."

***

"Sandy, comm line two for you."

"Thanks, Jimi." Sandy set down the filter canister he'd been working on and grabbed a towel to dry his hands as he headed for the nearest comm unit. Gesturing at Naslund, elbow-deep in the ship's water treatment system, to keep going, Sandy pressed the connect button. "D'abu here.

"Sandy, hi. It's Alex. What are you doing?"

Alex's voice carried and Nas looked up, speculation sparking to full-blown life instantly in his eyes. Weighing privacy against the pain-in-the-ass factor of going to the nearest private unit, Sandy decided to grit his teeth and try to keep the conversation short.

"Hey, Alex."

"Yeah, I… I just wondered if, maybe, you're coming by tonight?"

"I can't." Sandy glanced at Naslund, who wasn't even pretending to be focused on his work, listening with blatant interest. "I'm stuck on the ship tonight. I've got this job going that I can't walk away from and everybody figures I've just had three weeks of shore leave, so I'm getting no sympathy. What are you doing? A word of warning, though: you're on speaker and Naslund's listening to every lascivious word, so watch what you say."

"Oh. Well—" Sandy could hear the hesitation; could almost see Alex chewing his lower lip. "I was, I saw the other guys come in and I was… just hoping I'd see you."

The disappointment in Alex's voice sounded real and Sandy wondered who was listening in on Alex's end. Individual comm units weren't allowed in any of the performance rooms at *Nelly's*, so where was Alex calling from? "Me, too. I can't get away right now, though."

"That's too bad. Last night was…" Sandy closed his eyes and leaned his forehead on the comm unit as Alex's voice softened. Watch what you're saying, honey. "I really liked it."

Naslund's grin only got wider. The little fucker was really enjoying this. "Yeah, me, too. I'm sorry, babe, but I'm stuck. Hopefully, I'll get this finished soon, so hopefully tomorrow."

Sandy raised a hand to the comm unit, his fingers curling inward as though to stroke the words that emanated from it; caress the unit itself if he couldn't have Alex.

"Oh. Serious? That's too bad." Alex's voice dropped to a whisper. "I'd really like to see you."

Flashing back to sharing Alex's bed, Sandy scraped his fingertips over the half-dozen holes in the speaker panel. The sound quality was so-so, but he could still remember what Alex's voice sounded like from the adjoining pillow. "Me, too. I'm sorry, Alex."

They'd hardly done more than kiss, and even

that had been tentative and fraught with misunderstandings and false starts, but already Sandy thought of Alex as his and wasn't that crazy? This was just a game. A game they played for the benefit of Alex's employers and the rest of the people around him. Not that Sandy wouldn't like to make it real, but he had to keep in mind that it wasn't. Not yet, anyway.

"Maybe I could… forget it. Have a good night, Sandy. I hope your job goes okay. Comm me when you have a chance?"

Oh, hell. Sandy slumped against the bulkhead, folding his arms and tucking his hands beneath his armpits. Alex never asked for much. Watching him night after night at *Nelly's*, Sandy knew Alex worked hard and pulled his weight, rarely made a fuss. What had it cost Alex to find an available comm line and contact him?

"Listen," Sandy checked to see if Naslund was still listening and shot the man a look that said he'd remove the man's tonsils through his asshole if Nas didn't get back to work. "I can't leave the ship, but there's no rule that says you can't come here. I have to check on this water system every couple of hours until I get it up and running, but you could come and hang out in my quarters."

"Really? That'd be terrific. I'll stay out of your way, I promise. You'll hardly know I'm there. You're sure, now?"

"I'm sure." The little bloom of warmth in his gut told Sandy he was doing the right thing -- whatever the personal cost to himself. "You know how to get here?"

***

One down, two to go.

Two more sections of airlock and Alex would be off the station and on the *Vigilant*. Off Doradus for the first time in six months. Odd how he didn't remember being bothered by the small chambers in between sections before. He didn't remember being claustrophobic the last time, but the size of them, the thickness of the walls, was really getting to him.

Alex snorted. Maybe he should admit that the reason he didn't remember was because the last time he'd been through the airlocks he'd been coming down off the drugs, crashing hard, and the truth was he didn't remember much of anything from that period. Alternately burning up and freezing cold, Alex's only hazy recollection from that time was of ants -- the grotesque blue-green ants he'd thought were climbing out of his clothes, crawling on his skin, chewing the flesh from his bones. He'd scratched his skin raw, even after he'd landed on Doradus and Joe Sotheran had taken him in.

Shaking himself like a dog coming out of the water, Alex shoved the memories aside. That was all behind him now. He was doing okay. He had a job. A few friends. Sort of. Sandy wouldn't have agreed to help him if he was a total loser, so he had that going for him.

Sandy.

He was looking forward to being with Sandy like he hadn't looked forward to being with someone in… Alex searched his memory. A long time. Ever, maybe.

There had been Nick, of course. Alex could remember a time when he'd looked forward to seeing Nick so much that he'd practically vibrated with anticipation: scared, excited, his stomach doing somersaults. Nick had been dangerous and thrilling, and it made Alex laugh now to think about what a stupid hick kid he'd been about his first time. His first love.

Love.

Alex pulled the borrowed coat he wore closer and rolled his eyes at himself. Nobody was that naïve.

No one but him, that was.

A flicker of movement caught Alex's eye, making him sit up straighter. There wasn't much traffic at this hour, most people preferring to stick to a schedule that mimicked terrestrial Earth, so in the wee hours of the morning Alex had the chamber to himself.

Squinting, Alex tried to decide if -- yes, that was someone at the window -- the far window on the other side of the next chamber. A series of three airlocks separated the precious artificial atmosphere inside the rotating cylinder of the asteroid-turned-space-station from the void of space, and someone was at the window of the third, looking in at him.

Pushing himself to his feet, Alex approached the window. His distance vision stunk to begin with, and adding in the two sets of double-paned windows doomed him. It might be Sandy, though, so he gave a little wave before returning to his seat, self-conscious as hell.

He couldn't sit still. Alex jiggled his knees; bounced on the balls of his feet; crossed and uncrossed his arms. God, how long did this process take? Between the tram ride and the pressurized airlocks, it felt like he'd been traveling for days.

Oh, come on Alex. He's just a man. They all put their boots on one foot at a time.

Maybe.

Sandy was different. He just seemed so… decent. As if there was such a thing. Sandy would never— Alex shook his head again. No need to revisit those memories any more than necessary. They were even beginning to fade a little, so let them already.

Alex looked down at his feet, encased in the same pair of ordinary black work shoes he wore every day, and wished he had something a little nicer. He shouldn't worry about it, he knew. No one had to tell him about the futility of worrying about what couldn't be changed.

Still.

It would be nice, just for once, to be appreciated for who he was.

The magnetic lock clicked open and the door rolled slowly back.

Two down, one more to go.

***

"You made it."

The third and last door had finally opened and Sandy swept Alex into a hug, burying his face in Alex's hair; holding tight. Alex didn't know what do with his hands, but he was pretty sure he ought to do something with them, so he tried placing them carefully on Sandy's back.

Tongue-tied and shy suddenly, Alex fumbled for something to say. Anything. "Yeah." Oh, brilliant conversationalist.

Sandy had sounded truly busy, tied up with work, and probably didn't have time to waste keeping Alex company. It was too late to worry about that, though. He was here. Now what did they do about it?

Sandy pulled back, running his hands up Alex's arms, cupping Alex's face. A big man, Sandy had hands to match and they were enormous, easily spanning the back of Alex's head as his thumbs stroked circular patterns along Alex's jaw. "I'm glad. But you'd better kiss me if you want anyone to believe we're in love."

"In love?" Alex's mouth fell open.

"Yeah. We're crazy about each other." Eyes twinkling, Sandy gave Alex a rakish grin. Anyone looking at Sandy would no doubt believe him. Drawing closer, shoving the bulky borrowed jacket aside, Sandy's eyes got that hooded, I'm-thinking-of-sex look in them. "Now kiss me."

Hands pressed flat against Sandy's back, Alex was mesmerized by the look in Sandy's eyes. Suddenly aware of the proximity of Sandy's dick, a jolt of apprehension shot through Alex.

When Sandy's lips touched his, though, the apprehension turned into something else. Something different and much more interesting. The little tingle that had begun in Alex's groin, back at *Nelly's*, was back. What was even more strange about it was that Alex realized he liked it. Maybe even wanted some more of it.

Pressing closer, Alex gave up his mouth to Sandy's kiss; splayed his hands across the muscles of Sandy's back and let Sandy's tongue lick into him. A heartfelt groan gave Alex the confidence to chase after Sandy's tongue a little with his own as

Sandy's retreated.

Running his hands through Alex's hair, Sandy broke the kiss, pulling Alex deeper into his embrace, Sandy's heavy sigh bringing their bodies into even closer contact. Surprising himself by how much he liked it, Alex clasped his hands together behind Sandy's back and looked up. "In love, huh?"

"Oh, absolutely. Deeply. Wildly. Crazy in love." Sandy smiled and gave a little wink. When Alex smiled back, Sandy swung them in the direction of the ship, away from the airlock, and dropped an arm over Alex's shoulders. "C'mon. I'll show you where to stash your gear. Then you can decide if you want to eat, sleep, or just hang out."

"Gear?"

Sandy swung something in his free hand and Alex recognized his own carryall, obscured by the jacket that had landed on it. So dazzled by Sandy's greeting, he'd forgotten its very existence. "Oh, right."

Half expecting to see a crowd, Alex was a little let down that they made it all the way to Sandy's quarters without meeting a soul. Fitting his hand to a thermal imager, the door slid open for Sandy and he led Alex inside.

Not nearly as palatial as Alex had imagined, still, it was larger than Alex's own room back at *Nelly's*. The bed was huge. But, then, so was Sandy. A small table, a couple of chairs built on the same scale as the bed, a desk and a computer completed the furnishings.

"It's nice." Alex smiled encouragingly as he looked around.

"Not exactly the Governor's suite, but at least I don't have to share."

"Yeah, that would be bad. You're a little past it for the whole roommate bit."

Sandy head came up. "Hey. Watch who you're calling old there, junior."

"Oh, please. Would you get over yourself already?" Feeling lighthearted -- playful, even -- in a way that was totally new and unfamiliar, Alex nudged Sandy. "You know you're the hottest thing to hit town since portable virtual reality units. Don't try to play coy."

Laughing, Sandy nudged back. "Holy shit, I'd ask what you're smoking, but I thought you quit all that."

"You know I did. And watch who you're pushing there, old man. You have no idea who you're dealing with here. No idea at all." Alex got a lucky shot in, rocking Sandy back on his heels with a well-timed shove.

"You little—" Alex never even saw Sandy move. The next thing Alex knew he was falling backwards, bouncing a little on the firm mattress as Sandy followed him down. Caged between Sandy's arms, legs pinned by one of Sandy's, Alex gasped for air. Not even breathing hard, Sandy grinned down at him. "I'm sorry, what was that again? No idea? I'm saying I've got me some hot new stranger in my bed and it's looking mighty tasty."

A little thrill of terror washed over Alex, but it was gone so quickly, that what remained felt like a shot of pure adrenalin. The scent of Sandy's skin surrounded Alex, the intimate fragrance of the man floating up from the bed beneath them, earthy and sensuous. Grabbing Sandy's arms for leverage, Alex squirmed, the thought of Sandy pressing his full weight down on Alex unexpectedly exciting.

He was alone in Sandy's suite, pinned down by a man half-again his own size -- so why wasn't he terrified?

Because it was Sandy, of course.

Slowly, the leg pinning Alex shifted, until Sandy sat nearly astride Alex. With gradual, deliberate movements -- maintaining eye contact the whole time -- Sandy aligned their bodies so that their rapidly hardening dicks brushed. One slightly raised eyebrow seemed to ask permission and Alex's body responded for him with a tentative wriggle of his hips.

Just a tiny movement, really, but Alex was shocked. Shocked at himself and at Sandy, too, whose eyes sparked in response. A man like Sandy could have anyone he wanted; why was Sandy wasting time on someone like him?

Alex let his gaze slide away from Sandy's, to where his hands were inching their way up Sandy's arms; feeling their way past the elbows and up to those impressive biceps. "I like your arms."

Stupid. God, how inane. But something about Sandy being on top of him like that, touching him, did things to Alex's brain.

"I like yours, too. All of you, in fact. So pretty." Sandy smiled softly before lifting a hand to run a finger down Alex's nose, and then drag it across Alex's lower lip.

A little dazed by the wonder of it all, Alex got positively swooney when Sandy shifted his hips a little and dragged his dick over Alex's. So much so, that the swoosh of the door opening barely even registered with Alex's overwhelmed senses.

"Hey, chief! First cycle is finished. You wanna—? Whoa. Hey. Sorry, I guess not."

Chapter 8

"I'm really sorry about…"

Sandy took a few drops of water from the sample he'd drawn and dropped it onto the test cartridge. As he waited for the water to be drawn up into the chip's various reservoirs, he listened to Naslund's seventh or eighth fumbled apology with half an ear.

"… that. I had no idea."

"Nas?" Sandy kept his gaze fixed on the test cartridge. He focused on plugging it into the tester unit, because if he didn't he might have to kill Naslund. Wouldn't want to. Wasn't even sure a court would consider it murder, more like justifiable homicide.

"Yeah?"

"Shut up."

"But, Chief—"

Wrenching his gaze away from the test chip, he stared hard at Jacob Naslund's hastily turned back. The smaller man had turned abruptly and begun wiping away the excess water from the outside casing of the system's main bacteria culture chamber.

"Right. Shutting up, Chief."

Sandy knew he was close to losing it. He'd had Alex in his arms, in his bed. They'd nearly had intimate, genital to genital contact. The feel of Alex's tongue in his mouth, Alex's taste on his lips -- it was all still there. God, he didn't know how much more he could take before he snapped and did something that really freaked Alex out.

This made the second time Sandy had been forced by work to tear himself away from Alex and he didn't like it. Sandy'd never really been torn between duty and pleasure before. Although, what he felt for Alex didn't seem so much like pleasure as naked, elemental need. He needed to be close; needed to be a part of Alex, like he needed for Alex to be a part of him.

Uptake completed, Sandy ejected the test cartridge into the trash and plugged the tester into his mini comp to read the results. When the answering lights came up the right ratio of red to yellow, he judged that the cycling was progressing at an acceptable rate. The new strain of nitro-bacter he was culturing had come out of an experimental lab on 10-Hygiea, and the results so far had been beyond promising -- off-the-scale unbelievable was more like it. Both hardier and more efficient, it could handle a heavier load when converting nitrites to nitrates: about thirty percent more.

Since the *Vigilant* hadn't been designed to carry the size of crew they'd packed on to her when they'd fled Earth, it was a constant struggle to keep the life support systems from overloading and that had become the bane of Sandy's existence. Something like a more efficient water filtration system could mean longer trips between servicing and, not coincidentally, more profit for their fledgling company.

Sandy liked to eat, so profit was good.

"Hey, Chief."

"Yeah?"

Naslund stopped trying to pretend he was doing anything productive and leaned against the unit's culture chamber, towel now swinging easily from his fingertips. "I've got a question."

Apparently Naslund had a bigger pair of stones than Sandy'd given him credit for. Sandy didn't reply. Just narrowed his eyes in a look that said Nas had better tread carefully.

"I was just going to ask what you thought of the idea of installing a meat vat. We're going to be out of the Meal Ready Packs pretty soon. I was just thinking that if we could culture our own food on board ship it would, you know, solve a lot of problems."

Stomach rolling at just the thought, Sandy gave Nas points for improvisation. He'd opened his mouth to ask about Alex and probably only changed his mind at the look in Sandy's eyes. "I'm not putting one in unless we have to. Yeah, it would solve some problems, but it would just bring a set of new ones along with it. And then there's the smell."

"No, no, that's a myth. They don't smell at all -- I've been studying up on them." Naslund's pixie-like face lit up as he talked. "They're really kind of fascinating. I mean, growing bovine muscle tissue from a matrix of—"

"Fascinating. Oh, absolutely. I've got enough to deal with, without taking on any Frankenstein experiments. I've got engine nozzles to check. Life support needs to be cleaned -- and you know how much fun that is. There's the entire outer hull to check for anything the deflectors missed. My dance card is sufficiently filled, thank you."

"Okay. It was just an idea."

"What?" Sandy glanced up in time to catch Naslund's speculative gaze. "What's that mean?"

Nas tapped his fingers restlessly. "Nothing."

"Listen, I'm going to add a little more feedstock here, then go try to get some sleep. I'll be back in a couple of hours to check it again." Gathering his test supplies, Sandy rose to his feet.

"Should I see if Sutton can help me get started on life support?"

"Yeah, that'd be good. I'll see you later -- about oh-five-hundred?"

"Will do."

Sandy left, resisting the urge to jog back to his quarters, compromising with himself by holding it to a brisk walk. Once outside his quarters, Sandy paused to take a deep breath before entering the darkened room.

Gaze sweeping the room, Sandy passed over the empty bed, finally locating Alex in the corner in one of Sandy's jumbo-sized armchairs. Slumped sideways, neck bent at an awkward angle, Alex dozed. Sandy stifled the impulse to wrap his arms around the sleeping figure, opting instead to call from the safety of the doorway.

"Alex. Hey, Alex."

Alex's head jerked around, seeking the source of the noise, his expression relaxing once he located it. "Hey. Hi. Did I fall asleep? I'm sorry."

Sandy stepped forward, allowing the door to close behind him, and approached the chair. Squatting down, he ran two fingers up Alex's forearm, Alex's long-sleeved shirt uncharacteristically unbuttoned at the wrists.

"What are you doing in the chair? The bed's a little more comfortable."

"Oh, yeah, you're probably right. I didn't… I mean, I thought about it. But I forgot to ask and I didn't know if it would be okay. This is fine, really."

Unable to resist, Sandy raised his other hand, so that both hands rested on Alex's arms. He stroked lightly, savoring the feel of warm skin and soft hair under his fingertips. Aware that he risked tipping his hand, showing too much, Sandy fought the desire to touch more completely, to kiss, to press their bodies close.

Nodding in the direction of the bed, Sandy took a risk. "Want to come lie down with me? I've got a little break and I'm gonna to try to catch some sleep."

There were dark circles of fatigue under Alex's eyes, and small creases on his skin bore mute testimony to where his face had lain pressed against the chair back. "Yeah. I'd like that." A small smile played around the edges of his mouth. "You know, I slept the best I have in a long time with you, the other night."

Standing, Sandy covered the rush of emotion Alex's confession raised in him by letting his hands slide down to grip Alex's, pulling Alex to his feet. "Come on."

Sandy led the way to the bed, his blood flowing steadily south, hardening his dick the whole time. If he thought there was a hope in hell of hiding it he'd willingly suffer in silence, but there was no way Alex could miss the hard-on burgeoning in Sandy's pants. Gathering Alex to him, Sandy tried to leave a little room between his cock and Alex's ass as they spooned.

"Sandy?"

Why did the voice automatically drop to a whisper in the dark? Even though this was only semi-darkness, Alex's voice instinctively softened. Some remnant of tribe behavior from a more primitive time, probably. Sandy didn't know. "Yeah?" Having Alex in his arms was amazing. It was astonishing how something so simple could be so intensely satisfying.

"I like being here with you."

Sandy took another deep breath, the heat in his dick now matched by a more general warmth flowing through his entire being. "Me, too."

"I feel safe."

There was a lump in Sandy's throat now, keeping him from choking out more than a word or two. "Thanks."

"That probably sounds stupid, huh?"

"No, it doesn't."

"I'm really glad you're my friend."

"Me, too." Sandy spoke to the top of Alex's head, Alex tucked up against his body, his lips brushing Alex's hair with each word.

"Sandy?"

"Yeah?"

"I can feel your hard-on."

"Yeah, I bet. Hey, sorry about that." Time for some direct communication, maybe. "Look, Alex, I can't control that I get one when I'm around you, but I can control what I do about it. We can both go to sleep and nothing will happen. I promise."

Alex toyed with Sandy's hand where it rested, draped lightly across Alex's stomach. Just the thought of pressing on Alex's abdomen, maybe letting his hand stray down to cradle Alex's dick, while he pressed his aching cock against the crack of Alex's ass made Sandy's whole body quiver.

"Sandy?"

"Yeah?"

"It's not a problem. In fact, I'd kind of like to... Could I see it? If that's okay?"

Oh, fuck. What now, genius?

Sandy's hips flexed instinctively, arching forward at Alex's statement. He could control himself. He could do this. He could. "Sure." Rolling away, Sandy lay on his back in the darkened room. He still wore what served as his work uniform most days: a snug knit shirt and black BDUs, complete with regulation issue Teflar boots.

Alex turned to face Sandy, kneeling up, hands braced on his knees and reached with one tentative hand before hesitating. "Can I... is it okay if I... can I touch?"

Concentrating on controlling his breathing, Sandy tried to relax his jaw. "Okay."

The hovering hand dipped to the hem of Sandy's shirt, pushing it slowly up Sandy's body to bare his belly. Switching hands, Alex held the shirt out of the way while his fingers traced the tattoo that covered one half of Sandy's torso. "This is so amazing. This has significance, I'm sure." The feather light touch of Alex's fingers was torture; it lit fires beneath his skin and made Sandy long to grab the hand and shove it down his pants, where it belonged.

"It's a pe'a -- traditional Samoan tattoo."

"This is incredible." Alex rose to his knees, shoving the shirt up further, raising Sandy's arms over his head to remove it entirely. That his movements brought his crotch up to eye-level for Sandy was just more pain. "Oh, wow."

Although he'd lived with it since puberty and Sandy knew what his tattoo looked like, it gave him a feeling he couldn't quite name to experience it through Alex's eyes.

Alex raised his gaze to Sandy's, eyes alight. "Did it hurt?"

Memories of the exact sensation had faded, but Sandy recalled the stick he'd gripped in his teeth and the cloth he'd twisted between his hands when the pain had been at its most intense as the tufuga applied it.

"Little bit."

"How long did it take?" Alex was pouring over each of the different designs now, tracing the inverted triangles that represented sharks' teeth and strength; running a delicate finger over the half-circles topped by triangles symbolizing adversity; and the more intricate combinations that stood for frigate birds, or people holding hands in unity.

"About three months."

"Every day? For three months? What does it mean? How far down does it go? Can I see?"

Determined hands were unsnapping Sandy's pants, hooking clever fingers in the waistband and peeling them back, underwear and all.

"No, not every day; some days I had to heal in between. I did it to show that I honor my Samoan heritage. That I'm part of the community; that I suffered for my people."

"Oh, wow. That's… It's so pretty. Is that okay? Can I say it's pretty?"

Alex hand worked Sandy's pants open and

Sandy willingly lifted his hips to allow Alex to drag the clothing down his body, freeing his rigid cock. Sandy wasn't sure what Alex was calling pretty and he didn't much care. He was half-naked and Alex's hands were on him and that was all he needed to know.

***

Alex was pretty sure there must be a special place in hell for people who shamelessly took advantage of other people who were only trying to help them out, but he couldn't seem to stop himself. Big, gorgeous Sandy was laid out in front of his eyes and was letting him do pretty much whatever. The only problem was that Alex wasn't sure exactly what he wanted.

All of that beautiful, reddish-brown skin was so much more attractive than his own pale, fishbelly white. And those muscles. Oh, my. Alex ran his hands up Sandy's chest, testing the resilience of smooth skin over firm muscle. Letting them slide back down, Alex gave an experimental flick over Sandy's nipples and smiled to himself a little when Sandy reacted.

From his vantage point astride Sandy's legs, there was beautiful naked man as far as his eyes could see. This warrior, this man of honor, this stunning example of everything masculine that was good, had somehow fallen into Alex's life. For once fate had done something decent for him and there was no way he was going to ask questions -- take the chance on missing out by second-guessing the why of it.

"Sandy?"

Eyes closed, nostrils flaring with the slow, deliberate breaths he drew, Sandy didn't answer. Alex wasn't sure he'd even heard. It slowly dawned on Alex that maybe Sandy was doing what Alex used to do, and going away to somewhere in his mind; somewhere where what was happening to his body wasn't happening to his mind. Alex should stop.

He tried more urgently. "Sandy!"

No response. Just a slow breath in, then out.

Oh, crap. What should he do? What would he have wanted someone to do when he'd been in that position? Stop, of course, so he did. Alex carefully withdrew his hands and placed them on his own thighs.

He could still look, though, and he studied Sandy's body. Tried to, anyway. The skin he still wanted to touch some more. Maybe even sample. He'd had small tastes of Sandy's mouth, but his skin, with its pleasantly clean, musky scent of healthy male drew Alex. How weird was that? He wanted to press a finger into the broad expanse above Sandy's nipples, make a small indentation, then watch it spring back.

He'd like to trace a finger along Sandy's high forehead, where it gave way to the hairline. Alex wanted to get really close and examine Sandy's thin, perfectly arched eyebrows. Could they possibly be natural? Sandy didn't strike him as the type to indulge in excessive personal grooming, but how else could you explain them? They were nothing like Alex's own unruly messes.

Maybe because he was concentrating on the area, Alex spotted the minute fluttering of Sandy's eyelids immediately. They blinked rapidly and sprang open. "What are you doing?"

"Nothing. Just looking."

The two ridges between those fabulous eyebrows were back, as Sandy formed his words carefully -- like he was drunk, or drugged. "Why did you stop?"

"Because it looked like you weren't enjoying it. You were so tense, and you didn't answer when I said your name."

"It was fine. You can do anything you want."

Another area that Alex had never really taken his eyes off was Sandy's cock and it quivered as Sandy spoke, still hard and full, small droplets of semen bubbling up from its tip. Maybe he wanted Alex to touch him? Alex couldn't tell. Usually people told him exactly what they required, what they expected from him. This was difficult, trying to divine what someone wanted without words.

"Anything? But what do you want? Do you want me to touch your cock? Should I stroke you?"

Spreading his arms a bit, as though offering surrender, Sandy closed his eyes and settled more deeply into the mattress. "Whatever you want to do, Alex. Anything… nothing. It's up to you."

A dozen ideas popped into Alex's head, each one crazier than the last. Anything! Anything? That was too much freedom for any one person to handle. Too much responsibility. How could he possibly know what was okay with Sandy? What was acceptable and what was off limits?

He couldn't.

"Sandy, tell me what to do. What do you like? What would you like me to do to you?"

"Alex—" Sandy held out his hands, palms up. He seemed to expect something, so Alex placed his own hands in Sandy's. "I'll like almost anything you do, so what do you want to do?"

Alex gazed down at Sandy, his mind suddenly a blank. "I don't know. All of a sudden I can't think."

Curling his fingers inside Alex's, Sandy gave him an encouraging smile. "Can't think of anything at all? What about touching? I thought you wanted to touch my dick."

"Oh. Yeah, that's right, I did. May I?"

Sandy's smile became a shaky grin. "You want to play 'Mother, may I?' You definitely may."

The way the tension had been building, Sandy's remark drew a snort from Alex. "Don't make me laugh. I haven't thought of that game in years." Sandy just smiled back at him, cock full and weeping, body obviously humming, but doing nothing about it. "Okay, if that's how you want to play it."

Alex touched the sensitive head, running one finger around the flattened tip. Eyelids half-closed in pleasure, Sandy sucked in a breath, his belly tightening with the movement.

"Sandy, I'm going to put a hand on your dick. Is that okay?"

Sandy nodded affirmatively in a short, jerky movement, his gaze focused on Alex's hand as Alex moved it down the shaft and wrapped his fingers around Sandy's cock. Pausing to admire the view, Alex studied Sandy's ruddy brown cock, held in a cocoon of Alex's own making.

Nice.

He liked it.

Alex's gaze wandered down to Sandy's balls, drawn up tight against his body, only the smallest amount of hair on them. As a matter of fact, now that Alex thought about it, besides what was on his head, Sandy had almost no body hair.

"What about...? Can I touch your balls?"

Smile long gone, replaced now by a distant, unfocused look, Sandy nodded briefly. Just a quick jerk of his head, really.

Still holding Sandy's cock in one hand, Alex reached down to cradle Sandy's balls with the other. So soft. Warm and velvety, Alex couldn't get over the difference between what he felt while touching Sandy and everything else he'd felt in his life.

No, that wasn't it at all. It couldn't be the comparison to what he'd felt before, because he hadn't felt before. The difference was that now he felt something, when before he'd forced his body to do what it had to, while he kept his feelings safely hidden away.

The little ball of warmth that had started in Alex's chest had spread, so that now big chunks of him glowed, tingled, even. Cupping Sandy's balls, Alex squeezed a little -- compressed the soft skin as he carefully pumped Sandy's dick, until Sandy moaned and began rolling his head from one side to the other.

"Do you shave them? You don't shave— No, that's stupid. Forget I asked."

"Oh, God, Alex. That's..." The low, guttural moan that rumbled up from Sandy's chest was the sexiest thing Alex had ever heard. He'd done the same thing dozens, maybe hundreds of times before, and never felt a thing himself. It seemed somehow disloyal in Alex's mind to even think of those other times while he touched Sandy. It was exactly the same, but somehow it was nothing like any of the other times. Somehow, when Sandy groaned, Alex got a pleased little burst of pride in his chest

Lowering his head, Alex lapped delicately at Sandy's dick, stroked it as he tasted Sandy's essence and braced himself for the wave of revulsion that had been his unavoidable reaction for so long. Alex waited and, when it didn't come, he sat back for a moment and just looked. Eyes screwed tightly shut, hands clutching fistfuls of the bed cover, neck straining as Sandy's back arched, his entire body bowed up off the bed. Somehow, all of that rigid control gave Alex the courage to lower his head once again and take the length above his fist into his mouth.

The scent and taste remained reassuringly Sandy. It felt wrong to think of what he'd done back in his other life with dozens, hundreds, of nameless, faceless clients while he was touching Sandy, so Alex did his best to shove those thoughts aside and concentrate on Sandy. When he looked up the long expanse of Sandy's amazing body and glimpsed the face of his friend, it was somehow all different. Alex wanted to give back to Sandy. The feeling of friendship that had begun to grow in him, from the time of that first conversation back at *Nelly's*, changed everything.

Trying not to think too much, Alex concentrated on Sandy, on using his mouth the way he knew how to bring Sandy maximum pleasure. It was second nature to use his lips and tongue and hands together; to listen for the breathing to tell him when to speed up and when to slow down. Sandy was so quiet, though, it made the task that much more difficult.

"Alex, please… I want—"

Sandy's voice, so guttural, tortured-sounding, startled Alex. What was he doing wrong? He'd been watching. What sign had he missed? "What? What did I do? I'll stop."

Head thrown back, hands still clenching the rough fabric of the bedcover, Sandy's face gave nothing away and Alex began to panic.

"No, don't stop. Fuck me. I want you to fuck me."

Chapter 9

"This fucking sucks. I hate this shit."

"No kidding? Then why'd you volunteer?" Sandy didn't need to glance in Jimi Vilnius' direction to know what he'd see if he did: curly mop of dark red hair, more freckles and teeth than sense. Regardless of the subject under discussion, he'd be smiling.

"Who volunteered? I was asleep." Bitching and moaning, yet still smiling.

"Same thing. Next time don't sleep through a planning meeting."

"D'abu, this sucks. Do you know how many other things I'd rather be doing than checking the hull for flaws? I had plans."

That remark drew a snort from Sandy. "Yeah, you and me both, pal. Work comes first, last and always. You know that."

Vilnius finished pulling a black mesh skullcap over his hair, compressing its volume of waves and curls enough to fit under the exo-suit's helmet, and began checking his pockets for supplies. He looked up as he tucked tubes of vacuum-setting epoxy into his pockets. Another flash of that toothy grin, its prominent canines reminding Sandy as always of a vampiric horse. "So, uh, I heard you got something going with Alex the bartender. Hey, I say good for you. You work too hard as it is and I hardly ever see you hook up."

"So, you about ready? Where's your glue gun?" He wasn't about to discuss Alex with anyone, much less a greenie like Jimi Vilnius -- fifteen years Sandy's junior and resident team flake. The kid took the hint and shut up, silently holding up one of the epoxy extruders they'd become all too familiar with since arriving on Doradus. "Okay, let's hit it."

The transition chambers to the maintenance areas were smaller, so the wait time was a fraction of the amount of time needed for the ship-to-station or station-to-ship transfers. Still, since the inter-suit voice link lines were routed through Doradus' main communication system, Sandy didn't like to use them for anything not strictly business. Which meant that chit chat with Vilnius was out and left Sandy alone with his thoughts, something he'd been avoiding.

If he could somehow limit himself to thinking about the good parts of the previous night, he'd be happy to let his thoughts run on a continuous loop. Sandy would gladly relive over and over lying naked on his bed with Alex's hands and mouth on him. Even now, hours later, a ball of heat settled in Sandy's belly and made his dick throb as he pictured Alex sitting astride him, running those hands up and down his torso. Clever fingers had flicked at his nipples, which even now tightened again at just the memory.

Sandy'd wondered briefly at the possibility of cardiac arrest when Alex had gone down on him. Jesus fuck, but the feeling defied all description. Too intense. Too exciting. Too damn good.

And over too quickly.

How in the hell had he allowed himself to be so stupid? Sandy could ask himself the same question from now 'til eternity and never understand. He knew how skittish Alex was -- and who could blame the man? After the hell Alex had lived through, that he could still function, laugh, approximate a human being, was a miracle not many people could fully appreciate.

What kind of weak-willed individual had so little self-control that he'd let his mouth run away with him and say something as unbelievably, profoundly dumbass as Sandy had? What the hell had he been thinking? Who could blame Alex for freezing up the way he did? Sandy wanted to kick his own ass into next week.

"You okay?" Vilnius peered out from behind the clear visor of the exo-suit at him, freckles standing out starkly against pale skin.

"Yeah. Why?"

"I dunno. You made a weird sound -- like you were choking or something. Your suit okay?"

Oh, for fuck's sake. Now he was freaking out the newbie. Get a grip on yourself, you fucking moron. "Suit's great. Let's just focus on the job, okay?"

"Yeah, sure thing." Vilnius flinched and looked away.

Sandy shifted the glue gun he held from one hand to the other and back again. He turned it over and tried to read the serial number off the handle. Flicked the power switch on and off. On and off. Every time he let his hands fall idle, though, Alex's face -- with its shock slowly replaced first by horror, then by a blank stare -- took shape in his mind's eye.

Too bad he couldn't take the glue gun and burn the memory out.

Even if he could, that still wouldn't do anything for Alex. Alex would have to live with the memory of someone he trusted saying those things to him. "I like being with you, Sandy. I feel safe with you. I'm glad you're my friend." Some fucking friend.

The door slid open and he and Vilnius spent the better part of the next six hours tethered to long booms that swung out over the *Vigilant*, keeping the two of them from floating away into the black. Off balance and semi-nauseous, they crawled over the surface of the ship's hull scanning for flaws caused by collisions with microscopic specks of dust traveling at interplanetary speeds, until they were numb with it. Simultaneously nerve wracking and mind-warpingly tedious -- like pouring over the roof of a house with a magnifying glass -- it had to be done. By the time they had to return the rented suits, Sandy had a headache from eye strain and his fingers could barely grip the epoxy gun enough to hang onto it.

When the two men finally peeled off the helmets, it took a conscious effort for Sandy to blink his eyes, so dry and caked from the oxygen-rich mix pumped through the exo-suit. He rolled his head and rubbed at the tendons, stiff from holding his neck so long in one position. "I'm getting too old for this shit. I gotta start leaving the glamorous work like this to you young Turks."

Vilnius' grin was back as he pulled off his mesh cap and shook his head. "Oh, come on. Yeah, okay, it was kind of a pain. But we're done. I'm gonna grab a shower -- I know, a short one -- and something to eat. Unless Sarhaan or Kai has something else for me, Nas and I are going down to the Pike. You wanna come with?" This last was obviously an afterthought, strictly for the sake of sucking up to a more senior team member.

"No thanks. I've got things on board to take care of."

"All right. Go, buddy." The wicked slant of Vilnius' smile told Sandy where the kid's thoughts had immediately gone.

"I said some things, not someone."

"Sure, sure. I believe you." That ever-broadening grin belied the outward sincerity.

"Yeah, so … good job out there. Why don't you take off? Go have some fun before we start maintenance on life support tomorrow and life gets glorious again."

After parting ways with Vilnius, Sandy spent the walk back to his quarters ticking things off his mental to-do list and ignoring the quickening of his pulse. He had a thousand and one details to keep track of and the truth was he really couldn't afford a distraction the magnitude Alex was turning out to be. After another night spent staring at the wall instead of sleeping in Alex's arms, he was beat. The lack of sleep was accumulating and he hadn't been kidding when he'd told Vilnius he needed to start delegating some tasks.

As it turned out, though, he could have saved himself the worry.

Alex was gone.

For all he'd told himself he'd been expecting it, Sandy still couldn't help the lurch of disappointment when the door to his suite slid open and he saw the empty bed, not even Alex asleep in a chair. Nothing but an empty room, inhabited only by sterile furniture and a few remembrances of home, his note to Alex nowhere to be found.

Alex,

I have to work for a while, but I'll be back as soon as I can. Can you stay?

Sandy

The answer to that was blindingly obvious, judging by the silence in Sandy's quarters. Shit. He'd blown it with Alex and there was every possibility he wouldn't get a second chance.

Damn it.

Sandy mentally kicked himself for the hundredth time and scrubbed both hands over his face. The headache had settled into a steady, pounding rhythm behind his eyes, beating in time with the mocking chant of 'fuck me, fuck me, fuck me' that wouldn't stop circling in his brain.

Pinching the bridge of his nose gave him no relief, so Sandy tried pressing the heels of his hands into his eye sockets.

That helped a little.

He lowered his weary body into one of the oversized chairs he'd bought off a Euro transport ship that was getting out of the business, deciding if he couldn't push the thoughts out of his head, he might as well wallow in the memories.

Maybe they needed a thorough airing before they'd agree to an exorcism.

Fuck.

He'd been stupid, sure -- but, come on. How long was he supposed to hold out?

He'd been naked. Alex had been touching him. Putting his mouth on Sandy's dick, for God's sake. It had been beyond good. It was his most cherished fantasy coming true. That beautiful, precious, one-of-a-kind face with those sweet, soulful eyes had been gazing down on Sandy with a look that said they found him beautiful, too.

Alex had run his hands up and down Sandy's chest, he'd touched Sandy's cock like it was holy; caressed it with his mouth like--

Oh, fuck, what did it matter now how Alex had touched him?

How out of his head with pleasure Sandy'd been didn't make a bit of difference to Alex. Sandy'd begged Alex to fuck him and Alex had backed away like he'd had a beam rifle locked, loaded, and pointed at his head.

How was he supposed to come back from a fiasco like that?

***

"Hey Alex, hand me the knife?"

"Alex, I need two ales, a Milky Way martini, and an Idaho vodka, neat."

"Hey, can somebody -- anybody -- get me a Chardonnay and a dirty martini? Please? C'mon, you guys are killing me here."

Slapping the paring knife down on Teddy's side of the prep area, Alex pulled the wine bottle from the cooler and poured a wineglass two-thirds full. Picking up the cocktail shaker he'd momentarily abandoned, Alex shook it steadily several times while he pulled a martini glass from the freezer and strained the contents of the shaker into the glass. "There ya go, hon."

"You okay, Alex?"

Alex glanced over at Teddy, who seemed to be

having no trouble keeping up with the evening rush. "Yeah, fine. You got a second? Grab me an Idaho?"

Seconds later the requested drink appeared. "Here ya go."

"Thanks." Alex kept working; kept mixing drinks and pouring things from bottles and taps as fast as he could. If he kept working, kept going, he could focus on things like getting the proportions right and pleasing the wait staff and customers, rather than what a wreck he'd made of things with Sandy last night. He'd figure something out eventually, but for now he wanted a break from feeling like a miserable failure.

"Good thing you came in, man. Jared's okay, but he's no you." Teddy smiled and gave Alex a wink. He and Teddy made a good team and nights they worked together always went better, with faster service, happier customers, and better tips. "What happened there, anyway? I thought you had the night off."

Mixing a couple of Fahrenheit 451's, Alex responded. "Nothing. I just decided I liked eating. I got bills to pay off and I guess Joe's getting impatient."

"What about your new fella? He can't help out?"

"I haven't asked him." After scanning the room for the hundredth time -- still no Sandy -- Alex made a show of consulting his vid link for drink orders. Finding only a couple of orders for ale, he began pulling those. "He does too much already."

Teddy edged closer, his voice dropping to a confidential level. "How is… everything? Are you… I mean… is everything okay, you know, between you two?"

Alex overfilled the glass and searched for a towel to wipe it down. "I don't know. Pretty good, I guess."

"Really? Even the…" Teddy's brown eyes dominated his narrow face, overpowering his pale skin and fair hair. "I didn't think you ever wanted to get involved with anyone. That's all I've ever heard you say."

Shrugging, Alex met Teddy's gaze briefly before reaching for a glass to polish. Anything to keep his hands busy. "I know. But Sandy's different. He really goes out of his way to make sure I'm okay. You know? I'm not even sure why he's hanging around. He doesn't need my kind of grief."

"Maybe he likes you? I dunno. That's a lotta man -- you ever think you maybe shoulda started out with something a little smaller? More manageable? Like, what about the new guy?"

"Nick?" Alex's gaze shot to Teddy's, but Teddy was looking across to the doorway on the far side of the room where Nick lounged, talking to his partner, Joe Sotheran. Teddy braced himself with one hand on the bar, while the other was shoved deep in one pocket, giving his dick a discreet rub. "Uh, no." Alex didn't think he'd let any feeling bleed into his words, but Teddy's disbelieving gaze nonetheless swung in Alex's direction.

"O-kay. I hope you know what you're doing." Teddy took another glance in Nick and Joe's direction before reaching to pull down more martini glasses from overhead to fill with ice. "I wouldn't say no to some o' that, I'll tell you what."

"Knock yourself out."

"I just might." Teddy's voice dropped to a nearly inaudible murmur. "I just might at that."

***

It was a nice night for a walk.

Every night was a nice night for a walk on Doradus, but Alex tried not to let that discourage him. He'd finished work over an hour ago, but he hadn't wanted to go back to his room. Not yet. Alex didn't want to be anywhere anyone might think to look for him and *Nelly's* or his room would be the obvious go-to's when trying to track him down.

He could have hung out with Teddy, probably.

Like a lot of *Nelly's* employees, Teddy had a place of his own, just inside of the business-residential divide. Alex didn't think he could handle it though if he was hanging out with Teddy, trying to unwind, and Nick showed up. Teddy had some pretty weird ideas about what constituted a good time and the last thing Alex wanted was to be anywhere near those two when they thought no one was looking.

Shoving his hands in his pockets, Alex kept walking, his fingers worrying the pockets' contents.

What was he going to do about Sandy?

He really liked Sandy. He wanted to think that maybe Sandy liked him, too. Sandy was different. Alex trusted Sandy and he wasn't sure quite how that had happened.

The heels of his shoes made a hollow sound on the fake wood sidewalk as Alex walked, passing the mostly-closed businesses. A glowing red sign advertising rooms to rent by the hour made a jarring contrast to the darkened businesses on either side.

The more mundane offerings of clothes chemically-cleaned cheaply and specialty goods catering to assorted ethnic groups from Earth were gradually being infiltrated by other business capitalizing on the success of business like *Nelly's*. Nothing succeeded like success and everyone wanted a piece of it.

"Looking for something to do?"

A voice called softly from a doorway, startling Alex out of his daydream. A young man, dark-skinned like Sandy, but with a long, loose braid of hair hanging down to his waist, took a step out of the shadows. Alex took one look at the business' window display -- an empty chair was the only prop -- and flinched. "No, thanks."

Alex quickened his pace. Things were different on Doradus and no one would chase him down, but he wanted to be away from the pro and his business as fast as possible. The sex trade might be perfectly legal on Doradus -- well-paid and respected, even -- but the feeling that washed over Alex when his gaze met the boy's made his skin crawl.

A year ago that had been him.

Not exactly, but close enough.

This man probably set his own schedule, charged according to his own needs, decided who was an acceptable client and who didn't make it through the door.

Alex hadn't had any of those luxuries.

He wanted to slam the door on the memories that leaked through, but he couldn't. Sandy's voice in his head, asking Alex to fuck him, was there again and Alex knew he needed to find a way to resurrect enough of the old Alex to somehow make that happen.

A chill shook Alex's body and he chafed his upper arms with his hands. He'd worked hard to bury the Alex that had existed in that world -- only in that world -- for all of those months; months that had turned into years, until it was hard to remember a time when he had had control over his life and his body. When he hadn't been just an empty receptacle for the fantasies of anyone with money and connections.

Images bombarded his brain, skipping chaotically from person to event to act and back again. From his first, early weeks when he'd been in a state of shock, to later when the drugs and events had numbed him enough that it didn't hurt simply to breathe, to later still, after he'd existed so long without feeling that it had taken Liam to remind him what that was like.

Liam.

What an amazing amount of guile it must have taken to outwit the handlers. It was Liam that had finally, finally given Alex the courage to act, as well as suggesting to him an escape route. Too bad Alex hadn't figured things out in time to help Liam, but Alex told himself again that he'd done what he could.

Thinking about Liam brought up the feelings again, only this time they met and mixed with feelings about Sandy.

Why couldn't he ever seem to get anything right?

Why couldn't he do what he needed to do not to let people down?

Alex pulled his hands from his pockets again and rubbed his eyes. Damn C02 converters must be on the fritz again; suddenly his eyes were stinging and his nose was starting to run. With nothing else available, Alex wiped his nose on the back of one sleeve and sniffed hard.

Crap. He'd been wandering aimlessly since he got off work and he wasn't any closer to finding an answer. Too bad he couldn't ask Sandy what to do.

When the glow of lighted signs from dozens of small businesses, still lit at this hour, seeped into Alex's consciousness, he realized he'd walked further than he'd meant to.

The Pike.

Doradus' version of a sailor's fun zone.

Like Doradus itself wasn't enough of a huge R-and-R facility, the Pike had evolved as the place to go when your itch couldn't be satisfied anywhere else. Media pods, containing every electronic amusement imaginable and then some, were rentable by the hour. Entertainment included not only games and live news feeds from Mars, the moon, and Earth, but virtual reality chairs, where any experience desired could be experienced. For a price, of course, but that was to be expected.

Alex had heard about it from Teddy and some of the other employees at *Nelly's*, but he'd never ventured down before. Some instinct of self-preservation had warned him to stay away and Alex had heeded it. His brain and body had been fully occupied trying to heal; trying to figure out how life as an independent being worked.

Shrugging to himself, Alex kept walking.

He slowed a little, wanting to take in as much as he could as long as he was finally here.

Everywhere people were walking, looking for the perfect entertainment to fulfill their wants and needs. Miners and spacers made up the bulk of the people milling about, people eying each other as much as the booths and kiosks that crowded together, each competing for their share of the credits to be made.

For as much a piece of meat as he'd been treated like back on Earth, it still came as an occasional shock that the sex trade on Doradus was a respected profession, with a pay scale to match. The recreational time specialists -- or RaTS, as they were often referred to -- looked sleek and well-fed.

In direct contrast were the miners, who had neither the time nor access to facilities required to maintain a civilized look, except for their periodic trips to Doradus.

Spacers, on the other hand, had both -- they just didn't give a shit. They were as far as it was humanly possible to get from Earth, frequently due to a congenital dislike of rules and regulations. Toeing anyone's line of respectability, including those of hygiene and good manners, didn't appeal to them and they didn't care who knew it.

At *Nelly's*, decorum was maintained by a well-paid security team whose reputation for professionalism was as widely known as their accuracy with a weapon.

Out here, though, things were a little different.

So busy watching the crowd, Alex didn't see the space jockey whose shoulder he clipped. Just spun around on one heel, throwing his arms out to reach for something, anything, to catch himself.

"Nataka kushuka hapa!"

The back of his hand smacking something hard, Alex didn't have time to catch a breath before the tough-looking spacer was in his face, looking him up and down. He realized at nearly the same time that he hadn't fallen on his ass because helpful hands had caught him, and that the spacer must have changed his mind about something because his sneer had turned speculative.

"Pugunza bei kidogo,wijanga?"

Backing away was impossible; the hands supporting Alex also held him in place, and trying to tug his arms free proved fruitless. "Excuse me, I didn't see you. I'm so sorry. I don't speak … Kush?" Alex's attempt to twist free was as unsuccessful as trying to get a look at whoever restrained him. He craned his neck to no effect, his pulse picking up with every second he was held, unable to retreat.

"Rafiki sisemi kuKush." This time the normally lyrical Kush language came from behind Alex, its naturally sing-song rhythm coming out unusually harsh and guttural. *"Natango hatapa ni riyana. Chini?"*

Beginning to turn away now, the spacer's gaze flicked up to Alex's captor, before giving Alex a last look. *"Sijui sema."* And then he was gone.

Alex was tensing, preparing to fight in earnest to get away, now that the immediate threat was gone. But even as he gathered himself, he was released. Turning, he came face to face with the blond man with the ruined voice. The one who'd insulted Sandy. What was his name? Yeah, Bartok. The shithead.

"If you're trying to think of a way to thank me, I've got an idea."

Chapter 10

Sandy paused to check the pressure gauge next to the chamber window, found the results unacceptable again, and resumed pacing. He spent half his life these days, it seemed, in pressure chambers waiting to get to the other side. Rubbing a hand over the stubble on top of his head as he paced, he jingled the contents of his pocket with the other.

Damn it.

Glancing at the gauge for the third time in the last two minutes, Sandy willed it to move faster. Amped up and antsy were alien sensations to his body. He'd always been the deliberate one; cool and collected when everyone else was coming out of their skin. Partly his Samoan, Pacific Islander upbringing, partly just his nature, Sandy'd never been the nervous type.

He was on the edge of his control now, though, that was for sure. He'd had all day and half the night to think about Alex and how he'd messed that up. Going over and over it in his head, Sandy'd replayed the scene until it was burned into his brain. Every touch of Alex's hands, his mouth … God. The way he'd responded to Alex's touch; the way the slightest brush of Alex's fingertips over his nipples had lit fires in him.

The startled look on Alex's face, the way he'd scrambled off the bed, backing away until he'd been stopped by the bulkhead and couldn't go any further. The boneless slide to the floor, where Alex had sat, long arms wrapped protectively around his legs, compressed into the smallest amount of space he could physically manage.

Stop beating yourself up. You screwed up. Okay, so get past it and see what can be salvaged from it.

If this was a military operation, Sandy would look at his options and choose the one with the best chance of success. He'd have a plan B in mind, and probably a plan C, too. He'd also have his teammates to help him look for fresh angles; things he hadn't thought of; contingencies he ought to plan for.

This time he couldn't, though.

Not about Alex.

It was too personal. Too private. He didn't mind Sarhaan and Kai knowing his business. Hell, after they'd worked together so closely and so long, there wasn't much about his life they didn't know. Alex's business wasn't Sandy's to reveal, though. It was just barely possible that Alex didn't want the details of his personal life dissected like a training op debriefing. He might have a few things he wanted to keep to himself.

So Sandy was facing his problem head-on; tracking Alex down to try and straighten things out. Maybe Alex would tell him to fuck off; to go take his pathetic, needy self somewhere else to get his business take care of.

It was entirely possible.

The final door slid open at last and Sandy

headed down the ramp, intent on catching the tram into town. He'd tried repeatedly to comm Alex, but hadn't been able to reach him. Knowing that it was hours past Alex's usual quitting time and having logged enough time observing Alex to know the man liked his routine, the change in practice didn't reassure Sandy any. Alex liked to close the room down, get his clean up and prep for the next shift finished, then head back to his room; he wasn't at all prone to fits of impulse.

Climbing onto the tram, Sandy propped his feet on the opposing bench, folded his arms across his chest, and settled in for the seventeen minute ride into Doradus proper. He stared at the scuffed toes of his work boots with unseeing eyes as his thoughts again turned inward.

Alex struck Sandy as being something of a homebody, actually, and that got to Sandy-- right in the gut. Although he'd tried not to let himself get ahead of the game, Sandy had to admit he'd been fantasizing a little. Couldn't seem to help it. He'd been trying out different scenarios in his head -- ways how maybe he and Alex might be able to work something out.

There were so many obstacles in their way, though; to call the odds long was an understatement.

Sandy began to jiggle his feet, idly kicking one against the other, seemingly of their own accord.

Was what he wanted really so awful? So impossible to understand? What was so wrong with liking to be the one getting fucked, rather than the one doing the fucking? So he liked the feeling. So what?

After all this time, Sandy sighed inwardly and

shook his head a little at seeing his old enemy pop up again. Every time he thought he'd made peace with all of that...

He knew a lot of people didn't understand; would look at his size and height and peg him as being a particular way. He couldn't help it that he liked what he liked and Sandy didn't see why he should have to apologize for that.

Why couldn't it be just that simple?

It wasn't as though he never took the more active role.

Fucking was great. Sandy was a big fan. Sometimes there was nothing better than grabbing onto a set of lean hips and easing in to a tight ass bit by bit. Sinking in slowly then sliding out, groaning at the wicked sweet pleasure of it all. Letting the tempo gradually pick up until you were pounding away, grunting and swearing and slapping that ass.

Shit, yeah.

It was just that, more often than not, he preferred to be the one done to. It felt incredible and Sandy couldn't figure out what was so hard to understand about that.

People didn't understand, though.

Sai, for sure, hadn't.

Although Sandy'd tried his best to explain, words had never been his gift. He could look at most any machine put in front of him and tell in broad terms what it did, regardless of whether or not he'd ever seen it before. He could fix damn near anything with only the materials he had on hand. Could manufacture a tool or device to suit just about any purpose needed. But saying what was in his heart? Forget it.

The automated voice of the tram system called out the name of the stop nearest the entertainment district where *Nelly's* resided and Sandy got off. He didn't have much of a plan for finding Alex; he just figured he'd check in at *Nelly's* and make sure he hadn't missed the man there before heading out to search.

After confirming with Big Jay, the doorman, that Alex wasn't anywhere in *Nelly's*, Sandy began by following the same path he'd taken with Alex that first night. The rush of feeling that washed over him whenever he thought of taking Alex in his arms for the first time hit him again: how impossibly good it had felt to have Alex's body pressed close to his, to run his hands down the slim curves of Alex's backside and know he wasn't just imagining the whole thing -- that it was really Alex he was holding.

It occurred to Sandy that if he'd been a little less of a Boy Scout and given in to the urge to scan Alex's identi-chip into the *Vigilant*'s computer system when he'd had the chance, he'd be closing in on Alex's exact coordinates instead of wandering aimlessly through the night.

It would have been easy enough.

Just call up the data from when Alex had first come on board and link it to Alex's personal information. Kai wouldn't have thought twice about doing it, Sandy knew -- but then, Kai's background was intel.

Come to think of it, it probably wouldn't have taken Cal over fifteen minutes to hack into Doradus' computer system and download the information there. That would have meant asking Cal, though, and for a variety of reasons Sandy wasn't ready to have that conversation yet.

So Sandy kept going, widening his search area to another adjacent block, and then another. The glow of lights coming from the direction of the Pike was just becoming visible when Sandy spotted a familiar figure dressed in black. Sandy mentally committed himself to giving Alex a few lessons in street smarts when he saw how Alex walked -- his head down, thoughts obviously on something other than situational awareness.

"Feel like some company?"

Despite Sandy's deliberate attempt to pitch his voice low and unthreatening, Alex still jerked his head up, startled. "Hey. Sandy. What are you doing out here?"

That sounded a lot like pleasure in Alex's voice. Affection even, maybe, and Sandy chuckled a little that Alex could even ask the question. "Looking for you."

"Yeah? How come?" Alex smiled and Sandy was struck again at how radically it changed his face.

"'Cause maybe I wanted to see you. Ever think of that?" The distance between them narrowed until they stood only centimeters apart.

"Really?"

Alex's disbelief was a physical pain for Sandy. It took hold of his heart and squeezed, that anyone so good and perfect and unique could be so doubtful of something that simple.

"Yeah, really." Sandy reached out to touch -- he needed to touch -- to run a hand up Alex's arm. "Kiss me?"

"You don't have to. No one's watching."

"How about if I want to?" Sandy stepped closer

still, until he could feel the heat of Alex's body.

Lifting his gaze to meet Sandy's, Alex's voice dropped to a whisper. "Sure."

Raising one hand to tangle it in the softness of Alex's hair, Sandy slipped the other along Alex's waist, hooking his fingers in a belt loop as he lowered his head. As Sandy got close, Alex's eyes closed, hiding their clear blue color and something else along with them. Sandy wanted desperately to think it was welcome he'd seen flash there, but he couldn't be sure. So he closed his own eyes and lost himself in the feel of Alex's lips on his, in the silky slide of Alex's mouth opening to him.

Alex's hands came up and settled at Sandy's waist as their bodies pressed together, Sandy growing hungrier for the taste of Alex as the reality of touch, taste, and smell worked on him. His dick had gone hard at the first touch of Alex's hands on his body and all he wanted now was more.

More skin, bared to his touch.

More of that exotic, unique taste in his mouth.

And especially more of the hands, tentatively beginning to explore his body.

"Alex, can we go—"

"Is my place all right? Unless it's too small?" Face upturned, a little breathless, a little uncertain, Alex was irresistible. Not that Sandy wanted to try, but he knew he had to somehow.

"That's fine. Just to talk. I know you're not ready for anything to happen yet, but I want…" How to be honest without scaring Alex to death? "I want you to know you're safe with me. No pressure, okay? I don't want you to be afraid."

Alex reached up to touch Sandy's face. "I know. Come on -- let's go."

That small, half-smile had Sandy worried.

***

Just a little more of the sparkling water he'd grabbed from the bar to wash the aftertaste from his mouth and Alex felt better already. The little bloom of heat in his chest was spreading, chasing the butterflies he'd had earlier. Sneaking up the back stairs, Alex had tugged Sandy along, hurrying to get them to his room.

Inside now, Alex closed the door behind them and lit only the small reading light in the corner. Sandy looked wonderful and Alex had to tell him. "You look amazing."

"Thanks. Uh… can we… I think we need to talk. About the other night, I—"

Alex shushed Sandy with two fingers over the beautiful mouth. "That's okay. Really. Don't worry about it." He slipped his hands underneath Sandy's shirt, the smooth heat of Sandy's skin like silk under his fingertips. "So nice. You feel good."

"Alex, what are you--? Are you sure?"

"So sweet. You are so sweet, yes, I'm sure. The other night was bad. It was my fault. But it'll be okay now, I promise." He had to reach to fit his arms around Sandy's waist and place kisses along Sandy's neck, but it felt so good to press himself against all of that strength and goodness. So solid. So strong and sure -- like nothing Sandy could ever do was wrong.

"I don't know. Oh, baby, that feels so… Alex, I—"

"Ssh. Just let it feel good." Just like old times, Alex's dick was hard; he pushed closer, flexing his hips, and smiled at the answering rise of Sandy's hips. Dragging his cock teasingly back and forth across Sandy's, Alex kissed and nipped his way down Sandy's jaw until he reached that chiseled, beautiful mouth. "Kiss me. I want you to kiss me."

A pair of brawny arms came around Alex, nearly squeezing the breath from his lungs. "Alex. Baby, I thought you'd never-- God, I want you." Sandy's mouth sealed over Alex's, Sandy's tongue slipping eagerly inside.

Flashes of heat, like fire licking along Alex's skin, bloomed in little bursts everywhere inside him. For the first time in a long time, he knew he was beautiful and this magnificent warrior enfolding him in a crushing embrace was only the proof. Alex was beautiful and Sandy was perfect and the two of them belonged together -- together in bed.

"Come to bed, Sandy. I need you. Please?"

Sandy opened heavy-lidded eyes to gaze down at him, lowered those big hands to cup and then squeeze his ass, before dropping kisses on his face. "Honey, are you sure? Is this really what -- do you really want this?"

Slipping out of Sandy's arms, Alex dropped to his knees, trailing his hands down Sandy's chest on the way to press his mouth against Sandy's fly. Breathing hot air from his lungs onto the cock straining hard against the cloth constraints, Alex dragged his teeth across the hard bulge that lay beneath.

Sandy groaned and arched against his mouth. Pulling back a little, Alex ran his hands along the backs of Sandy's powerful legs, up to that round, perfect ass. "Of course I want you. How could I not? You're so beautiful. So everything I want. Come to bed." Rising, Alex suited actions to words, tugging Sandy toward the bed. It was too small, of course, but it would have to do.

Eyes glowing, Sandy let Alex lead him.

"Oh, baby. Are you sure?" Following Alex down onto the bed, Sandy laced their fingers together. "Alex."

Spreading his legs as he drew them up, Alex took Sandy's weight, sinking down deep into the mattress. "Sandy. So prettyprettypretty. Kiss me." Arching his neck as Sandy began to feast on it, Alex squirmed, savoring the feeling of all that sheer size pressing him down, savoring the heat and scent of Sandy and the incredible feel of Sandy's dick stroking his as Sandy began rocking against him.

"So beautiful. I want you. I want—" A deep, luxurious kiss cut off Sandy's murmuring and the slide of Sandy's tongue into Alex's mouth sent shivers racing up his spine.

Letting his hands roam over the broad expanse of Sandy's back, Alex -- impatient for the feel of skin on skin -- pulled at Sandy's shirt. "Off. Please. Want to feel you."

Sandy sat up to comply and Alex immediately missed the feel of him. But the sight was almost worth it as Sandy tugged his shirt up over his head and that amazing, tattooed torso was revealed. Alex reached out unthinkingly, not even considering resisting the need to touch. "Tell me again."

"What?"

"What's this called?"

"A *pe'a*. It's not a real one, though."

Running his fingers over the rows of dark green symbols, unable to take his gaze off them, Alex didn't understand. "What do you mean? It looks perfectly real to me."

"A real *pe'a* runs side-to-side, from here," Sandy gestured to a point at mid-waist, "to here." He indicated an area above his knee. "Not vertical, like mine."

"I don't care -- it's beautiful. You're beautiful." Alex had never meant anything more sincerely in his life. Sandy was gorgeous. So beautiful and so much of him it was hard to take in all at once.

"Oh, Alex, no. It's you. You're the one."

Alex smiled up into Sandy's eyes and stretched sinuously against the coverlet. "Help me take my shirt off. My pants, shoes, everything. I want to bc naked with you."

Sandy went to work on Alex's shirt, his big fingers moving quickly over the buttons to tug it off. For such a large man he moved gracefully, hands slipping easily beneath Alex's waistband to undo the belt and pants to remove those, too, dropping kisses on Alex's stomach along the way.

When Alex was finally naked, a long sigh eased out of Sandy. Nearly silent, it matched perfectly the soft, awed look in Sandy's eyes as his gaze traveled over Alex's body. Sandy's lips parted, his jaw moved subtly, but no sounds came out. He sat, frozen, kneeling atop Alex's outstretched legs.

"Sandy. Please?" Alex lifted his arms, opening them to Sandy.

"Baby. Alex, I… God." Gathering Alex in his arms, Sandy rolled, cushioning the impact with his body as they fell against the wall Alex's bed crowded next to.

Suddenly on top of Sandy looking down, Alex freed his arms and pushed himself up. "What do you want, Sandy? Tell me. Please. Tell me what you want. You feel so good. I'll do anything, anything you want. Just tell me."

"Alex… anything. This is already more than I planned on. Just lie with me. Hold me. Let me hold you."

Sandy tried to pull Alex close, but Alex had a better idea. Bracing his arms beside Sandy's head -- outside of Sandy's broad shoulders was out of the question -- Alex nipped at Sandy's lips. He licked at Sandy's mouth before twisting his neck a bit to take one of Sandy's tiny dark nipples between his teeth. Biting down briefly, Alex flicked his tongue over it, sucked it hard into his mouth as Sandy's groans filled his ears.

"I think I know what you want, Sandy. I want to give it to you. Please, can I give it to you? I want to fuck you. Will you let me? Sandy, will you let me?" The idea of being inside Sandy was irresistible -- inevitable. Why had he even hesitated before?

Why didn't matter any more. They were here now and Alex wanted to give it to Sandy almost as much as he sensed Sandy wanted it. He kissed Sandy again, his tongue sliding smoothly between Sandy's teeth.

Sandy moaned and arched beneath him, gripping his hips in large hands and grinding up against him. "Baby, you know I do. I want you. God, I want you. If you—"

"I do." As hard as Sandy now, Alex's erection pressed against Sandy. Only Sandy was still wearing his pants and his belt buckle was digging painfully into Alex's cock.

A little pain was nothing, though. His real problem was what to do for lube. Alex hadn't needed it since he'd been on Doradus. Maybe…? No. Sandy didn't seem the type to carry it on him.

Wait.

The hygiene station.

Perfect.

"Sandy, wait a minute." Alex hopped off the bed, taking a lingering look at Sandy as he did. So big, so gorgeous, so naked. And Alex was about to make him so, so happy.

The massage oil he'd borrowed from Teddy and never returned ought to work. Alex rummaged beneath the sink until he found it and dashed back. Sandy was not only still there, he'd removed his pants.

Perfect.

Slicking himself up, Alex climbed back onto the bed. Kneeling between Sandy's sprawled legs, Alex spread some of the oil on Sandy. "How do you want it?"

Sandy looked ready. His chest rose and fell, his nostrils flaring as he gazed back at Alex with eyes half-closed. "Anything you want to do will be good for me."

"I hope you mean that, because I'm not the most experienced at this side of things. You'll say something if I do it wrong?"

"You couldn't do it wrong for me."

Oh. Sandy's smile was so sweet. So sweet. If Sandy wanted it -- and if, for some inexplicable reason he wanted it from Alex -- Alex was going to do whatever it took to satisfy him.

Chapter 11

As Alex pressed up against his body, Sandy tried to unwind, but relaxing was a joke. It was Alex, and the reality of it was... it all meant too much to Sandy. Alex pressed harder and Sandy's body gave way, allowing Alex entrance; the feeling was nothing less than magical.

In a long, smooth glide, Alex eased in, not especially thick but wonderfully long, and Sandy groaned at the sensation. Being fucked was usually good, sometimes great, and, very occasionally, fantastic. The fact that it was Alex, and not some random guy he'd picked up on leave, already pushed it into the category of fantastic. Then Alex began to move and Sandy's higher thought processes shut down.

The sweet slide of Alex's dick out, then in again, sent waves of sensation shimmering through Sandy's body. Alex's chest rested against his legs, which were folded back and spread as wide as he could get them. One of Alex's hands gripped his knee, while the other stroked restlessly up and down his thigh; all the while incoherent groans of pleasure poured out of his mouth.

Just enough of the civilized man remained of Sandy that remembered to think of Alex. "Are you okay? Is it good?"

Alex began moving faster, pumping steadily in and out of Sandy's ass. "Oh, God. Baby, yeah. So good."

"Good. That's good."

Something nagged at the back of Sandy's brain. Something wasn't right… Alex… something. It was all too much for Sandy to think about right now, though. Finally, he was exactly where he wanted to be, doing exactly what he wanted, with the only person he wanted to be with.

"Alex, I—" Sandy wanted to ask, wanted Alex to… but Alex was already… Sandy should just…

"What? Is it all wrong? What do you need?" Slowing down now, Alex was gripping his legs like they were lifelines.

"Nothing. Just…" Sandy tried to get Alex to meet his eyes, but Alex's gaze flitted restlessly, never settling long in one place. Unable to force the words out, Sandy reached for Alex's hand, bringing it down to touch his dick. Holding Alex's hand inside his own, Sandy folded the long fingers around his cock and nearly lost his mind at the intensity of the pleasure. "Like that. Could you just--?"

"Sure. Of course."

Trying to time his stroking of Sandy's dick to counterpoint his thrusts in and out of Sandy's ass, Alex bit his lip in concentration. The last thing Sandy saw before his eyes slid shut was Alex's slightly irregular bottom teeth sinking into the lush fullness of his upper lip.

Sandy's hand rode Alex's as Alex stroked him and the pleasure was too much. Overwhelmed, he came, warm jets of jism hitting his chest as he clenched hard around Alex's dick inside him.

Alex continued to ride him, although more slowly now. Sandy gradually pried his eyes open to watch that long torso, so beautifully furred with a surprisingly lush happy trail that led down to the darker hair of his groin. Back slightly arched, Alex's head fell back, accenting the long line of his body; from his thighs, up his elongated chest, to the bend of his long, elegant neck.

His body undulating with each slow, luxurious snap of his hips, Alex looked dazed. Preoccupied, almost.

"Alex?"

"Mmmhmm?"

Sandy took the hand still enclosed in his own and brought it to his lips. The scent of Alex's skin, mingled with his own, tantalized Sandy's senses. First placing a brief kiss on Alex's knuckles, Sandy licked at one finger. "That was amazing." Drawing the finger into his mouth, Sandy sucked on it for a moment, smiling to himself when Alex's head came up and his eyes opened a sliver.

"Yeah?" A small smile played about Alex's mouth. "Want to see what else I can do?"

"Does it involve you coming and the two of us going to sleep?" As Sandy's body came down from its high and the best post-sex lassitude he'd ever experienced settled over him, the effects of a long day began to catch up to him. He'd go all night if Alex wanted to, but what Sandy really wanted was to hold Alex in his arms and get a little rest.

Alex sobered. "Is that what you want? To go to sleep? 'Cause I feel like I could go all night."

"I think you already have. What time is it?"

"I don't know. Umm… like, four maybe?"

Sandy smiled at the small wrinkle of worry that

settled between Alex's eyebrows. Smiled, until the magnitude of what they'd done sank into Sandy's consciousness and his own worried frown appeared. "Are you okay, baby? This was a lot for you, I know."

"I'm fine. It was great. Do you want to do it again?"

Whoa. Things were really starting to not add up in Sandy's head. Alex's smile was a shade too bright and, now that he didn't have the claws of need digging into him, Sandy could focus more on Alex, on the look in his eyes and the way his body moved. It suddenly occurred to Sandy that the way Alex had been behaving was more than just a case of whistling past the graveyard.

"I definitely do, but that can wait. Do you—Can you…Can you come, do you think?"

It was gone as quickly as it came, and Sandy still wasn't sure exactly what he'd seen, but something like -- anxiety? fear? surprise, definitely -- had raced across Alex's face.

"Oh, sure. Absolutely. Now, right?"

Sandy's gut twisted a little tighter with dread. "Whenever. It doesn't matter."

Leaning forward, Alex dropped his head a little and, eyes closing, began to move faster inside Sandy. Sandy couldn't explain it, but he knew that Alex was going somewhere in his own head and even as Sandy wondered where that was, he wasn't sure he could handle knowing.

Regardless, Alex's body moved beautifully and Sandy couldn't help reacting. He rubbed his hands up and down Alex's forearms, where they rested alongside his body. He ran his gaze over Alex's body, so beautiful, so perfect, so utterly Alex.

Sandy lifted his head and tried to catch Alex's mouth with his own, moaning at the pleasure of Alex's mouth on his as Alex fucked him hard.

Stiffening suddenly, Alex flinched; he pulled away, whispering a soft "ah" into Sandy's mouth, his hips jerking erratically as he came. When Alex's eyes finally opened again, Sandy's chest tightened at the guarded look in them. "How was it -- okay? Was it, I mean, did you like it?"

Sandy buried a hand in Alex's hair, burrowing under it to rest against the warm, damp skin he found at the nape. "It was perfect, baby. You were perfect."

***

When he woke later, Sandy's back was chilled and he wished whoever was making that racket would stop. Turning over, he reached out with an arm, feeling for Alex in the semi-darkness.

Nothing.

Dog-tired and wanting just a little more sleep, Sandy dragged his head off the pillow, locating the source of the noise and Alex in the same spot. "Baby, what are you doing?"

Down on his knees, Alex's head snapped up. "I'm sorry. I thought I was being quiet."

"No, not so much. What are you doing?"

"Cleaning." Eyes wide, chewing on his lip, Alex was the picture of guilt.

Sandy decided he must be more tired than he realized, because Alex's answer didn't even begin to make sense. "Cleaning? At..." Sandy searched for the clock. Locating it, things made even less sense. "...five-thirty in the morning?"

Dressed in the same threadbare sleep outfit he'd worn the first time Sandy had stayed, Alex rubbed at his nose with the back of a gloved hand. "I was too wound up to sleep and I started thinking about what a mess the bathroom is. It's really small and you'd think it would be easier to keep clean, but it just isn't. So, anyway, I was thinking about what a mess it is and how I didn't want you to see it. You know? So I thought I could get things cleaned up a little and then when you woke up it'd be nice, 'cause I didn't want you to think I was a slob or… you know… messy, or anything."

Rubbing a hand over gritty eyes, Sandy added up the clues, not liking the direction they were leading him, but unable to come up with any alternative that made sense. "I don't think you're a slob, I promise. Come back to bed?"

Gaze bouncing around the tiny wash area, then the rest of the apartment, Alex got up. "Okay." He pulled the cheap rubber gloves off his hands and, after stashing them and the scrub brush under the sink, Alex cast a final glance over his shoulder at the toilet he'd been scouring and climbed into bed.

Sandy gathered Alex to him, spreading the thin coverlet over them both and closed his eyes as Alex settled in against him. "Your feet are cold." It was a random thought, absently voiced, but Sandy could have kicked himself when Alex immediately moved so that the offending body parts no longer touched him. "I didn't mind. Really."

Gradually Alex burrowed closer, his arms folded close to his sides, head tucked under Sandy's chin. "You're nice and warm."

"Go to sleep, baby." It was good having Alex in his arms, close like this. The same thing, only in a real bed with decent sheets and blankets would be even better, but for now Sandy would take what he could get.

After he'd gotten just a little more sleep, he'd figure out what to do about getting Alex off whatever drugs he'd taken.

***

"Alex. Alex, baby, I've got to go."

Alex winced and pulled a pillow over his head. Even the rustling of the sheets hurt -- like his skull was too small and his brains were being squeezed out at the seams. He moaned a little, but that hurt, too, so he tried waving off the voice with one hand.

The realization that it was Sandy gradually seeped into Alex's consciousness.

Cool fingers stroked his nape. It felt divine, even though the scraping sound still reverberated around Alex's head. "The ship commed and I've gotta go. I'll be back as soon as I can. Will you be okay?"

Speaking was out of the question and even just nodding sounded painful, so Alex formed an anemic thumbs-up sign with one hand. The bed shifted as Sandy leaned over and placed a kiss on the base of his neck, Alex ignored the reality of a gesture that shot daggers of pain through his brain because he adored the concept so much.

"Talk to you soon." The bed shifted again and after a few seconds the apartment door closed.

Alex slid back down into the darkness.

***

"So, what was wrong with the last place?"

Alex took one look at Shae's cute little face, with its scrunched up button nose, fall of golden red hair shimmering with the aftershocks of a head tilt, and hated him. "Because it was all wrong. It was too small. There was no view; it was dark and ugly. How could you not see that?"

Sipping at his coffee, Shae drummed his fingers on the little tabletop between them, probably fed up with not only Alex, but the whole venture. Apartment hunting on Doradus Station was always difficult and Alex had only reluctantly agreed to team up with Shae after succumbing to the logic that pooled resources would give them more options. If just looking for somewhere to live was any measure of how they'd do as roommates, it was probably better to just give up now, as far as Alex was concerned.

"Huh. See, I didn't think it was all that bad. You're not going to get much of a view with what we're prepared to pay. Same goes for size -- we can't afford much. But it had two rooms for sleeping, a kitchen, and a communal room. Not a bad deal, all in all."

Shae's delicate shrug only accentuated his petite frame. It was all Alex could do not to slap that smug little face, so he spooned more sugar into his latte and tried to not to lose it. Why had he never noticed how irritating Shae was with his northwestern accent and his 'if only you were as cute as me' demeanor? If the annoyance factor was this high after one four-hour stretch together, what would living with it be like? And did Alex really want Shae listening in when he and Sandy were together?

"Did you see how thin the walls were? They were practically transparent. I don't know about you, but I'd like at least the illusion of privacy. What?"

"Nothing. Just… you're kinda bitchy today. Something up with you?"

It didn't help that Shae was right. "I'm just… tired. I didn't get a lot of sleep last night." Alex stirred his coffee, licking foam off the spoon before setting it aside.

"I'm tellin' ya, maybe you shoulda started with something a little easier to handle. Did you ever think of that? That's a lot of boyfriend you managed to land, pardner."

Alex set down his coffee in mid-sip and glared. "What is it with you people? What? Do you all get together and dissect my love life for fun? Just shut up, all right?"

"Whoa. Jesus, Alex. I didn't…" Shae was looking at him like he'd sprouted horns or something.

"Listen. I don't think this is going to work out. I'll see you back at work, okay?" Standing, Alex was torn between storming out and wasting a good latte. He didn't make enough credits to feel okay about leaving a perfectly good drink. Besides, he needed the caffeine, so he chugged the rest and then left.

Alex shoved his hands in his pockets and hit the sidewalk. He felt crappy. Mad at Shae. Mad at himself. Second-guessing himself over last night.

Had it been okay?

Was Sandy pleased?

Would he hear from Sandy again?

His thoughts were spinning, circling back

endlessly over last night's events. Alex walked, head down, thoughts focused on his memories of the previous evening. Sandy's skin was so smooth. Alex had licked those tiny nipples and held that taut flesh between his hands. So rosy brown. And so much of it. Sandy was amazing.

He'd actually…It was a little scary to even remember it, but… he'd held Sandy's hips between his hands and pushed inside.

How incredible.

The feeling had been— Alex closed his eyes for a moment, recalling the exact sensation as he'd eased inside. He'd been held snug by hot, tight walls. Not since… not since Liam.

Sandy had been different, though.

Just the fact of it being Sandy had made it profoundly different. Nothing bad could happen to him when he was with Sandy. And the fact that it was Sandy urging him on, coaxing him in, was… it was kind of… kind of hot.

How funny that he had to search to identify the feeling.

Thinking about it now, Alex got a little tingle and rubbed his dick surreptitiously through his pants pocket. Passing his fingers over the tip, he got a little thrill that reminded him of Sandy. It was nothing like being held in Sandy's arms, though.

The man was so big.

Alex was tall, but Sandy was taller. Taller and about three times as wide. And thick. God, his thighs were huge, heavy with muscle, and just a little crinkly hair. Alex had wrapped his arms around them and—

"Alex. Hey. What's up, man?"

Blinking, Alex pulled up and tried to focus.

"Kai. Hey, yourself."

Tall, lean, dangerous-looking Kai Xuwicha -- XO and second in command of the *Vigilant* -- stood directly in Alex's path.

"What are you doing up and around this time of day?" Kai's smile was always a little wry. Like laughing was a luxury he couldn't quite afford.

"Now that's not nice. I don't know who's been spreading those rumors, but—"

"Alex, you forget who you're talking to. I know you, doll. We go way back."

"Yeah. Right. I forgot." Alex's smile faded. Kai was right -- he did know Alex.

"So. Where you headed?"

Kai didn't budge, so Alex stepped to the side. "Back to my place. I think I'll try to get a nap in before work tonight. I'm still a little wiped."

"Yeah? You out for…? What are you out for?" Kai tilted his head, looking about as harmless as a curious cat. Pure panther was more like it.

Alex shrugged. "Oh, just thought I'd see about getting my own place. It's starting to feel a little cramped at *Nelly's*."

Smiling, Kai didn't look at all smug or knowing and Alex could have kissed him for it. "Yeah. I can imagine. Find anything?"

"No. Everything's so expensive. Anything I could afford I didn't want and everything I wanted was way out of my price range."

"That's too bad." Turning, Kai fell in beside Alex. "Headed this way? Want some company?"

"Sure." They walked, Alex realizing only belatedly that the path they followed led to both *Nelly's* and the team's office in the business district. "Have you seen Sandy this morning?" Oh, crap. Alex wanted to kick himself, but the words had slipped out without his conscious permission.

Alex didn't like Kai's roll of the eyes.

"Yeah, poor guy."

"What's the matter? Is he okay? He's not sick—?"

"Nah. Just up to his ass in alligators." Shaking his head, Alex peered at Kai, trying to understand. "He's been working on the water system. Had this big overhaul underway, thought he had it all under control when he… well, I guess he was with you last night?"

Alex nodded, biting his lip. This didn't sound good.

Kai sighed. "So, it has some problems. It would have been good if Sandy'd been on board last night -- he might have caught the problem in time. But, he wasn't and he didn't. It's not the end of the world; he just has to start all over from scratch, basically. He's not going to be a happy camper 'til that thing's up and running. Mainly because the whole ship's dependent on it and Sarhaan and everyone else's going to be breathing down his neck 'til it's fixed."

Mulling the problem over, Alex wished he had more of his brain to work with. Everything felt like mush inside his head when he tried to use it. "Is he in trouble?" Alex chanced a look at Kai, walking silently beside him, and wished he hadn't. Kai didn't look happy.

"Well, he and Sarhaan have seen happier times together, definitely."

Wincing, Alex confessed instantly. "It's my fault. He was with me. I shouldn't have let him stay. Tell them it's my fault."

"Sandy's a big boy. If that's what he had his mind set on, you couldn't have stopped him." The side of Kai's mouth kicked up in a small smile. "Don't worry about it, Alex. Sandy'll get it fixed and he'll be back before you know it."

Not at all sure he believed Kai, Alex looked down and watched the sidewalk disappear under his feet as he walked. "I hope so."

Chapter 12

"So. How's it coming?"

Sandy looked up. He gave Sarhaan credit for not giving him more shit than absolutely necessary and this time Sandy appreciated it even more than usual. He glanced around the room -- dining hall was too dignified a term for the communal eating area -- and swallowed the last mouthful of ale in his glass before answering. "It's coming."

Pulling out a chair, Sarhaan turned it around and straddled it, propping his elbows on the seatback. He sat looking for several seconds before picking a piece of lint off his sleeve and glancing up casually. "Catching a break before you go back?"

Sandy thought about it and nodded. "Pretty much." He looked at his old friend and decided to let the undercurrents go unaddressed for the moment.

"Big fucking job, man."

Settling back into his chair, Sandy massaged his temple with one hand. "No shit."

"How's it coming?"

"Like I said, it's coming."

Sarhaan sat up a little. "Help me out here and give me number. I don't even care what the number is. Just something."

"Sixty percent, maybe. I'd say definitely over half-way -- God willing and the river don't rise."

"Okay, that's good. What else do you need to get the job done? You need help besides Naslund?"

"Nah, we're okay. In fact, most of the cleaning and prep that we did the first time doesn't need to be redone; it's still good. I could probably handle it myself if you need Nas for something else."

"Not necessary. I don't want you stretched any thinner than you already are."

That last comment caught Sandy's attention. "You don't have to baby-sit me, Sarhaan. I can do my job."

Suddenly Sarhaan's gaze was glued to the empty ale bottle that sat on the table. He reached out one hand and began rocking the bottle in circles. Stalling. "I didn't say you couldn't." Sarhaan's gaze flicked up to meet Sandy's. Withdrawing the hand that toyed with the bottle, he used it to smooth the close-cut beard he'd worn for as long as Sandy had known him. "I don't think you can do two jobs at the same time, though."

"Two jobs?"

"Chief engineer on the *Vigilant* and personal bodyguard."

Well. He really must be preoccupied if he hadn't seen that one coming. "You want me out, just say the word, Sarhaan."

Sandy'd known Sarhaan for a lot of years. Long enough to be able to spot the flicker of surprise that flashed through his eyes before he covered it up by looking down at the ale bottle again.

"I didn't say that. You know I don't want you out, D'abu. I want you here, doing your job. We're all in this together and a lot of people are counting on you."

Every bit the commanding officer now, Sarhaan hadn't been when they'd run for their lives from a Republican Army that had turned on its own, but he'd grown into the role as the months had worn on. Gazing back at the man who'd been not just his comrade but his friend, too, Sandy weighed his loyalties. "Yeah, people are. You asked me to look out for Alex. Remember that? So what are you saying -- job over? Mission accomplished?"

"I'm saying I need to know what your priorities are. Doing your job, making sure this bucket of bolts doesn't fall out of the sky and us with it? Or getting some tail?"

Anger -- instant and visceral -- flashed through him. Half-way out of his chair before he caught himself, Sandy had the bottle clenched tight in his hand.

No. Oh, no, no.

Forcing himself to sit down, Sandy drew in a long breath before trusting himself to speak. "That's pretty funny coming from you."

"You think so?"

"Considering you not only brought your boyfriend on board, you put him on the payroll and gave everyone else one more mouth to feed." Sandy knew he ought to stop -- bite his tongue until tempers were cooler. But, damn it, who did Alex have to stand up for him? "And considering Alex wouldn't be in the position he is if you and Kai had kept your promises way back when."

Sarhaan's eyes narrowed and his jaw tensed. When he finally spoke, his words were slow and measured. "You, my friend, are very, very close to the line. You do not want to cross it, believe me."

"Oh, please. Are you trying to intimidate me? You can't be serious."

Far from backing down, Sarhaan leaned forward hard on the chair back, crowding in close to the table. "D'abu, listen to me. I've known you a long time. You've saved my butt and I've saved yours. We make a damn good team." Bracing an elbow on the table, Sarhaan edged closer still. "But I need to know if your head's in the game. Too many people are counting on you."

Not about to let Sarhaan think he had the upper hand, Sandy leaned in, too. "Listen, old friend, I am not about to sit here and swallow a bunch of 'do as I say, not as I do' advice from somebody who was in my shoes not that long ago."

"Oh, really. And what shoes would those be?"

"Overmatched and clueless."

That threw Sarhaan back in his seat. Both hands braced on the table, he sat staring at Sandy for a long moment, before the tension in his body began to ebb and a small smile began to play about one side of his mouth. "No shit?"

"No shit."

Unbelievably, Sarhaan began to chuckle. What began as short bursts ran together until his shoulders shook and eventually Sarhaan was wiping his eyes with his thumbs. "Oh, this is sweet. In fact, it's beautiful." The belly laughs had subsided into irregular bouts of repressed hilarity, with Sarhaan going off into another fit of laughter every time he so much as glanced Sandy's way.

"Yeah? Well, fuck you, pal. I'm glad you're enjoying it, 'cause it's killing me."

"No, no. Sorry, man. It's just, you're always mister calm-cool-and-collected. No man too big, no situation too tough for you to handle. It's just too beautiful to see you finally taking your lumps like the rest of us."

"What do you mean 'finally'?' Sandy made a conscious effort to relax his grip on the ale bottle and set it carefully back on the table.

"I mean, you just seem to sail through stuff pretty easily. Water off a duck's back. Nothing ever seems to get to you."

"Not everything. Or don't you remember Sai?"

"Sure I do." Sarhaan paused, taking a long look at Sandy. "I wasn't sure you did. You never talk about her."

Sandy shrugged. He never knew what to say. "I'm not exactly proud of it, if you know what I mean."

"You did the best you could. What else were you supposed to do?"

"How about stick by her? Do the right thing."

Catching Sandy's gaze, Sarhaan fixed him with a hard stare. "You got something against living? Because if you'd stayed with her -- 'done the right thing' -- you never would have run with us. You would have stayed and you'd have been killed, just like Salinas, just like Procter, and just like all the rest. I remember them, too."

Sandy nodded. "My head says it was the right thing to do. I couldn't ever give her what she needed. She couldn't… I didn't…" Putting it into words and speaking those words, to even just one person, brought all the shame and pain rushing back, like it was yesterday and not years ago. "She thought I was fa'afafine. It's a Samoan thing. You wouldn't understand."

"What about Alex? Does he understand?"

Lifting his gaze from where his finger absently traced a stain in the tabletop, Sandy tried to read his friend's face. "I don't know. Alex has a lot of things going on in his head -- makes it hard for him to focus."

"Listen, your business is your business. When I asked you to keep an eye on Alex, that's all I meant. Just watch out for him; try to be there if he needs help. Not that he'd ever ask. But if it's more than that, then I'm happy for you. Both of you. You're both past due for a decent break, I'd say."

"Don't hold your breath." Sandy hated self-pity, but the sullen tone in his voice was unmistakable.

"Too early to plan for a spring wedding?"

"Probably. But it's not too late for me to take this bottle and shove it up your ass."

"Huh. Appreciate the offer, but I think I need to check with Caleb first. You know we agreed to be exclusive and I'm pretty sure he'd consider that violating—"

"Yeah, violate this, pal." He gestured with one hand.

"Whoa, whoa. What's with all the aggression? Xuwicha said you finally got laid last night." Sarhaan's smile was only faintly mocking; ten-percent just-fucking-with-Sandy to ninety-percent faked utter sincerity.

"You know what? Just fuck off -- both of you." Sandy rose to leave. "I'll be in life support if you need me. I want to get this thing done right this time. A lot of other things could use my attention right now."

"Okay. Say the word if you need any more help, all right? And, uh, D'abu?"

Half-way to the door, Sandy turned back.

"Yeah?"

Sarhaan blew him a kiss. "Good night, sweetheart."

Sandy resumed his walk, not bothering to watch for the reaction as he gestured with both hands this time, Sarhaan's laughter echoing after him.

***

When Sandy finally rolled into his rack, fourteen hours had elapsed and it was a full cycle-and-a-half since he'd left Alex's bed. Scrubbing his gritty eyes with a thumb and forefinger, Sandy closed his eyes for a moment while he punched in Alex's co-ords on his comm unit.

No signal.

Damn it.

Now that he had the filtration system beaten into submission, Sandy had a few hours to call his own before he had to get started on the next task. The entire time he'd been focused on getting the new water system going, the Alex situation had been running on a loop in the back of his mind. Sandy'd had plenty of time to think about all the things he'd done wrong, the ways he'd put his own needs ahead of Alex's, and the things he could have handled better.

Mostly, though, it had been the look in Alex's eyes that had kept coming back to him. The squirrelly way Alex's gaze had bounced around the room, never lighting anywhere for long; the uncontrolled babbling about anything and everything.

It killed Sandy -- fucking killed him -- to see Alex that way. To see Alex reduced to that level by the drugs that had been used for so long to control him. And to know that it had been the pressure Sandy had put on Alex that had led him back to them.

Shit.

Why couldn't he have just kept his mouth shut instead of saying what he had? Poor Alex. Of course Alex had try to do what he could to make Sandy happy. Sandy knew that Alex felt beholden to him. He knew that. So what had he done? Just put Alex in the position of knowing that the one thing he could do to make Sandy happy was the very thing Alex had sworn off of. Way to fucking go, buddy.

Sandy tried comming again, but still no dice.

Where the hell was--? Check the time, genius. How about at work?

That was another thing Sandy had to work on: finding Alex a new place of employment. That had to work on Alex's head, seeing the floor shows at *Nelly's* every night.

Alex was smart. There had to be some other way he could make a living.

Needing to see Alex, talk to him, pet him -- no, keep your damn hands off him. That's how you got him into this mess -- Sandy let out an exasperated sigh at the thought of everything that was involved in getting to see Alex. Waiting through the airlock system again. Climbing onto the tram for the long, circuitous ride from the docking station to the city proper. The walk from the tram station to *Nelly's*. Fuck. He was rapidly learning to hate the whole tediously drawn out process.

Alternately cussing and muttering, Sandy cast a weary glance at his pillow and hoisted himself up.

Five minutes later, after throwing on fresh clothes and checking the tram schedule, Sandy made his way down the corridor to the first set of airlock doors.

***

"Shots up."

Slapping the two drinks on the bar, Alex checked his monitor for the next order, more to confirm than anything else. Two ales, a gin and tonic, and one tequila shot. Pouring the shot one-handed, he set the first of the two ale glasses beneath the spigot and let it begin to fill. The shot was finished first, so Alex started on the G-and-T while the alc poured.

The place was busy. As busy as Alex had seen it in a while. Amateur night always drew a crowd and nowhere more than the men-with-men room. Seemed like every guy from here to the Horsehead Nebula thought he had what it took to go pro.

Glancing briefly up at moans from the stage, Alex snorted. He'd seen the guy in the middle trying out last month and here he was back again. Starting the second ale, Alex gave the guy's technique a cursory review. More enthusiasm than finesse, the poor shmuck apparently harbored expert aspirations when he wasn't even a gifted amateur. He'd never make it to the pros if he couldn't go any deeper on a cock than that.

"Shae, order's up." Alex pulled down glasses for the two martinis due up next and began measuring the vodka. The four drinks from the previous order sat unclaimed. "Shae, order's up!"

Scanning the room, Alex's gaze quickly located

the missing server. Near the back, away from the noise and lights of the stage, Shae stood deep in conversation with Nick. Head tilted, eyes intent, Shae seemed to hang on Nick's every word. Nick bent attentively low over the much shorter Shae, one hand resting on the bare skin of Shae's lower back as they talked.

"Hey Alex, watch what you're doing."

So busy watching Nick and Shae, it took Alex a moment for Teddy's warning to register. Tearing his gaze away, Alex realized he'd been so distracted that he'd over-poured the vodka, wasting more than a shot's worth. "Thanks, Teddy." Alex quickly cleaned up and started the drinks over but the image of Nick, flirtatious and intent on seduction, wouldn't leave his head.

Alex knew that look. He knew the exact shade of blue of Nick's eyes. He'd been on the receiving end of that devastatingly wicked grin. He'd let himself be lulled by the promises made by those inviting pink lips.

"Hey, barkeep. Can I get an ale when you're done there, maybe?"

The voice was distinctive, so much so that visual identification wasn't really necessary. Still, sliding his gaze sideways, Alex fought to keep a neutral expression on his face. Bartok, everyone's friendly neighborhood drug connection. "You bet." Alex swung his gaze back to the task at hand, then on further to his right to see whether or not Teddy was within earshot. "That it? Just an ale?"

The sandy-haired man grinned amiably at him. "I can't think of anything else. Can you?"

"No. I can't." Beyond Bartok, Shae smiled teasingly up at Nick, whose hand slid easily down the slope of Shae's ass as Shae turned to go.

"I'll be here for a while -- if you think of anything."

Alex started the ale as Bartok's hand tapped the bar restlessly, turning something half-hidden in his hand end over end. Smiling a little too smugly, Shae picked up his order, a little extra sway in his hips as he walked away. Nick only added to Alex's hell by coming to stand behind the bar and watch the bartenders work.

"Get you something tonight, boss?"

Nick tossed him a variation of the same smile he'd given Shae moments ago, this one with the same easygoing charm, but minus the heat. "They're keeping you busy tonight, huh?"

Setting Bartok's ale in front of him, Alex held out his hand for the man's credit chip and came away with the chip, plus a little something extra. Alex palmed them both.

"Yeah, but nothing we can't handle." He glanced down at Teddy's end of the bar, then quickly back to the hand that held Bartok's card. Alex's stomach rolled at the small packet tucked discreetly beneath the card. Two small crystals, pink in color, the color that gave the drug its name: pink diamond. "Receipts should be good tonight."

Alex nearly came out of his skin when a hand clapped down on his shoulder. "I'll get out of your way and let you get back to it, then."

"You bet." So grateful that Nick was leaving, it was only when he gulped a hurried breath that Alex identified the light-headed sensation overwhelming him as the effects of stress. Nick's departure brought it down a notch below overload, but Alex's heart still pounded and he couldn't seem to catch his breath.

"Well, well. Aren't you the popular girl at the dance tonight?"

Alex looked at Bartok and tried to figure out what the hell he was talking about. Bartok just smirked, though, and cast his gaze in the direction of the door. Following the direction of Bartok's gaze, Alex looked in time to see Sandy making his way across the room.

The little leap of happiness in Alex's chest was immediately quashed by guilt over what he held in his hand.

Sandy didn't approve.

But Sandy didn't understand.

Crap.

Swiping the card, Alex rang up Bartok's drink and handed both items back to the man. Bartok's eyes barely flickered. Just glanced down before pocketing both. "Not what you're looking for tonight?"

Sandy was just meters away now.

"Some other time, maybe."

It was eerie, the way crowds seemed to part for Sandy as if by magic, almost. There was no mistaking either the power behind the muscle or the determination in his dark eyes.

Now that Alex knew Sandy a little better, he could see how it was all tempered by the man's innate decency, the gentleness of his manner. Sometimes it was hard to remember that not everyone could see that, though. They just saw the potential for murder and mayhem and got the hell out of the man's way.

Taking the spot that miraculously opened, Sandy bellied up to the bar. He leaned over, letting his elbows take his weight, and gazed at Alex. Despite the serious look, Alex's insides melted and his dick stirred, going all tingly. The moans from the stage and the crowd noise all faded as Alex's world narrowed to just the beautiful man centimeters away from him.

"Hey, baby. You got a minute?"

"Of course." Alex spoke without thinking, not that consideration would change the answer. He checked the traffic on the other side of the bar; Teddy would be swamped if he left for too long. "Only for a minute, though? We're pretty busy."

"Yeah, I figured that out all by myself." Coming around the end of the bar, Sandy followed Alex's lead into the liquor closet. Dark and cramped, it held the expensive wines and thousand-credit bottles of alcohol for the high rollers. "Kiss?"

Swamped by Sandy's nearness, senses filled with the scent and sight of him, Alex could only manage a guttural, "Sure." His nod was cut off by Sandy's mouth coming down on his, and those big hands settled on his hips.

The heat of Sandy's body drew him in and Alex pressed close, only to pull back, worried about sullying Sandy with the residue of sugar and lime and the smell of stale beer. Sandy just made a happy noise deep in his throat, though, and pulled Alex back in. "You feel good. I'm sorry I didn't get back sooner. Lotta shit to get done."

Wrapping one arm around his back, Sandy pressed their lower bodies together and the electrifying feel of Sandy's dick rubbing against his made Alex groan. Sandy leaned back against the door, put both hands under Alex's ass and lifted, his hips rocking as he moved Alex over him. Alex wrapped his arms around Sandy's shoulders and hung on; resting his forehead on Sandy's shoulder, a whispered, "Sandy," the best he could do.

"Alex, you gotta stop distracting me. I came to talk, I swear."

Laughing weakly, Alex closed his eyes and let the feelings take him over. Warmth and lust and affection and trust and sex. He wanted to melt all over Sandy and be absorbed directly through Sandy's skin.

He wanted to be naked.

He wanted to fuck.

A fist pounded on the door Sandy leaned against. "Alex! Get your ass out here, I'm gettin' killed, man. Come on."

"Crap. We need to talk, Alex." The only light came from an ancient illuma-box overhead, but when Alex opened his eyes, the lines of fatigue above Sandy's eyes and beside his mouth were starkly obvious. "If I buy the house a round, will that get us some time?"

Alex gasped at Sandy's offer. "You can't! You can't afford that." His feet touched the ground again as Sandy eased him back down.

"This is important. How soon can you get off duty?"

More pounding. Teddy. "For fuck's sake, Alex. Come on!"

"You look like you could use some sleep. Why don't you use my room? Get some rest while I finish my shift. I'll come up when I'm off work. You look beat." Alex used his thumb to try to smooth the lines over Sandy's brow, the other hand stroking the one running vertically alongside Sandy's mouth.

"If that's what it takes. We need some time alone -- just you and me -- to talk."

"Sure. Whatever you say."

"No, not whatever I say. Alex…" Dark eyes serious, Sandy opened the door and stepped out. "You'll come straight up when you're off duty?"

The heat of Sandy's hand where it rested on his hip warmed him and revived the tingling in his dick. Alex nodded. "Of course. Go now, okay?" He gave Sandy a shove and paused to retie his server's apron a little looser, all the better to hide his hard-on.

Alex was studying the video display for the next several drink orders when Joe Sotheran's faintly Euro-bloc accent penetrated his focus. "Alex, I'd like to see you in my office when you've finished your shift."

Hands clasped loosely in front of him, Alex's boss gazed at him stoically while his new business partner scanned the room with a restless gaze. Looking for Shae, perhaps? Alex glanced from one to the other, possible scenarios racing through his head. This had better not be another attempt to pressure him into performing. He'd do every other job conceivable before he'd do that.

Chapter 13

Sandy decided he really must be tired if having a drink at the bar and watching Alex work didn't sound good to him. The watching Alex part was fine; but the music, the heat and noise generated by that many bodies all in one place didn't appeal to him at all. Besides, it wasn't like he needed any more experience in the unfulfilled longing department. Trying to catch a little nap in Alex's room might be the smart thing after all.

Taking a last look before he left, Sandy's gaze was drawn to the reach of Alex's long arms as he pulled down wine glasses from the overhead rack. The loose, billowy clothing couldn't completely hide the lines of Alex's body, not to Sandy's eyes, and especially not now that he'd seen them up close and naked. He'd love to be running his hands up the sides of Alex's waist, cupping Alex's ass in his hands like he had in the storage room.

Sandy shook his head in an attempt to keep the images from taking hold and forced his feet to get moving. Not only could he use the rest, but it would help pass the time until Alex's shift was over and he could join Sandy up in Alex's room. Maybe Sandy could convince Alex to lie down with him. There was no rule that he knew of that said they couldn't talk just as well from a horizontal position as a vertical one.

Working his way toward the door, Sandy took minor note of the stage show. He usually didn't need a program to figure out the night's theme, but he had to admit that tonight's had him stumped. It looked like… historic musicians, maybe? Spandex and high heels, sure -- seen it dozens of times. The powdered wig on the guy topping was a new one, though. And what the hell was the cross-dresser doing in there, anyway? At least, he thought it was a cross-dresser. Hoped so, anyway.

Sandy paused to consider other possibilities, still partly occupied with the problem of what to do about Alex.

How could Alex ever hope to overcome his past when he was still surrounded by the free market equivalent of what he had lived involuntarily for too many years? Sandy could look at the performers on stage and keep in mind that -- with the exception of the occasional amateur night -- these people were not only voluntary participants, they had taken part in a highly competitive selection process and won out over fierce competition. These were well-paid professionals who didn't have to do what they were doing for a moment longer than they wanted to.

Was Alex's mind capable of making that distinction, though?

He'd been taken young, before his attitudes and feelings about sex had had a chance to fully develop. He'd been kept against his will, a modern day sex slave centuries after anything close had been outlawed. Could he watch night after night, people having sex -- not because they felt anything for each other, or even just because it felt good, but for money -- and not be reminded of what he'd experienced?

Sandy didn't see how he possibly could.

If Sandy wanted to have anything more with Alex than the friendship they'd developed from opposite sides of the bar in the man-on-man room at *Nelly's* -- and he did -- it increasingly seemed as though they'd need to find Alex a new job.

What could Alex do, though?

Most of life on Doradus was service oriented. Doradus had begun life as a place to service interplanetary mining and transport ships working the asteroid belt. Everyone knew the story of how billionaire J. Gage Burnette had gambled early on that asteroid mining would be the next big thing and built stations catering to the industry. The half-dozen stations scattered throughout the belt had quickly become vitally important to the people who'd been willing to give up the security of a post-revolutionary Earth to seek their fortunes in space.

What Burnette hadn't foreseen, though, was the difficulty of maintaining control over installations at the farthest reaches of human influence. It hadn't taken any time at all for the crews recruited to run the stations to appreciate the unique positions of power they held and begin conducting their own business on the side -- business that had rapidly outpaced their original missions and become too lucrative to ignore. In slightly less than a decade, the stations broke away from the control of their home world and declared themselves independent entities.

Sure, Burnette had more money than God, but the distances involved made bringing in an army impractical. Eventually a way would be found to bring the rebel stations to heel again, but for now it was the jagged edge of the frontier and every man had better look out for himself.

Sandy threaded his way through the crowded lobby, heading toward the staff exit of *Nelly's*. Whatever special Sotheran was running tonight had the place more crowded than the hold of a Republican penal transport; the room was packed. Maybe they were offering one-credit blowjobs on the het stage, because the crowd was thickest around that room; so thick that Sandy had difficulty navigating a straight path and found himself first jostled and then carried along by the crowd.

The door to the staff quarters was in sight, though, and Sandy was lowering his shoulder, making a concerted effort to move that way when a hand grabbed his arm just above the elbow. Sandy's reflexive move backward was countered by the jab of hard metal against his ribs.

Nelly's security staff was slipping if anyone had made it through with a weapon.

"You'll come quietly if you like your boyfriend's face the way it looks now."

A matching prod on his left made Sandy pause. A quick glance over first one shoulder, then the other revealed a pair of small but tough-looking Euro types -- one dark, one fair-skinned dirty blond -- blocking him in. Being outnumbered didn't worry him. Typical Euro bloc thugs, they were the dregs of the criminal classes -- cheap, interchangeable, and easily replaced. The human equivalent of a Saturday Night Special and everyone's go-to when a job was likely to get messy.

The weapons were a complicating factor, though, because sure as shit some bystanders were going to get in the way. Sandy didn't know whether to believe them about Alex. That part was just as likely to be an empty threat as not.

Just that few seconds' pause was enough. Two more of the Euros' buddies appeared, twitchy and irritable; exactly the type to take out a couple of collateral targets. The crowd behind the new pair melted away and a disembodied hand shoved Sandy through a bank of voluminous curtains that hid a door to the outside.

"Good evening. I apologize for the abruptness of my manner, but my business is urgent and it was absolutely vital that I speak with you immediately."

Sandy jerked his arm free and turned to face the new voice, shifting to balance himself on the balls of his feet. New guy made it five to one -- not insurmountable numbers, although the weapons added to the equation. He'd gotten used to life on Doradus and stopped carrying a weapon. Used to his size, if not the reputation of his ship and teammates, smoothing the way, Sandy had to admit these guys didn't look impressed.

The one calling the shots was only slightly taller; a little less lean and a lot more polished than the ones holding the weapons. The flat nose and burn scars screamed old guard Securitate; most likely one of the dozens of ex-secret police turned freelance now making money in the free market economy of the post-revolutionary era.

"I was just fine. As it happens, I'm not on duty right now. So if you'd like to talk to me, why don't you come around to my storefront tomorrow? If you want to talk business, I'll be able to quote you prices better from there, anyway. Now if you'll excuse me, I'd like to get on with my evening."

"I'm so sorry, but I'll have to insist on your indulging me for just a bit longer, I'm afraid. Dov?"

In the instant it took Sandy to recognize the last word as a name, the thug to Sandy's right and behind took a step back. Another poke to Sandy's ribs from the left stole his attention briefly as the guy on the right came back, putting his weight behind a two-handed swing. The crack and thud, followed by searing pain in his knee told Sandy the joint, and probably a good bit of the cartilage, was gone.

He brought his arms up, but the two goons who'd stood guard alongside their leader moved in quickly, twisting them out and to the side in order to bring maximum discomfort.

"Mr. D'abu—"

So they knew his name. They probably knew all about him, then.

"Mr. D'abu, please. As is sometimes the nature of business, this will necessarily be unpleasant. Please understand that that is all it is -- business."

What the fuck? He'd never seen these guys before. Seen plenty like 'em, but not these particular ones. Sandy shook his head, fighting back the nausea. "What kind of business? We turn you down for a job or something? Beat you to a deal? What?"

His answer was a small shrug, the raising of an eyebrow, as though it was an insignificant thing they discussed. "I and my associates have put a good deal of effort into -- please, Mr. D'abu, don't attempt that." He'd been checking the positioning of the guys holding him when the goon with the blackjack stepped up again, this time swinging hard into Sandy's ribs. "It is possible that you remind my man Dov here of someone from his past whom he did not like very well. He seems to be more enthusiastic than usual tonight. Tell me, how do your ribs feel?"

"Br--broken."

It was true. What could have been a knife in his side, but was probably a broken rib or two, made a nice counterbalance to the agony in Sandy's knee. He'd been dinged up pretty good more than once during his time in the Marines, but this one was going to leave a mark, he was sure.

"I am sorry." A slight grimace accompanied the delivery and Sandy almost believed the man, whoever he was. "History teaches us, though, that messages delivered sans… gravitas… frequently are not accepted with the appropriate level of seriousness."

"Message?" It hurt too much to draw a deep breath, so Sandy's question came out more wheeze than speech. His shoulders and elbows weren't too happy about the pressure being put on them, either.

"As I was saying, my associates and I have put a substantial effort into building our business. You and your friends are now attempting to cut into that business. I'm sure you can appreciate our concern."

"You want to talk business? We'll talk business with you. Maybe we can work out territories."

The one on Sandy's left gave a savage twist to Sandy's wrist and more bad news in the form of a subtle little pop sent Sandy to his knees.

"I'm so sorry Mr. D'abu, but my associates simply cannot accept a compromise on the subject. You and your friends must cease and desist immediately or more unpleasantness will follow. Do you understand?"

His shoulder threatening to dislocate, Sandy stared back. Besides the fact that pain was hampering his breathing, he knew a rhetorical question when he heard one.

Hands clasped in front of him, the man had an air of seriousness and regret, almost, about his long face as he nodded again in the direction of his chief enforcer. "Dov, please explain to Mr. D'abu how important it is to us that his associates appreciate our position."

Bracing himself for another assault with the stick, Sandy never saw the fist that connected with the side of his head and cheek. His last thought before he slid into the darkness was that there must've been a pair of old fashioned brass knuckles behind it.

***

"You wanted to see me, Joe?"

Alex hoped this wouldn't take long. He wanted to get back to his room as soon as he could so that he could curl up with Sandy and get some sleep. Poor Sandy had looked beat. Maybe Alex could distract Sandy from whatever it was he wanted to talk about so that they could just hold each other and not think. That would be nice. But first he had to get through whatever the boss had on his mind.

"Please sit down, Alex." Sitting behind his

desk, Joe Sotheran looked all business. A computer screen off to one side scrolled numbers across its face; each line a different color, the numbers updated and constantly changing. Obviously reflecting the different rooms, Alex guessed that the fluctuating numbers probably reflected attendance, while the rising numbers were most likely either gross income or possibly net, adjusted to take expenses into account and give a truer picture of profits. "Interested?"

Tearing his gaze away from the accounts screen, Alex looked back at Joe. "Hmm? Well, yes, actually. The different colors are each a different room?"

"On this screen, yes. We've also got real-time numbers on each of the private rooms, the wait staff, the performers, even the bar staff. "

"Performers? You keep track of who's on stage?"

"Of course. We know the take by hour depending on who's on stage, who's working the crowd, and who's behind the bar. We're entirely market driven. Whatever's bringing in the profits is what we want to highlight, and perhaps think about bringing in more of."

"That's so interesting. I had no idea."

Joe was smiling, even nodding a bit. "I hadn't realized until recently what a head you have for business, either."

Scouring his memory, Alex tried to figure out what Joe could possibly be talking about. Head for business? He was decent with numbers, sure. But, other than the fact that it came in handy for dividing up the tips and calculating how many supplies to lay in, Alex didn't see what that had to do with anything.

"For business?"

Alex's thoughts flashed to Sandy, imagining him upstairs in Alex's bed, his large frame dwarfing the room's meager dimensions. In a few minutes Alex would be up there, too. He pictured them lying face to face, both naked, his arms looped around Sandy's neck, their lower bodies rocking and bumping languidly against each other. They'd be feeding each other slow, wet kisses, of course. His dick twitched sympathetically even as Alex's brain tried valiantly to focus on the conversation at hand.

"Yes. We hadn't realized that you, in fact, had your own business interests." Hands clasped quietly on the desk, Joe leaned forward, his gaze pinning Alex.

"I do?" Had he been daydreaming and missed something? Some critical piece of conversation that made everything make sense?

"Yes, and unfortunately, Alex, the terms of your employment at *Durty Nelly's* prohibit the conducting of personal business whilst on the job. Do you understand?"

Alex gazed back at Joe, fidgeted in his chair, and wondered if he was having some kind of adverse reaction that made all regular conversation seem like gibberish. Conducting personal business on *Nelly's* time? "Do you mean taking a break to talk to my boyfriend?"

An expression of mild discomfort -- pain, almost -- crossed Joe's face and it was his boss' turn to shift in his seat. "No, actually. Although that does bring us to the second point I need to bring to your attention. You are aware of the prohibition against allowing non-employees into secure areas of the business, aren't you?"

"Secure areas?"

"Yes. Specifically, the wine vault. You were observed entering it with a customer and not emerging for several minutes."

"Oh, but—" Alex was speechless. This was ridiculous. "But it was just Sandy. He's not going to steal anything. All we did was talk."

Joe sighed. "Of course I believe you. However... we have established rules in place for a reason and it's my job to make sure the rules are enforced equally. I can't make exceptions for one employee and not be expected to make exceptions for others. You do see that, don't you?"

"Joe, this is ridiculous. I had a break coming and I needed a quiet place to have a quick conversation with my boyfriend. We talked, that's all. Nothing was damaged. In fact, I didn't even take the whole break, since Teddy was busy and asked me to come back early. What's the big deal?"

His expression growing increasingly troubled, Joe glanced at the computer readout, down at his hands, then back at Alex. "Alex, I'm going to call Nick in now. He has information that I think can shed some light on this conversation."

"Nick?" Oh, no. Alex had heard this song before and he didn't like the ending. "What's he got to do with this?"

Pressing a comm button on the desk, Joe called Nick into the room.

Waves of dread washed over Alex. His stomach turned over and he was afraid he was going to throw up. The parallels to another time weighed

Alex down, threatening to crush him under their combined weight.

Nick entered through the same door Alex had used, closing it behind him. The snick of the magnetic lock clicking into place completed Alex's sense of inevitable doom.

"Nick, could you show Alex what you showed me earlier?"

Joe made room for Nick behind the desk, sliding his chair back to allow Nick access. Pressing a few keys with one hand, Nick looked up from behind a fall of blond hair that Alex knew from experience was softer and smoother than any silk ever made. Was that regret Alex read there? Or guilt?

Pushing one last button, Nick stepped back and the computer screen switched from a rainbow of scrolling numbers to a view of the bar -- Alex's normal work station -- taken by a camera Alex had never known was there. The time marked on the screen was a few hours earlier and Alex saw himself on the screen; watched as the screen Alex accepted payment from Dave Bartok.

Alex had been there.

He knew what had happened.

Still, to see it on screen in full color and three dimensions made it seem somehow unreal.

Nick pressed a few more buttons and the camera focused in on Alex's hand as he reached into his work apron, withdrew a small packet, and handed it back to Bartok along with his credit chip.

"Do you deny that that's you in the video?"

Do you dispute that that is you in the picture? Years might have passed since he heard those words. He might be millions of miles away from

Earth and his wasted youth -- the man he was now might be as far from a struggling student and musician as it was possible to be -- but suddenly Alex was sixteen all over again and the sense of betrayal was as fresh as if it was yesterday. *Do you deny that that is you performing that disgusting and unnatural act?*

Alex's face heated and he knew his cheeks were flushing as red as the stripes of his boss' shirt. He bowed his head, resting his chin on his clenched fist.

"Alex?"

Alex looked up, determined not to let them see they'd gotten to him. He'd be damned if he'd relive that scenario again. He'd only just gotten away. Only just begun to break free of the nightmare that he had been forced into. Alex wanted a life -- a real life -- and if he had anything to say about it, it would somehow include Sandy. "What?"

"While you're not prohibited from having another job, at *Nelly's* we can't have employees doing anything other than their assigned job functions. *Nelly's* has a well-deserved reputation for excellence, due in large part to well trained employees performing their duties to the best of their capabilities. We simply can't have employees doing what you did. Is that completely clear?"

"Absolutely. But, Joe... I don't care what it looks like on that video. I wasn't doing business. Bartok offered, I refused. It was as simple as that."

"Really? A simple case of mistaken identity? Mr. Bartok mistook you for a customer, perhaps?"

Alex flushed. He knew he looked guilty as hell. "Something like that."

"Then, this isn't you, either?"

More video, this time taken down in the Pike. Alex remembered glancing around for security types and, right on cue, the man on the screen turned and looked into the camera. Dave Bartok again, handing Alex a small packet and Alex giving him credits.

Alex could only stare at the display. Watch himself, not that long ago and at the same time a lifetime ago, pocket the drugs and walk away.

Was it stupid? Sure. But he'd do it again in a heartbeat, because taking it had let him be close to Sandy. Even high as a kite, it had been the best night of his life. He and Sandy had been as close as two people could be and it had been nothing short of amazing. For as much sex as Alex had had in his life, it was as close to making love as he'd ever come -- maybe ever would come.

The video stopped, frozen on Alex's very recognizable back, and Alex could only manage a small bitter smile as he rounded on Nick. "Nice to see you haven't lost your touch. Still selling people out to help your own interests. This time you haven't even got the excuse that you're saving your own skin. What does this get you, bonus credits with your new partner? Trading favors with the local security chief? What? Tell me. What did it get you, Nick?"

Maybe Nick had grown up some, too, because he at least had the grace to look abashed. "That was a long time ago, Alex. You don't think I'd go back and do things differently if I had the chance? Because I would. Seth Loftin brought this to us. He was concerned."

"Thanks, but I'm not quite as naïve as I used to be, Nick. Ten years being used like a sex doll will do that to you. Do you have any idea of the things I've done?" Just saying the words opened the door a tiny crack. Despair welled up inside him and Alex fought to stuff it back down. If he let it out, even for an instant, he'd be lost, so he reached again for the numbness that had gotten him through so much. Don't think. Don't feel. Just keep moving. "Forget it. Consideration for others never was your best subject."

"I'm sorry you've had a difficult time in the past, Alex." Joe Sotheran's tone was so matter-of-fact that Alex could only stare in amazement. What would it take to touch the human soul behind that cold-blooded exterior? If there even was one to touch. "Be that as it may, rules are rules and I'm afraid we've no choice but to terminate your employment."

Chapter 14

"Can't this thing go any faster? Kai, talk to the man; see what you can do. Jimi, how's he doing?"

"Not good. There's not much we can do for him out here."

Sandy wished everyone would cut the chatter and just take the bloody knife out of his ribs. Make that knives -- plural. Maybe he could roll onto his side and—

"Whoa, buddy. Sandy, don't move. Sarhaan, help me."

Problem now was, no air. Every shallow breath he took hurt more than the last. He'd take the pain, if only it brought oxygen with it.

Prying one eye open, Sandy found Sarhaan watching him, brow furrowed with worry. "Sandy, you awake? Talk to me, big guy."

"Can't. Breathe."

"Shit. Jimi, what've you got? Says he can't breathe."

Vilnius, looking all business, joined Sarhaan, so that the faces of concerned teammates bent over him were all Sandy could see. "I'm doing the best I can, but I don't have a lot of options until we get him back to the ship. I don't want to have to do this on a tram in motion if I don't have to. Sandy, I need you to lie still. Can you do that for me?"

Tram in motion? That might explain his nausea. His knee was on fire -- throbbing and hot -- his sides ached. But the thing that had him teetering on the edge of panic was the fact that he couldn't draw breath. His chest hurt like hell and his lungs were screaming. "Breath. Air."

"Fuck." Vilnius again. Good kid. Sandy hoped he knew what he was doing. "Sarhaan, I'm gonna have to stick him. I don't think I have a choice here."

"Stick him? What the--? Is he turning blue?"

"We're at least another ten minutes out. Jimi, can he make it that long?"

Voices. Sandy couldn't tell who was who. Kai, maybe?

"I'm gonna do it, Sarhaan, or it's gonna get ugly. Here, hold his shirt back for me." Someone swabbed Sandy's chest with something cold.

"What's that?"

"Just some local anesthetic. Then the catheter. Close your eyes and relax, Sandy. This should help." A pinprick jabbed Sandy in the chest, a little below his collarbone. "Can you feel that?"

Sandy heard more than felt the thumping at the site of the needle jab. No air. He tried a head shake.

"Good. Eyes closed, now. Think about something nice. Think about home. Think about Alex. Sarhaan, pinch his hand, hard. Right there between his thumb and his, yeah, like that."

What did his hand have to do with anything? Vilnius must be leaning on him with a pen or something. The pressure built. A weight on his chest. Built some more. Suddenly it was gone. Part of his chest gave way and this time when he tried to draw breath into his starving lungs it worked.

"Okay, better. That's better. Did you hear that, Sarhaan? That should help. I think this'll hold him until we get him on board."

***

"You make a shitty invalid, you know that, D'abu?"

"So let me out, then." Sandy glared at Kai.

"Tú comprends, you're still fucked up?" Kai stared back impassively.

"I'm all better. See?" Pushing himself upright, Sandy swung his legs over the side of the infirmary bed, only flinching a little at the twinges of pain in his leg and back.

"Better, sure. But you, my friend, are still far from well. The shape you're in, I think Jimi here could kick your ass."

The affronted look on Vilnius' face made Sandy laugh, which in turn triggered a bout of coughing. Pressing a hand to the side he'd collapsed the lung on, he kept it there until the coughing fit passed. Sandy didn't care how long he'd spent in re-gen -- he still felt like shit. His knee was maybe eighty-percent and he'd gotten winded just going to the head.

Vilnius scanned the metabolic readout from the telemetry and got his serious look on again. "Chief, you could really stand one more pass through the machine. You need it to--"

"No! Definitely, no. I've already had all I can take of playing dead man; I can't lie still another minute. I'm going stir crazy. What I need is to get out of here." Sandy fit his actions to match his words, sliding off the bed and heading for the locker holding his clothes.

Pulling off the sick bay clothes, he wadded them into a ball and tossed them into an open laundry bag, then stepped into his pants. Or tried to. He had to sit down first to do it, but he finally got his pants on. "And to talk to Alex. Who was the last person to talk to him?"

Sandy tugged a clean shirt over his head and looked around for his boots. He was pulling on the second sock when something in the quality of the silence struck him as odd. When he looked up, Vilnius was gone and Kai was standing with his arms folded across his chest. Sandy knew that look and it was rarely a good thing.

"Kai… What aren't you telling me?"

"We're not sure where he is, Sandy. No one's seen him since the night you got ambushed."

***

"What do you mean you haven't looked?" Sandy's temper was rising along with his volume and if someone didn't start giving him some answers he liked, things were likely to take a turn.

"I never said that. I said it wasn't our top priority." Kai's easy slouch as he walked belied his attention to the conversation. He might look calm, but Sandy knew that any periods of true relaxation were few and far between for the team's XO. "It's on my list of things I'd like to know -- it's just not number one."

"That's just great." Sandy headed in the direction of Sarhaan's quarters as fast as his throbbing knee allowed. He needed to find Alex and the thought of all the time that had been wasted while he floated in limbo... God only knew what had happened. "I hope finding out who made unauthorized modifications to my anatomy is one of them."

Walking beside Sandy, Kai's athletic stride had never looked more effortless. Sandy had never envied the man his lean, wiry build more. "That'd be one, definitely."

"What they wanted should be another one. To send a message, obviously, but what did they want? Something about cutting in on their business -- but that doesn't make any sense. There must be a hundred ships hauling cargo and transporting people."

Kai only nodded and looked thoughtful as they arrived at Sarhaan's door. "I think the four of us should talk this over before you go taking off. More and more this sounds like it affects the whole crew; the business. We need to deal with it as a team."

"Four of us?" Sandy palmed the thermal-imaging lock, entering as the door slid open. Sarhaan stood with one arm braced against his desk, the other against the big chair that sat behind it, bracketing Caleb. Perched on the edge of the big chair, Caleb sat, his hands moving quickly over the keyboard of Sarhaan's computer. "Ah."

"Caleb's been helping gather the intel. He's been checking station security computers for information and we've got a few leads."

Sarhaan and Cal looked up. Even without Sarhaan's possessive, protective body language, Sandy would have spotted the connection between them. Their closeness was obvious in the easy familiarity -- comfort evident in their physicality.

Maybe someday…

"Hey, Sandy." Caleb smiled and sat back, one hand dropping to rest against Sarhaan's knee, as though touching Sarhaan was its normal resting state.

Sarhaan glanced up, acknowledging Sandy's presence with a nod before returning to gaze at the computer screen. "Come look at this. This is pretty interesting. How are the ribs today?"

After first flicking a glance in Kai's direction, Sandy crossed the room, rounding the desk even as Cal tilted the screen for easier viewing. "They're okay. My knee's still crap, but I'm done lying around in sick bay. What'm I looking at?"

"I heard you'd finally had enough. You going to try to heal on your own, then?" Sarhaan's hand now rested against the back of Cal's neck, absently rubbing a strand of Cal's hair between his thumb and forefinger.

"I can't sit still any more. I'm already too far behind to lose any more time. And what's this I hear that no one's talked to Alex since I got laid out?"

Sarhaan and Kai made eye contact.

Caleb wiped a hand on a pant leg.

It was finally Sarhaan that broke the silence. "We're looking for him, don't worry. Caleb's been monitoring the exit logs and he hasn't left the station."

"That's it? That's all you've got? What about *Nelly's*? What does Sotheran say?"

"Everyone's favorite nightclub owner isn't talking. Claims he can't violate company confidentiality agreements."

"That's horseshit. I'll go down there and violate

something, and I won't be the least bit confidential about it when I do."

"Sandy, take a look at this." Cal drew his attention back to the computer readout. "Is this the guy you had the run-in with?"

One look at the picture and Sandy knew. The man who'd been running the show out back of *Nelly's* had been a few years older, a little more the worse for wear, but definitely the same man in the picture. "Vasiliy Brasov. That's the one."

"Wanted by both the Republic and the Euros, he fought extradition until he could buy his way off world. He's ex-Andryusha. He disappeared around the time of the collapse of the European Union and, until now, he'd been presumed dead."

Caleb leaned back, resting against Sarhaan's legs, looking so comfortable and secure that resentment flared in Sandy's gut. Why should he be safe and sound while Alex was still out there, God only knew where?

Sandy looked to Kai, who'd been suspiciously quiet until now. Kai was the one with the background in intel; shouldn't he be at least involved this conversation? "What do you think? Know him?"

Folding his arms, Kai shifted his weight onto one foot, looking singularly unimpressed. "I know his type. Those old school hard-guy types -- the 'yushas, the Stasis, Te-Wu -- they'd usually rather gut you than deal with you, so you're probably lucky to be here."

"What does that mean for us then?" Sarhaan's hands rested on Cal's shoulders now and Sandy knew exactly what was going through his head.

Kai looked first at the screen and then at each of

them in turn. "It means, I think we've got an old fashioned turf war on our hands."

***

"Okay, so this all goes to the laundry on Green?" Alex shouldered the giant bag of soiled laundry and headed for the door.

Mid-morning and Henry was only just climbing out of bed. Tousled and sleepy-eyed, looking years younger than Alex knew him to be, the slender Asian man finger-combed his waist length hair as he yawned and waited for his cup of tea to cool. "Mmmhmm . Be sure and tell them it's mine, okay? I throw them a freebie once a month or so and they give me a better rate."

"You're kidding." Stopping to stare, Alex gazed at Henry and reassessed.

"Nope." Henry shrugged. "Arkady -- the owner -- he's not very demanding. He's easy to please and it's no big deal to me."

"Wow. I wouldn't think…"

In the midst of logging in to the morning news feed, Henry paused. "What?"

"I just…" Alex was unsure just how candid he could be. "Never mind. I'll see you later."

"What's on your mind, Alex? Don't be afraid to say what you really think."

Picking up the scent of Henry's jasmine tea as he pursed his lips and blew across the top, Alex weighed exactly how far he could trust the man. Was Alex entitled to any respect as a no longer practicing member of the brotherhood? "I'm just surprised that you'd work for free. I don't think I would."

"Have you given any more thought to--?"

"No." Alex cut Henry off. "Definitely not. That answer won't change."

"Well, to me it's all the same. I could work for credits or I could barter for services. Besides, it saves us both on processing fees this way."

"I guess."

"No luck finding anything new yet?" Henry stirred his tea and took a cautious sip, watching Alex over the rim.

"No. I've got an interview at the *Busted Flush* in a few hours, though -- keep your fingers crossed for me. You're going to want your couch back sooner or later, I imagine."

"Don't worry about it. You're no trouble at all, hon, I told you. It's kind of nice having company, actually. And," Henry glanced at the bag of laundry Alex still held, "it's definitely not bad having someone to take care of the mundane tasks."

"I guess that's my hint to get going. Besides, I want to have time to come back and clean up before my interview."

Henry grinned, his dark eyes sparkling. "Why? Have you been in the place lately? They don't call it the Flush for nothing, you know. Somebody ought to flush it."

"It's money. Credits." Alex glanced at the couch that had been his bed over the past several nights. "I need to pay my own way."

"Yeah, I know." Before turning back to his news feed, Henry smiled encouragingly. "Let me know if you want help with your hair or anything. For the interview."

"Thanks."

Mulling over his list of things to do, Alex made his way down the stairs and out to the street. Henry lived over his business, sharing a four-plex with two other freelance recreation specialists and a guy who worked for station security. A nice enough set up, Alex could see getting something like that for—

He'd almost said Sandy and him.

He really missed Sandy.

It had been four days since Alex had been fired. It had also been four days since he'd heard from Sandy. Coincidence? Maybe. Maybe Sandy didn't want anything to with him any more. Or maybe he'd gotten tired of waiting.

By the time Alex had gotten back to his room -- escorted by *Nelly's* security staff, just long enough to gather his things and get out -- Sandy had been gone. Alex wondered what Sandy thought about why Alex had been delayed. Did he think Alex had decided to work late? That he'd rather be doing anything besides be alone with Sandy? Or had he figured out that Alex had gotten high and was appropriately disgusted?

Why hadn't Sandy returned any of his messages, though? Should he have gone to see Sandy on the ship?

Alex shook his head. The drugs might have been a mistake. Aside from losing his job over it, he couldn't tell what Sandy had thought about the whole experience. He'd never cared enough before to notice, but Alex couldn't remember a lot about the night. Maybe the difference was, he'd never wanted to remember before.

The laundry on Green wasn't hard to find and Alex dropped off Henry's laundry, giving the man behind the counter the location code for Henry's apartment instead of Henry's personal ID number. The man took the bag, running a speculative glance over Alex as he did.

Whatever.

The disgusting little weasel could hope for anything he liked, but all he was getting from Alex was a bag of dirty laundry.

Leaving the shop, Alex stopped to consider. The station's lighting had brightened to simulate late morning. The foot traffic was still sparse, but people were beginning to stir and move about. It might be a good time to stop in a few businesses -- see who might be looking for help. The only problem was, knowing how to mix drinks and give a world class blowjob were about all he really had as far as certifications.

While he was still willing to get behind a bar and make small talk to coax the customers into spending more, he wasn't willing to give up control over his body, not now when he'd only just gotten it back.

"Mr. Valentine, a moment of your time?"

Mr. Valentine?

No one called him by his last name. In fact, it had been so long since he'd even heard it that it had taken Alex a moment to realize that whoever it was meant him and not his father.

Alex turned. He wasn't far from the Pike and these men looked like they might have just come from there.

Different.

Outsiders.

There were three of them. Not the usual miners, spacers, or station-dwellers, Alex had never seen them before. So different from the well-heeled, sophisticated types that had been his main clientele back on Earth, these men looked… smudged. Dirty. Not their clothes or their skin, though. The men themselves, somehow.

Alex looked at them warily. "Who's asking?"

"Mr. Valentine, may I call you Alex? No need to be so formal."

"Have we met?" Could he have—? He didn't think so, but it wasn't out of the question. There'd been too many to say for sure.

A little shorter than Alex, but older, the man looked weary; as though he'd seen too much. Yeah, well, so had Alex.

"Not officially. Our mutual acquaintances have spoken of you so often, though. So fondly. I feel as though we're old friends."

This was getting weirder by the moment. If Alex had learned one thing over the years, it was reading people. His survival had depended on it and he had by God survived.

"Who are you? What do you want?"

"Done with the pleasantries, then? Straight to business? Very well, then." The man's smile faded. "What we want is for you and your friends to stop mucking about in our business. We've worked too long to let some small time operators from a dingy little backwater operation like this get in the way."

"Huh?" Alex stared at the man. His expression was too deadly serious to think he might be joking. "I'm not-- I don't-- I think you must have me confused with someone else. I'm a bartender. Was a bartender. Now I'm unemployed."

"Yes, yes, we know all about your little job at the nightclub. We've talked to some of your associates and word is getting out."

While their leader was talking, the two others -- obviously underlings -- moved around to flank Alex, so that he was now effectively surrounded. He tried to back up, but the two thugs closed ranks on him. Adrenalin spiked in Alex's blood and his heart picked up speed.

"Look, there's obviously a mistake here. I don't know what you're talking about, but I'm a threat to no one's business. I just..." Alex raised a hand to run it through his hair and one of the goons stuck a weapon in Alex's side -- a warning not to move -- and Alex froze. He had no idea what kind of weapon it was, but it felt extreme and Alex wasn't going to argue.

"Be very careful with your movements, if you would. My man Dov here is a notoriously poor judge of character; prone to acting first and questioning later. Problematic, but so difficult to train out of people, I find."

"Okay, now. Hold on. I really think you've got me mistaken for someone else. Can we just talk about this some more, Mr.—" He didn't know the man's name. Alex tried lowering the hand he'd raised to his head and got a jab in the side for his trouble.

"Vasily Brasov." The man's lips hadn't moved. The voice was familiar. Unaccented. The thoughts all collided in Alex's brain simultaneously.

Sandy!

Alex tried to look without moving his body too much. He craned his neck and found Sandy, with only one man for back up, standing a few meters behind him.

"Mr. D'abu." Brasov smiled and Alex got the

impression that for this man, the fun was just beginning. "And looking very resilient, may I say? I'm most impressed."

Alex must have unconsciously relaxed, because he got another poke with the weapon. Straightening, he turned his head, his gaze meeting Sandy's and he couldn't help but smile.

Sandy didn't blink. "I told you we could talk business, but first you need to stop harassing my people."

"I would like that, but a good businessman knows when the advantage is his, and any failure to exploit that advantage would simply be poor business practice. Unacceptable. Or do you not agree, Mr. D'abu?"

"I believe I see your point." Sandy's lips quirked. "But a businessman should also appreciate the importance of preparation in advance of any negotiation."

From behind him, Brasov's arm was twisted backward, while a disembodied hand pressed a pistol to the base of his skull as, from out of the shadows behind him, Kai Xuwicha stepped forward.

"Hello, Vasya. Just like old times, eh?"

Chapter 15

Brasov froze and Sandy could breathe again.

It chilled Sandy's blood to see Alex caught between a stone-cold killer like Brasov and his two thugs. Sandy'd slipped into fighting mode without a second thought, like slipping on a comfortable old coat, and it felt good to be back in action. Everything had been relaxed and easy, a walk in the park -- until he'd recognized the posture of men carrying concealed weapons and realized those weapons were trained on Alex.

Life was fragile. Terrifyingly easy to snuff out. He had to get Alex out of there.

"Who is that? Xuwicha? Is that you? How do you come to be involved in this shabby business, my old friend?"

"Who it is doesn't matter. All you need to know is that the pistol he's holding to your head is locked and loaded. Tell your associates to step away or my colleague will be forced to deliver a little message of our own -- gravitas, no extra charge."

"Disgraceful that someone with your abilities should be reduced to consorting with such second-rate criminals. You were always so much classier than that."

Nothing in Brasov's body language betrayed the pressure being put on his shoulder. He smiled and chatted as though catching up with an old acquaintance who had a gun pressed to his skull was an everyday thing.

Who knew?

Maybe it was.

Kai's narrow face twisted into a facsimile of a smile. "Tell your friends to back off and we can all go for a drink. Talk over better days. Tell you what, Vasya -- I'll even buy the first round."

Even from this distance, Sandy could see the calculation in Brasov's eyes and his gut clenched. This was where things would either go smooth and everyone walked away clean, or where a limited-phase energy pulse slammed into Brasov's brain pan and things got messy. An expensive cleaning bill would be the least of their worries if they had to discharge a weapon within the station.

"Dov, Arkady, allow Mr. Valentine to rejoin his friends. We can talk more about this later."

The two gunmen relaxed their posture and stepped back, allowing Alex to move for the first time since Sandy arrived. His gaze darting between the two sides, Alex took two hesitant steps before breaking into a run and within seconds Sandy was wrapping a protective arm around Alex as he buried his face against Sandy's shoulder. While Sandy murmured quiet reassurances, Kai lowered his weapon and stepped back. Brasov turned and the two men exchanged greetings like a pair of long-lost brothers.

***

"What the hell were you thinking?"

Sandy tried to keep his tone even, but the fear

was gone and in its place now was something hotter; something that felt a little like anger. They had retreated to VSS, Inc.'s offices, specifically, the apartment above it. Naslund was relaxing downstairs -- looking at porn again, probably -- while Kai played old home week with the criminal who had ordered a charged weapon held to Alex's head.

Alex's eyes widened and he held on to Sandy's arms as they gripped Alex's shoulders. "About what?"

"About anything. Were you thinking at all? Wandering the streets like some idiot child. You could have been killed. Do you know how close you came just now?"

"I wasn't wandering the streets, I was helping out a friend. I thought it was the least I could do after he was nice enough to let me sleep at his place."

Sandy brushed the hair out of Alex's eyes and tried to read what was behind them. "Is that where you've been? What's the matter with your place?"

Looking away, Alex shifted beneath Sandy's hands and made a half-hearted attempt to break free. "They fired me. Since the room at *Nelly's* came with the job… no job, no room."

"What do you mean they fired you?" The idea of someone having Alex and letting him get away made no sense.

"They fired me. Let me go. Terminated my employment. They gave me ten minutes to collect my things and then they showed me the door. I'm done. I have no job." The jaw was firm, as unyielding as the set of the mouth. It was the look in Alex's eyes, too bleak and hopeless for just the loss of a job. "What am I going to do, Sandy?"

"Oh, baby. Baby, c'mere." Sandy opened his arms and Alex moved in. Sandy raised his chin to make room as Alex slipped his arms around Sandy's waist and settled in against the wide chest. "Did Sotheran do it himself?"

"Yeah." Alex nodded and Sandy stroked his hair, combing his fingers through the silky dark strands.

"When?"

"The night I saw you at *Nelly's*. Four days ago, I think. You wanted to talk and you went up to my room to wait, but when I finally got there, you weren't there -- when they walked me up." Alex untucked his head and leaned back, gazing up at Sandy. "Where'd you go?"

Sandy sighed, trying to decide how much to tell Alex. "I, um, I got waylaid. Why didn't you comm me?"

"I did."

"Oh." Feeling like the lowest life form on terra, Sandy closed his eyes and wrapped his arms tighter around Alex. "God, I'm sorry. Shit. I should've thought…"

"It's okay." It was the defeated little shrug that did Sandy in. "I handled it."

"Sure, by yourself. You shoulda had me -- Sarhaan, Kai, at the very least -- helping. Sleeping on some stranger's couch. You did sleep on the couch -- right?"

"Yes, Mother, I slept on the couch."

"Well, don't say it like it's completely ridiculous. You're a good-looking guy with a great body. Of course he'd want you." Sandy tilted Alex's head back, pushing the hair off Alex's forehead with one hand to get a clear view of those blue eyes. “Who wouldn’t?”

“Astonishing, isn’t it, how many are able to resist my exotic allure?”

Alex might be mocking, but Sandy wasn’t. “Yeah, it is. I don’t know how anyone could look at you and not want you. If they talked to you -- got to know you, even a little -- then it’s even more unbelievable.”

“I think you must’ve taken one too many blows to the head, Sandy. That, or there’s something off with your eyes.”

“There’s nothing wrong with my eyes. I can see just fine.” He wanted to kiss Alex, ached to, so much that holding back caused a physical pain in his chest. Those eyes. That mouth. The smooth, pale skin with the tiny scar high on one cheek. “Alex—”

Sandy gave up fighting, closed his eyes and leaned down, tilting his head to find the perfect angle to kiss perfect Alex’s perfect mouth. Alex wasn’t panicking, but Sandy took things slowly nevertheless as he moved in, teasing Alex’s spare upper lip, drawing it in between his teeth. Alex’s hands at the small of his back gripped the material of his shirt. As Sandy leaned forward, their lower bodies pressed together and he groaned at the glorious pressure of Alex’s hardening dick pressing on his.

Letting his hands slide down Alex’s body, Sandy gripped Alex’s arms and pulled the man closer for a more thorough kiss. He loved the way Alex tasted, smelled, felt in his arms. Sandy needed to get closer, couldn’t seem to get close enough. He wanted to be right next to Alex’s body, skin to skin, to hold that slim body between his hands as they rolled across the bed. As they fucked.

Sandy broke away, came back for another kiss, slid a hand down to cup Alex's ass and press him closer. He groaned and kissed Alex again. "Alex. God, you feel good. Oh, yeah."

"Sandy, hold me." Alex wrapped his arms around Sandy's neck and squeezed. Lifting himself up onto his toes, Alex would have climbed into Sandy's lap if they'd been sitting. Instead, he wrapped one leg around Sandy, rubbing his now fully erect cock against Sandy's.

Alex was tall, but Sandy was both taller and heavier, so having Alex lean his full weight on Sandy wasn't a problem. Except that there was no reason for this awkward fumbling when there was a perfectly good bed at hand. This was the same apartment, after all, that Sandy had used for the months the guys had been gone on the run to 10-Hygiea.

Sliding his hands down to Alex's ass again, Sandy lifted Alex and walked them both backward toward the bed. "I want to lie down with you. Hold you." The backs of Sandy's legs now touched the bed and all he could think of was the last time they'd been in a bed together. "Will you?"

"Mmmhmm." Alex squeezed with his legs as he leaned back in Sandy's arms. "Just hold me?"

"Whatever you want. Hang on." As carefully as he could, Sandy lowered them both to the bed, enjoying the view of Alex smiling cautiously down at him. When Alex's smile slowly faded, Sandy realized he'd just been sitting, staring. "What is it?"

"Are you going to take your shirt off?" Alex's fingers were teasing Sandy's hairline at the nape of his neck, stroking delicately, sending shivers up Sandy's spine.

"I could do that." Sandy was leaning back, his hands bracing their combined weight and gravity was his friend, because it pressed Alex's cock deliciously down on his.

"Mmmhmm. I want to see it again."

"It's the tattoo, isn't it?" Trying to keep it light, Sandy smiled. Knowing Alex might bolt at any minute if he moved too fast, Sandy kept his gaze fastened on Alex's face as he unbuttoned the shirt. Alex's gaze never moved from the section of skin revealed by each successive closure unbuttoned. "I think you've got a tattoo fetish."

Alex didn't respond, just reached out one tentative hand, only to stop millimeters from Sandy's chest. Raising his gaze to Sandy's for the first time, the glow in Alex's eyes took Sandy's breath away and Sandy knew what the question would be. "May I?"

Sandy could only nod.

Alex's touch was so faint, so tantalizing, Sandy wondered for a moment if he only imagined it. It didn't matter, though -- his nipples hardened to a sweet ache anyway when he finally shrugged his shirt all the way off and he was bare before Alex's gaze.

"Why doesn't it go all the way around?" Alex was running his fingers over Sandy's skin, tracing the designs again, letting his fingers trail upward, beginning at the beltline and leaving a trail of sensation in their wake.

"The, uh, the *tufuga* -- the elder who did the

tattoo -- he wouldn't do it the traditional way. The old way." His dick was painfully hard, too, and Sandy was having a hard time concentrating on anything beyond Alex's touch and where it might go next. "Said since we were pushed off the islands, it wasn't right to do it the old way. So instead of a horizontal band around the body, he did a vertical band. Something about… God."

"What do you mean pushed off?" Alex's fingers trailed lightly over Sandy's belly, stroking small, repetitive motions across the short lines near the waistband.

"Alex, that's…"

"What?" Alex stopped.

"Don't stop. I'll keep talking if you keep touching me."

"Deal." Continuing the maddeningly delicate tracing, Alex followed the outline of Sandy's tattoo, his touch much too light. Preoccupied by imagining where Alex's fingers might go next, Alex's reminder came as a frustrating distraction. "You're not talking."

"Right, um. So, because we didn't have the land any more, he couldn't do it the old way. The traditional way. So he did it the same, only different."

Lying back on the bed, Sandy reached for his belt buckle, only to have Alex brush his hands away. "Let me."

Alex's voice was soft, as soft as his fingers when he reached under Sandy's waistband and grazed the sensitive head of Sandy's dick and the concept of rational speech evaporated. "Oh, Alex. Just—"

"Just…?"

Sandy raised his heavy eyelids, moving his gaze to Alex's hands moving so seductively near his cock. Alex looked into it -- like he was enjoying what he was doing. Alex would have learned how to fake responses with a high degree of believability. "Just anything."

"Really? Do you mean it? Because… because I'd really like to… "

Alex's gaze never strayed far from Sandy's belly, the tattoo, where the tip of Sandy's dick was just visible over the waistband of his pants. The seconds ticked by as Alex stared.

"Do it."

That got Alex's attention. "Do what? You don't even know what I'm thinking."

"Doesn't matter. Do it."

"Yeah?" Trailing two more tormenting fingers down the center of Sandy's chest, over his belly button, until they reached the snap of Sandy's pants, Alex's face broke into a cautious smile. "This is going to be so hot."

***

A feeling of wonder slipped over Alex as he gazed down at Sandy. Every time he thought he couldn't be any more amazed, Sandy proved him wrong. So beautiful. So incredibly giving. So sexy.

Alex closed his eyes to better concentrate on how impossibly good touching Sandy felt. From his position straddling Sandy, Alex flexed his hips and realized his problem immediately: he had too many clothes on. Dropping a quick kiss on Sandy's mouth, grinding his groin against Sandy as he did so, Alex pushed himself away.

"Where're you going?" Sandy's gritty, guttural tone sent heat flashing through Alex.

Sandy was hot.

Desperate.

It was Alex who was doing it to him.

"Don't worry. I'll be right back." Alex stood and quickly shoved his pants and shoes off, yanking his shirt over his head and dropping it where he stood. In seconds he was climbing back on the bed.

The first thing he did was remove Sandy's hand from where it had strayed to stroke his own cock. "If you want something to do with your hands, put them here." Alex took Sandy's hands in his and placed them firmly on his own butt. Sandy's fingers immediately sank into the skin, digging into the muscles beneath, making Alex whimper.

"Like that?"

"Perfect. Now don't move them." Alex lined his body up with Sandy's so that their dicks lay next to each other, touching, and flexed his hips again. Sandy's quick intake of breath told Alex that it must feel nearly as good to Sandy as it did to him, so Alex stroked again. The sight was nearly as entrancing as the feeling, their two cocks touching. The sheer intimacy of it took his breath away.

He placed his hand on both cocks, spanning them, pressing them closer together, and groaned.

"Alex." Sandy was panting, his thumbs digging into Alex's hips.

"What?"

Eyes shut tight, Sandy's head pressed back into the mattress, the tendons in his neck straining with the effort. "You're killing me. You know that. And, no, don't stop. Don't you dare."

"Okay." Alex began to move, stroking up into his own hand, where it grasped two hard cocks. He tried using both hands and the additional pressure was incredible, but when Sandy jerked and nearly dumped him off the bed, Alex put one hand back on the bed for balance.

He experimented.

He put one hand beside Sandy's shoulder, flexing with his hips and pumping his hand simultaneously. He needed to lean forward, though, and found that by rising up on his knees a bit he found a new angle that created the most amazing friction.

"Alex, yeah, like that. That's… God." His face pulled taut with tension, Sandy choked out his words, but Alex couldn't stop. It felt too good, The two of them -- together -- it was the most personal, intimate thing Alex had ever been involved in.

And so incredibly hot.

It was unbearably hot.

"Sandy."

Alex gazed down at his hand, holding the two of them together, at Sandy's gloriously straining body, that face a mask of overpowering pleasure. Alex came. His long spurts of semen splattering his hand, their dicks, Sandy's chest. As Alex's come rained down on them both, Sandy climaxed and sprays of hot, salty jism went everywhere.

Staying where he was as random tremors wracked their bodies, Alex could only smile. He couldn't escape the thought that somehow his pleasure had actually heightened Sandy's. That Sandy had gotten off on Alex's orgasm, and it was a revelation.

Leaning forward, Alex licked a fleck of come

from Sandy's chin. Found another on his neck and tasted it, lapping delicately at the salty taste, distinguishing easily between the flavors of sweat and semen.

"C'm'ere." Sandy's hand moved from Alex's waist to his shoulder, tugging, and Alex reluctantly leaned sideways to slide off, settling on Sandy's outstretched arm. Pressing a kiss to Alex's forehead, Sandy draped his arm over Alex, drawing his lover close and Alex relaxed into him.

The collective heat from their bodies kept Alex warm in the relative cool of the room, but he would have stayed close even without the chill. Plastered against Sandy's side, he breathed in the scents of skin and sex as he traced the designs on Sandy's skin through the slide of fluids combined there.

"Always with the tattoo. Would you even give me the time of day if I didn't have it?"

Alex craned his head back, checking Sandy's face. Something about the small smile there failed to reassure. "You're kidding, right? Are you kidding?"

"A little. I guess. I'm really not sure." Sandy's hand stroked idly back and forth across Alex's back, scratching beneath his shoulder blade and sending shivers up his spine.

"You can't be serious. How could you think something like that could even make a difference? It's who you are. You're so different -- inside -- from anyone I've ever met, I think."

"How am I different? How can you say that when I'm using you to get off, just like everyone else in your past did?"

"Is that how you see yourself? I… that's so wrong. You treat me better than anyone else in my life ever has. You ask me if something is all right and I feel like my answer makes a difference to you. Like if I said it wasn't, you'd change what you were doing, or stop altogether. No one's ever done that for me before."

Pulling him closer, Sandy pressed another kiss to the top of his head. "You ought to have so much. I just wish I could give you everything you should have."

"You give me too much. More than I deserve."

"Hey, D'abu!" Jacob Naslund's voice carried clearly from the bottom of the stairs. Beside Alex, Sandy stifled a curse.

"What's up, Nas?"

There was a long pause, and then Naslund's careful response: "Uh, how do you want me to answer that?"

Sandy sat up, scratching a spot above his temple, his gaze coming to rest on Alex. "Okay, let me rephrase: what can I do for you?"

"Listen, if you guys have, uh, finished your talk, Sarhaan needs you back at the ship. That thing he and Xuwicha were working on looks like it's going to happen, so he wants to make sure everything's ready to fly."

Alex looked away. If the crew was about to ship out again, Sandy would likely go with them this time, so he needed to get used to life without Sandy to lean on again.

"Yeah, right. Okay. With you in ten." Sandy's hand cupped Alex's shoulder. "You're coming with, right?"

Unable to hide his response, Alex's gaze flew to Sandy's face. Only a few seconds of Sandy's expectant gaze was all Alex could handle, though.

Circling his hand over the ridge of muscle that bridged Sandy's stomach and his hip bone, Alex stalled. "I, um…"

"I want you to come with us. I'll sleep a lot better if I know where you are." The worry was obvious in Sandy's voice and Alex hated being one more thing Sandy had to be concerned about. "Alex?"

"You don't have to worry about me, Sandy. I've got a place to stay for the time being. I'll get something better, as soon as I find another job. I'll be okay." Alex kept his face turned away. Maybe if he didn't look Sandy in the eye...

"Alex." Sandy sighed. "I don't want to tell you what to do. You don't have to do anything to please me, God knows. But I'm serious: it would be a big weight off if I knew for sure that you were someplace safe while you looked. In fact, Caleb could probably help you. He kicks ass on the computer and I'm sure he wouldn't mind."

His face concealed, Alex pressed his lips together and thought. Being with Sandy for more than just a couple of hours in the evening would be great. But part of his new life was learning to stand on his own, not cadging off friends, taking advantage of their generous natures. He'd already done too much of that.

"Sandy, you don't have to—"

"I know I don't have to, but I want to. I really mean it when I say it would go a long way toward letting me be more effective on the job. Besides," Sandy sifted a hand through Alex's hair, the smile in his voice obvious. "I like spending time with you and, pardon my ego here, but I think I might even be good for you. I know you're good for me."

Alex couldn't help an answering smile at that and hid his face against Sandy's side. "You don't have to protect me, Sandy. I know you don't think so, but I really can manage things on my own. I appreciate the offer, though."

Rolled suddenly on his back at that, Alex had nowhere to hide from the intensity of Sandy's stare. "You are bound and determined not to let anyone do anything for you, aren't you?"

"You're going to get wrinkles if you keep giving me that face, you know." Alex reached around the powerful arms holding him down to touch Sandy's face, first tracing the deep grooves between Sandy's perfect eyebrows, then the lines bracketing his suddenly stern mouth.

"Don't try to change the subject, Valentine. I know you've got your reasons, but let me help."

The effect of those dark eyes on Alex was powerful. They made him want to do or say whatever it took made Sandy happy. But he needed to do what was right for him, too. "Sandy, it's just… I have to start doing some things for myself. You know?"

"I know you do. And you're already doing more for yourself, every day. It's not weakness to let your friends help you out, you know. It's like me and the guys: we all help each other. Sometimes I need a hand, sometimes it might be you; but we're there for each other. I want to be there for you, Alex. Let me. Please."

The seconds ticked by as Alex searched for an argument Sandy would respect. He didn't have Sandy's years of military training. All he had was whatever brains and instincts he'd been born with, and the survival techniques he'd picked up along the way. The trouble was, Alex couldn't rely on his instincts when it came to Sandy. When his wants dovetailed so perfectly with what Sandy was asking him to do, how could he possibly trust himself to do the right thing?

"Yo, D'abu! Your ten's up. Can we get it in gear, you think?"

Sandy didn't so much as blink in acknowledgement of Naslund's plea. Just watched Alex and waited.

Chapter 16

"So then D'abu tells the guy, 'Better make those orders To Go'."

Sandy laughed as hard as anyone, regardless of the fact that the joke was on him. You wouldn't know it to look at him, but Vilnius was a funny little sonofabitch. Something about the freckles and red hair gave him an innocent look that let him get away with things he probably shouldn't and the group was having a good chuckle at Sandy's expense.

Sandy didn't care -- he had broad shoulders.

Besides, he felt great. Their first multi-trip contract secured and the crew was celebrating. Surrounded by friends, drinks flowing freely, Sandy was relaxed and nothing could piss him off tonight.

Leaning over, he spoke quietly in Alex's ear. "How're you doing? Want something else to drink?"

"No, I'm okay." When he drew back to look at Sandy, Alex's smile was a glorious thing, carefree and sweet. If Sandy thought he detected a warmth in those beautiful blue eyes, no one else had to know. It was his own little fantasy, to nurture as he pleased. "How about you? How are you doing?"

"I'm doing great." As he again whispered in

Alex's ear, this time the nearness of Alex's neck, bared and vulnerable, drew Sandy irresistibly. He leaned further and took a bite, holding on briefly before trailing kisses up the length of Alex's neck.

"Stop that! People are looking."

Alex sounded scandalized and Sandy had to laugh. The man could work nightly in what amounted to a high class brothel, watching every sex act imaginable until he'd become virtually immune to shock, but an innocent kiss or two on the neck had him gasping in distress. "Don't worry, sweetheart. No one cares."

"Jeez, D'abu. Get a room, would you, you two?" Again, Vilnius' air of aggrieved propriety made Sandy smile.

Once it started, of course, Naslund couldn't resist chiming in. "God, first Sarhaan and Cal, now you. What is it about this boat? How come everybody on it's getting laid but me?"

Gaze pinned on Sandy, obviously distressed, Alex froze at Sandy's side. Damn mess hall chairs kept him from pulling Alex closer -- why had he never noticed the pressing need for booths before? Draping his arm protectively across Alex's shoulders would have to do. "Fuck off, Naslund. Seriously, if you can't get laid on Doradus, there's something tragically wrong with you."

Vilnius laughed along. "Yeah. Deeply disturbed."

"Maybe if I didn't spend three out of every four cycles stuck on this fucking ship I could make some progress. I didn't see anything happening for you until you got left behind this last go-'round." Rocked back on two legs, Naslund balanced his chair while holding a beer in one hand and the table with the other. Nas' general lack of stature and complete absence of body fat ensured he was usually the winner in the race to get hammered, although Cal occasionally gave him a run for his money, and tonight was no exception.

"Children, children, settle down. Play nicely or I'll be forced to separate you." When had Sarhaan arrived? Late as usual, with Caleb still straightening his clothes and hair mussed, they might as well have been wearing a sign. Shuffling chairs, the group made room around the table for Cal and Sarhaan. "Alex. Good to see you. I'm glad you could join us."

An adorable blush flushing his cheeks a deeper pink than usual, Alex smiled shyly, acknowledging the comment before looking away. Sandy wouldn't have believed it if he hadn't seen it with his own eyes. "Me, too. You wouldn't believe what it took. I practically had to hog-tie him to get him here."

"Oh, for fuck's sake, D'abu. Keep your kinks to yourself, would you?" Naslund looked equal parts repelled and fascinated.

Sandy laughed. "Spite and jealousy, Naslund. Nothing but spite and jealousy."

"Hi, Alex. I'm glad Sandy talked you into coming aboard." Settled in next to Sarhaan, Caleb looked relaxed and happy -- content with who and where he was. His welcoming attitude toward Alex made Sandy even more disposed to like him than usual.

"Thanks." Again, Alex smiled briefly and looked down, fiddling with the edge of the buttoned tunic he wore.

Sandy cocked his head a bit, trying to figure out what was going on with Alex. He knew everyone at the table. Hell, he'd met them all dozens of times at *Nelly's*. Waited on them. Shot the shit, exchanging banter and insults in equal amounts. So what was up with the blushes and shy glances?

"Alex?" Angling his body a bit, Sandy threaded his hand through Alex's hair, gently encouraging Alex to raise his chin a bit. When he finally raised his gaze to meet Sandy's, the blue of Alex's eyes, the wounded soul he saw there, sobered Sandy instantly. "What is it, baby?"

Shaking his head mutely, Alex stared back, silently pleading.

But for what?

"Want to leave?" Sandy was vaguely aware of the hum of conversation continuing without them, but he didn't waste another moment's thought on it. His friends would understand.

"It's up to you. Whatever you want."

Still lost in the incredible blue of Alex's eyes, Sandy leaned closer until his forehead touched Alex's. Stealing a quick kiss, he took another read of Alex's eyes before turning back to the group. "Listen, as fun as this has been, we've got to go."

Naslund opened his mouth, only to turn on Cal, seated next to him. "Ow! What was that for? Fuck."

Caleb didn't spare Nas a glance, just smiled at Sandy and Alex. "See you guys later, then."

Relaxed, his arm slung comfortably across Caleb's shoulders, Sarhaan echoed Caleb's words. "Yeah, catch you later."

"Alex?" Sandy stood, holding Alex's chair for him. Alex rose, relief plain on his beautiful face.

Once out of the mess and headed down the hall toward his quarters, Alex stopped, tugging on

Sandy's arm. "Listen, if you want to stay…" Alex shrugged. "Don't worry about me. Go back and hang out. I'll be fine on my own."

"It's no big deal. I've seen way more of those guys than I ever wanted to -- the past few months, especially. If you're done, that's fine with me."

"You're not just saying that, are you? Because you would, I know you."

Dressed in his characteristic black, Alex's eyes stood out against his pale skin, their naturally dark lashes framing the blue of his eyes. Sandy wanted to pull him close for a kiss; to run a hand down to caress the firm backside he knew lurked beneath the artfully draped clothes Alex wore like a disguise.

"I have to choose between a smoky room, filled with a bunch of smelly, drunken coworkers, versus going back to my room with a good-looking armful of man that I'm crazy about? Gee, let me think."

Alex ducked his head again.

"Alex?"

"You don't have to say things like that, Sandy."

Touching Alex's face, Sandy brushed back the hair that had fallen over Alex's eye. "Let me guess. You're talking about the 'good-looking' part? Or the 'crazy about' part?"

Alex glanced around and Sandy tried to see it through Alex's eyes. A warship, utilitarian and stark, but home now. The bulkheads, a dull, gunmetal gray, the deck, a dark, metallic-looking grating, as synthetic as the air they breathed, it wasn't much to offer someone looking to build a new future.

"I have a mirror, Sandy. I know what I look like."

"Then you must know why I'm attracted to you." Dropping his arm around Alex's shoulders again, Sandy got them moving once more in the direction of his cabin.

"Not really."

"No idea at all?"

"Huh-uh."

"Alex, Alex, Alex." The sigh in Sandy's voice wasn't feigned.

"What?"

"What am I going to do with you?" They were stopped outside Sandy's quarters now. Sandy palmed the keypad and let them in.

Alex just shrugged and looked around. Again, not much to offer, but for the moment, it was the best Sandy could do. "I'm no bargain, that's for sure."

"Maybe not. But you're still the only one I want." Approaching from behind, Sandy rested his hands on Alex's shoulder, thrilled when Alex neither flinched nor shrugged him off. Sandy took it as a good sign and tried for a little more. "You know what I'd really like?"

Shaking his head, Alex looked over at Sandy's hand on one shoulder. "To fuck me?"

Sandy flinched at Alex's matter-of-fact answer. Of course. For too long, that's all anyone had wanted from him. "Not exactly. Here… would you come lie down with me?"

"Sure. Whatever you want."

Sandy sighed. He'd get Alex to stop saying that eventually. But first he'd have to change Alex's way of thinking.

"Would you mind if we took your shirt off first?" Leading Alex to the bed, Sandy sat down, letting Alex stand before him. Sandy rested his hands on Alex's hips, smiling encouragingly up at his lover.

His face a blank, Alex shook his head again.

Alex was tall and Sandy had to sit up straight to reach the buttons of Alex's shirt. One by one Sandy slipped his fingers inside and slid a button free, savoring the look on Alex's face whenever Sandy touched a sensitive spot. "Put your hands on my shoulders?"

Doing as he was bid, Alex placed his hands on Sandy, gazing down as Sandy slowly undid his shirt. Once open, Sandy pushed the two halves apart, running his fingers down the tantalizing trail of dark hair he found there, petting and stroking until he couldn't stand it any more and had to bury his face in it.

"I'm too hairy. I hate it."

Pulling Alex closer, into the opening made by his spread thighs, Sandy looked up, brushing his fingers over Alex's nipples until they tightened into hard little points. "I like it. If you even think about shaving it, or lasering, I'll…"

"You'll what?" A small smile threatened to break through Alex's expression as he gazed down at Sandy.

"I'll be mad, that's what. So don't even think about it."

"It's my body. Can't I shave it if I want to?"

Damn it, Alex was right. Sandy wrapped his arms around Alex's waist, resting his head against Alex's stomach. After a moment, Sandy looked up. "Of course you can. You're right. It's your body -- do anything you want."

Taking Sandy's head in his hands, Alex tilted it

back. "You're a good guy, you know that, Mr. D'abu?"

"Mr. D'abu? No one's called me that since... since I went into the Marines, probably."

"Really? What do they call you?"

"D'abu. Chief. Sandy." Alex was dragging fingernails over Sandy's buzz-cut hair, sending shivers racing over his scalp and down his spine. He closed his eyes and leaned into it. "A few more that don't bear repeating. Hey, cut that out."

"Cut what out?"

"Stop, you know, rubbing me; doing for me. It's my turn now." Fighting the melting sensation brought on by Alex's hands on his hair, Sandy forced his eyes open and attempted a glare.

"Oops. Sorry."

"You're not sorry. Look at you."

"What?"

"Forget it. I'm not falling for the innocent act."

"Positive?" Alex's dimple was showing again and the hint of a twinkle was back in his eye. If there'd been a particle of doubt in Sandy's mind before -- any at all -- it was gone in that moment.

No more hiding from it.

He was utterly, completely in love. "I'm positive. Now, get down here on the bed with me."

***

"Aren't you tired? You must be tired. Wouldn't you like to, I don't know, catch a nap? I could rub your back for you." Sandy's head between his hands, Alex rubbed his thumbs back and forth across the short, bristly hairs at Sandy's temples.

His eyes half-closed, Sandy sighed. "I gotta tell

ya, sleep is the last thing on my mind right now. What would it take to get you down here on the bed? I'd pay extra if the shirt came off."

Alex paused for a moment, his breath catching in his throat.

Sandy's eyes flew open. "Shit. I'm sorry. I didn't mean—"

"No. No. I know you didn't. I shouldn't be so sensitive. I'm sorry, Sandy." What an idiot. Of course Sandy didn't mean anything by it. Sandy would never make a deliberately hurtful remark.

"Aw, shit, I'm sorry. That was just stupid. I didn't mean—"

"It's okay. Here, let me lie down." Quickly slipping his shirt off, Alex laid it down on the nearest chair. The same one he'd slept in last time he visited Sandy, it was big and oversized -- like everything about the man.

One knee and one hand on the bed, a cloud of butterflies exploded in Alex's stomach. He could really use something about now. Just a little something to keep him loose, relaxed. In the moment instead of in his head, like now, mentally running through a list of his inadequacies.

Looping his arms around Sandy's neck, Alex swallowed nervously. Sandy put a hand on Alex's waist and smiled into his eyes. "I'm glad you decided to come, after all. I like having you here."

Sandy closed his eyes and kissed Alex. Alex let his own eyes drift closed and kissed back, heat blooming in a dozen places. Under his skin. Everywhere their bodies touched. Mostly in his dick, though. Just the feel of Sandy under his hands was amazing. Alex couldn't get over how much there was of the man, or how beautiful every inch was. Sandy was no dummy. He'd figure out pretty soon that Alex was all flash and no substance. At least when Alex had a little help, he could be funny -- entertaining, even.

"You're too nice." Alex pulled back, wanting another look. He couldn't get over how gorgeous Sandy was. "You let people take advantage of your good nature."

Sandy's belly laugh vibrated up Alex's body. "Oh, yeah. I hear that a lot."

"They do." Alex overruled Sandy's denial. "The team works you to death. You let strays like me take up whatever free time you do get. When do you ever take time for just you? To do what you want to do?"

Suddenly serious, Sandy ran a hand through Alex's hair before sliding it down to Alex's ass, pressing their lower bodies together. "Would you believe that's what I'm doing right now? There's no place else I'd rather be right now. Alex, would you—? Here." Using just his arms, Sandy lifted Alex while sliding under at the same time, until Alex sat atop Sandy. "Much better."

Sandy smiled up at him, running those big hands up Alex's arms, down his chest. Alex sucked in a breath when Sandy pinched his nipples.

"Sandy."

Sliding his hands over Alex's thighs, Sandy just watched and breathed. "Yeah?"

"Why…?" Alex paused. He had a million questions for Sandy and he wasn't at all sure he wanted the answers. Why was Sandy wasting time on him, when the guy could have anyone on the station? Guys who didn't have half the problems or a quarter of the baggage Alex did.

What did Sandy want from him anyway if not sex? They'd done a little -- fooled around some. Not nearly enough to satisfy a man with Sandy's desires, Alex was pretty sure. He'd watched Sandy eat and drink -- those types of appetites were frequently matched by the other kind. Someone like Sandy wouldn't be satisfied for long with handjobs and dry-humping.

Sandy didn't like the drugs, either. What if that was what it took for Alex to be a full participant?

Rubbing his hands in a circular motion, Sandy gradually worked his way back up Alex's thighs, until Sandy's thumbs were brushing the growing bulge in Alex's pants. "Don't ask why, Alex. A man can do what he wants, but he can't will what he wants."

"But Sandy…" Sandy's eyelids were looking sleepy again, gaze taking on a glazed look, as though he was looking into Alex's soul. What could Sandy possibly see that pleased him? That didn't disgust and repulse him?

"Alex, it doesn't matter. None of it matters. Your past. What everybody else thinks. The only thing that matters is what we want and need -- and if we think we can find it together."

"Sandy." Alex ran fingers over Sandy's face, over his cheekbones, down his nose, across his spare upper lip. Sandy's tongue flicked out, catching a bit of his moving finger.

"Alex…?" Sandy's eyes drew him. The heat and need.

"Huh, what?"

"Can you come closer?'

"I think so."

No hint of a smile, but Sandy's nostrils flared a

bit as his gaze sharpened.

Leaning down to brace his forearms alongside Sandy's head, Alex closed his eyes and kissed Sandy, his cock finding delicious pressure from Sandy's. Sandy's tongue stroked into his mouth and Alex leaned into it, losing himself in Sandy's heat and taste and smell. Rocking his hips against Sandy's, want washed over him.

"Sandy, I want…" Alex kissed Sandy. Hungry little kisses on his mouth and chin. "Would you mind?"

With a dazed look in his eyes, Sandy put his hands on Alex's hips, holding them still to grind against. "Mind? What?"

He'd never asked for anything like this before, so before he could think better of it, Alex blurted it out. "Could you be on top? I'd like to try that with you."

Sandy paused. "On top? Sure. Absolutely. But… are you sure? I'd think… Serious?" Sandy's voice trailed off and Alex could practically see him puzzling it out in his head.

"Could we just try it? I trust you. I think -- I think it'll be okay."

"Sure, honey. Anything you want. I think we'll have to take our pants off first, though." Sandy smiled and Alex could only nod.

It took Alex by surprise, how much he hated to move and lose contact with Sandy's heat, because it took a conscious effort on his part to force himself off. Watching Sandy the whole time, Alex swung a leg off and rolled to his back, wriggling out of his pants along the way. The flex of muscle in Sandy's arms as he did the same was riveting, the rippling motion drawing Alex's eye, only to find himself distracted in the next moment by flexing of Sandy's well-developed pecs. "Oh, yeah, Sandy, that's… oh, my."

Sandy smiled at him, filling Alex's field of vision as he climbed over, bracketing Alex's head with his formidable arms. Spreading his legs, Sandy brought his lower body into contact with Alex, his balls making contact a moment before his erect cock slid next to Alex's. "Still okay?"

Alex nodded and placed a finger over Sandy's mouth. "It's okay. And you can stop asking me that every fifteen seconds."

"Are you sure, Alex? I… I don't ever want to do anything that makes you uncomfortable. I l—" Pausing, Sandy looked up at the ceiling for a moment. When he looked back, his dark eyes were serious and the lines furrowing his brows were back. "I care about you. I want whatever we do together to be what you want. What you're comfortable with."

Lifting a hand to stroke the grooves of worry on Sandy's face, Alex tried to match Sandy's solemn tone, to let Sandy know that he was serious, too. "I think I'm getting that, finally. Because you know what else I'd like?"

"What?"

"I'd like to know what it's like to make love. I want to know what it feels like to have someone inside me that knows me and, like you say, maybe cares about me a little."

Alex glanced away as he spoke, focusing on a column of drawers built into the wall, afraid of what he might read in Sandy's expression. Was what he wanted too much? Probably. But Sandy was the most generous person Alex had ever known. If he couldn't ask Sandy, there really was no one else.

Alongside Alex's dick, Sandy's jerked as Sandy's hips did a slow roll and Alex forced his gaze back to Sandy, letting it move gradually up Sandy's chest, until it reached Sandy's face. Staring hard, Sandy was scanning Alex's face with that laser beam look of his until gradually it softened.

"Oh, honey. I would… I'm sorry, I have to ask: are you sure?"

"If you don't mind. If you don't want to, I—"

Sandy cut him off with a kiss, tongue filling his mouth, passion obvious. After a ravishingly thorough kiss, Sandy pulled back. "Of course I want to. I'm just afraid once I start, I won't ever want to stop."

Chapter 17

Trying not to be obvious about it, Sandy kept an eye on Alex as he reached for the brand new tube of lube in his nightstand drawer. A few unsuccessful experiments at *Nelly's* aside, Sandy hadn't needed any for a while and he'd had to purchase some at a place he'd seen down in the Pike. He was thumbing the cap off as Alex watched his face when Sandy caught himself. "I'd like to know what it's like to make love."

The man had said make love, not fuck him senseless.

Sandy recapped the tube and set it aside.

He couldn't resist another thrust of his hips, though, the rush of feeling as Alex's dick rubbed against his incredible. Licking into Alex's mouth, Sandy savored Alex's breathless acquiescence, the way Alex closed his eyes and kissed Sandy back. Lowering his body, Sandy slid his chest against Alex's, the surprisingly lush thatch of hair there sending a jolt of electricity through him as his sensitized nipples brushed over it.

Sandy gave in to the urge to taste, licking and nipping at Alex's own pink little nipples. Running his hands down Alex's sides, Sandy grabbed handfuls of smooth skin, delighting in the silky feel of it beneath his hands as he buried his nose in

Alex's chest.

Alex groaned, his hands on Sandy's scalp, sending shivers down Sandy's spine as he raked his short nails through Sandy's hair. "Oh, Sandy. That's..."

Sandy was kissing down Alex's stomach, making Alex flinch and jerk as he ran his tongue around Alex's navel. His hands already wandering lower, Sandy pushed himself down the bed, all the better to reach Alex's cock. One hand cradling Alex's balls, Alex's sighs got louder when -- after encouraging Alex up onto his side -- Sandy got comfortable and took Alex into his mouth.

"Sandy, oh God, you—"

His mouth filled with cock, Sandy could only moan in agreement. So good. So right. Sandy used his tongue to slide along the side and press on the sensitive underside as he pulled his head back a bit to suck on the tip. He wanted it all, though, not just the end. So Sandy took it all back in, wrapping an arm around Alex's ass and wallowing in the satisfaction of having Alex so completely fill his senses.

Sandy settled in, working Alex steadily, quickly, drawing on Alex's cock until Alex's balls began to tighten. Slowing down, Sandy pulled his mouth off, using only his tongue to take long, slow swipes at the sides and shaft while his hand drifted down the crack of Alex's ass to tease along another front.

Mumbling breathless, incoherent bits of encouragement, Alex reached for Sandy, trying to get his hands between Sandy's legs, but Sandy evaded him. This needed to last a while and if Alex got that mouth on him, it would be over in minutes, if not seconds, so Sandy angled his lower body away from Alex's reach.

"Sandy." Alex's frustrated wail only told Sandy what he wanted to know. Taking Alex into his mouth again, Sandy lavished attention on Alex, worshipping Alex's cock while he squeezed and fondled the sensitive balls. Easing off the pressure with his hand, Sandy concentrated on the taste and feel of Alex's cock, but too soon the quickening signs of Alex's approaching climax were back and Sandy pulled away again.

"But, Sandy… I was so close."

Pushing himself up, Sandy smiled a little at Alex and the picture of frustrated pleasure he made. A few more kisses, planted in random spots over Alex's body as he turned himself around, and Sandy was rolling Alex onto his stomach.
"Because it's too soon. You're not ready yet."

Alex whimpered into the bedclothes, clutching handfuls of the coverlet to himself. "I'm ready, I promise I'm ready."

"Have you ever taken hours to come?"

Trying to look over his shoulder at Sandy, Alex paused. "Me, personally? No. Never. What would be the point of that?"

Moving to straddle Alex's back, Sandy leaned down to whisper in Alex's ear. "Because when you finally do, when you're wrung out and spent and your lover finally lets you -- it's spectacular." Leaning closer, Sandy kissed below Alex's ear; continued kissing down below Alex's jaw, nuzzled Alex's bristly cheek with its beginnings of a beard.

"Right now, just a regular orgasm would do for me. Really. Save the special one for my birthday, just..." Sandy was inching backward, his own rigid cock sliding down over Alex's ass as he kissed and licked his way down Alex's back. When Sandy's dick slid into the crease of Alex's ass, Alex's breath caught and speech halted completely.

Sandy kept going, sliding lower as his fingers came back to flirt with Alex's puckered pink hole. "Just what?"

"Huh?"

Smiling, Sandy got comfortable again, spreading Alex's legs to give himself more room. "You were saying, 'just.'" Alex's body finally open and available to him, Sandy lowered his head again and began exploring with his tongue.

"Wh-what are you doing?"

Alex's flustered little stutter was completely charming and Sandy paused for a moment to smile. "You don't mean that literally, do you? You're not actually asking what I'm doing, right?" Alex's skin was soft and the scent of him was a little more intense, but it was clean and musky and tempting as all hell.

"I... But, I...oh."

Sandy always could resist anything but temptation and had gone back to teasing Alex with his lips and tongue, even as he stroked Alex's waist and ass with feather-light touches of his fingers. Alex's 'oh' was a sigh of pleasure as Sandy pressed the tip of his tongue into the sensitive nerve endings at the entrance to Alex's body.

"I love everything about you, baby. Not just your dick. Everything."

"Oh, mmm, S-sandy." Alex burrowed in against the coverlet, shifting a bit from side to side, trying to get some friction on his cock, probably. Sandy continued using his mouth to tease Alex, backing off and resting his head against the smooth curve of Alex's ass when Alex's moans got higher in pitch or started coming too close together, letting Alex come back down almost to baseline before building him back up again.

When Sandy added a finger to the teasing, Alex nearly came up off the bed the first time Sandy hit his sweet spot. "Sandy?"

"Yeah, baby?"

"Any, uh, any time now. I think, I'm pretty sure, yeah… oh! Sweet Jesus, that was close." Sandy was stroking inside Alex now and Alex was thrusting his ass back and up against Sandy's hand, as much as Sandy would let him, anyway.

Sandy dragged things out a bit more, but he was more than ready and Alex seemed receptive. "I think you're ready. How would you like it? Hand? Mouth?"

"Dick? Can I have your dick?"

"Sure." Closing his eyes for a second against the rush of pleasure, Sandy withdrew his finger, placing a last kiss on Alex's ass before wiping his hand and reaching for the lube again. "Absolutely."

His hands shaking a bit, Sandy stroked some of the cool gel over his aching cock, so far past hard it was nearly ossified. Adding some more lube to his hand, Sandy eased his fingers into Alex's body, smiling at the bone-deep satisfaction of Alex pushing back onto him, seeking his touch.

Edging up close to Alex, Sandy ran a hand down Alex's spine, ending with an appreciative palm against Alex's ass. "Alex, tell me if—"

"Sandy, shut up already and give it to me. I want it." Ass in the air, head resting on his folded arms, Alex's words were muffled but audible.

When he finally pushed inside, if Sandy thought he detected a momentary shudder from Alex, he told himself it was the good kind. As carefully as he could manage, Sandy began working himself in when Alex suddenly pushed back hard until Alex's ass rested against his hips and he was all the way in.

Hands on Alex's hips, a jolt of pleasure rocked Sandy to his core and, even as he tried to imprint the moment on his memory, he was pulling out so that he could do it again.

Easy.

Easy, now.

Sandy tried talking to himself, but it didn't do a damn bit of good.

He wanted to be careful.

He wanted to take his time, make sure everything was okay with Alex.

Only Alex wasn't listening, and Sandy's body for damn sure wasn't listening. Alex was moaning and pushing back with every thrust of Sandy inside him, and Sandy was grunting and slamming into Alex like a sailor on shore leave with a three-credit whore.

Alex pushed up onto his forearms -- still offering his ass to Sandy -- and began working his cock with one hand. Working himself, Alex matched his rhythm to Sandy's, fisting his own dick feverishly while Sandy pumped into him hard.

"Harder. Just a little. Yeah, like that, give it to me. Sandy."

Alex's body shook in a quick, halting rhythm as he came and it was too much for Sandy. The sight of Alex's beautiful body, the thought of him coming from something Sandy had done… Two, three more strokes and Sandy was coming, too, pumping himself into Alex's gorgeous ass as Alex shuddered and groaned, slowly slumping forward onto his face.

Gradually melting, when Sandy slipped out he rolled to his side, taking Alex with him. Draping an arm across Alex's waist, he held Alex close, placing lazy, replete kisses over Alex's back and shoulder. Sandy shifted the arm under his head and ran his fingers through Alex's sweat-dampened hair, as he caught his breath and soaked in the feelings he hesitated to put names to.

Love.

Tenderness.

Sandy cringed inwardly at the vulnerability those words implied. But what else could he do? He felt how he felt and all there was to do about it was figure out a way to make it work.

***

"Are you hungry? Want to go down to the -- unh -- mess and get something to eat?" Alex didn't answer. That is, unless shaking his head counted. "What about coffee? You've got to be ready for some -- oh, fuck, Jesus -- coffee."

Smiling with his eyes, Alex looked up from between Sandy's legs and took another long, bobbing pull with his mouth on Sandy's cock. Alex wasn't sure how this little test of wills had begun, but Sandy was determined to get them down to the mess hall for food and Alex was just as determined to keep Sandy to himself. Sandy was due for some time of his own, the way the crew had been working him, and Alex was going to see to it that he got it.

So Alex concentrated on his best combination of techniques to get Sandy off. Strong suction with lots of tongue, interspersed with some loving attention paid to the sensitive head area, then back to the shaft to swallow it all down. A hand adding a twisting motion as he jacked the shaft. Press two fingers behind the balls when he wasn't mouthing or licking them.

Alex had to give Sandy credit -- he was holding firm to his plan, doing his best to concentrate while Alex was doing his best to distract. "Oh, sweet— Let me just check in and then we can— Shit. Fuck, yeah. Yeah, oh, that's—"

Sandy came in strong spurts and the warm, salty fluid hit the back of his throat and slid down. Alex stayed where he was, stroking Sandy's thighs and milking the last of Sandy's climax as the thick fingers sifted through his mess of morning hair.

When Sandy's hand slipped beneath his chin, lifting it up, Alex finally let go of Sandy's spent cock. "You're bad for my productivity, you know that?"

"Oh, I don't know. I'd say you were pretty darned productive just now, as a matter of fact." Sandy's smile was rueful, but Alex just grinned back at him. "Way, way above average -- take the word of a professional on that one."

Alex realized his mistake when Sandy's smile, small to begin with, faded even more. Why couldn't he learn even a little tact, damn it?

Maybe Sandy could be the one to teach Alex, because he didn't say a word, just tugged on Alex's arm and gathered Alex to him. Running his hand through Alex's hair, Sandy started at the nape, raking upward with his fingers against its natural fall. When he reached the top, he slipped his hand out and started over at the bottom. Over and over again.

They lay that way for a while, Sandy petting Alex's hair and Alex, tucked up under Sandy's arm, tracing Sandy's tattoo across his beautifully broad chest again. Alex was determined to understand what the symbols meant, if he had to ask Sandy every day to explain them again.

"Alex?"

"Hmm? What? Don't stop -- that feels good." Sandy resumed stroking Alex's hair again and Alex hugged Sandy close, luxuriating in the feeling of being safe. Sheltered. He'd always wanted his very own white knight. Alex tilted his head back, all the better to take in the rugged beauty of Sandy's face. Planting a kiss on Sandy's chiseled jaw, he rested his head on Sandy's shoulder again.

All of that smooth, warm skin to snuggle up to; his very own personal space-heater. Alex had never associated being naked with a feeling of security before. Before Sandy, he doubted he could even hold the two thoughts in his head at the same time. "So, what were you going to say?"

"Just..." Sandy, unsure of himself? What was that about? "What would you think about moving in here?"

Alex laughed. "Isn't that what I just did, pretty much?"

"Not just as a temporary thing, though. I mean, what if you stayed?" The hand stroking Alex's hair paused. "You'd have more time to look around for a good job, instead of feeling pressured to take the first thing you found, if you didn't have to worry about paying rent."

"That's… wow. I don't know what to say."

"Say yes."

"But…" Alex tried to read Sandy's expression, but he was wearing what Alex thought of as his soldier look. Stone-faced. "I can't let you do that, Sandy. You've done too much already. I just need a place for a few nights until I get a -- Oh, crap! What time is it?"

"I don't know. Fourteen-hundred, maybe? Uh… yeah, fourteen-twenty-five."

Alex scrambled out of bed and began frantically searching for his clothes. "Crap, crap, crap. Sandy, where're my shoes? Damn it. I'm late!"

Rolling out of bed, Sandy reached under the mattress' small overhang. "Right here. What are you late for?"

"The interview. At *The Busted Flush*." Having hurriedly climbed into his pants, Alex stuffed an arm into one of the uncooperative shirt's sleeves. "I can finish buttoning on my way to the tram. Quick! Hand me my shoes. Aw, damn it! I need this job."

His stomach suddenly a ball of anxiety, Alex shoved his feet into his shoes and looked around. What else did he need? A coat? Probably wouldn't hurt to wear one. His hair was a mess, no doubt. Shit. Henry had offered to help him with his hair. Wouldn't make enough difference to matter anyway. No big loss there.

"The interview? What interview? Here." Pants and shoes on, Sandy stood, offering a comb with one hand while he reached for his shirt with the other. "I'm coming with you. How long do you think it will take?"

"I have no idea. Probably not all that long. They'll already have my work record -- not much to write home about there. I mix a few drinks for them. Maybe take a math test. Sandy, don't worry about it. I'll be fine. I'll just comm them on the way, explain that I'll be a little late."

"Calm down, okay? You're not doing yourself any favors by giving yourself a heart attack." Mostly dressed himself now, Sandy took Alex's chin in one hand, the other resting on Alex's shoulder. "I've been in the Flush and they'd be lucky to have you, so don't stress, all right? Getting yourself all excited won't get you there any faster. Ever heard the saying, 'Make haste slowly'?"

"No."

"It means move ahead, but do it deliberately. You'll be fine. Besides, I'm going to come along, too. Don't worry -- I'll wait outside. All right?"

It was easy to see what made Sandy such a good leader. That big hand on his shoulder felt like it was the only thing keeping Alex's mind and body from separating, the sensation of calm flowing into him through it was almost palpable.

Alex had to reach up in order to loop his arms around Sandy's neck and lock them in place. Resting his head on Sandy's powerful chest, even for just a moment, was reassuring and when he leaned back, breathing deeply as he let his lower body come into contact with Sandy's again, Alex smiled up into Sandy's eyes. "Thanks. You're the best. I don't deserve you. Listen, Sandy, you don't have to do that, though. Just walk me to the thing -- the whatever -- the tram. I'll be fine."

Sandy looked doubtful. "I don't know. I think

I'd better come with you."

"I'm not some stupid kid, you know. I think I can make it from the tram to the saloon."

Not budging a millimeter, Sandy took Alex's chin in his hand again. "I didn't say you were, honey, but that doesn't mean that there aren't bad guys out there who'd take you out without blinking an eye. Everybody can use a friend. There's no shame in wanting a little company."

"Yeah, you're right." Alex got a funny feeling in his chest at the idea that Sandy was offering friendship to him -- to the guy who didn't know much of anything except sex and booze. He brushed a finger over Sandy's stern mouth. "I'd like it if you were my friend."

"Good. So let's quit wasting time and get you over to your new job." Sandy dropped a quick kiss on Alex's mouth and, caught off guard, Alex staggered a little beneath the force of it.

Out the door and headed down the hall now, Alex continued to argue his point. "Sandy, I'm sure you have more important things to do than play my chauffeur. Like, why don't you take a nap or something? You'd probably like to catch up on some of your sleep."

An arm looped casually around his shoulder, Sandy argued right back. "I'm sure Sarhaan and Kai will find some pain-in-the-ass job or other for me -- as soon as they manage to track me down. In the meantime, though, I want to spend some time with you. If that's okay with you?"

"Sandy, you know I—"

The heavy thunk of boots pounding on the metal grating below their feet reached them and Sandy turned to face the oncoming rush. Instantly on alert, Sandy'd already stepped between whatever it was and Alex when the details of Naslund's breathless shout told them it was friendly.

"Chief! Thank God! Can you come quick? The water treatment system's exploded. There's water everywhere. We need you to triage!"

"Goddammit. Shit. Fuck. What happened?"

"I don't know, but there's water all gushing and Kai says you're the only one who knows what's critical to save now and what we can fix later. Chief, *please!*"

Alex realized his hands clutched the loose fabric of Sandy's shirt, the urgency in Jake Naslund's voice coming through loud and clear and transmitting itself to Alex and Sandy. Sandy glanced down, craning his neck around, seeking Alex's gaze with his own. "Alex, shit, I think I gotta go. I've got to go take care of this."

"I told you, don't worry about me. I'll be fine. Unless they want me to start right away, I'll be back after the interview." Naslund was inching closer, as though prepared to pry Sandy loose if he had to, and all but vibrating with anxiety. Smiling understandingly at Sandy's teammate, Alex placed a hand on Sandy's chest. "It's okay. Go save the day."

Sandy stared hard at Alex, covering Alex's hand with one of his own. "Okay. You'll come straight back?"

"Yes, mother." Alex couldn't resist a smile at Sandy's over-protectiveness.

"Be careful, would you? I'm not fooling around, here."

"Chief, please." Naslund actually reached out to

Sandy's arm now, for emphasis.

"Okay. I'll be fine. Now go."

Giving Alex's hand a final squeeze, Sandy took off -- in the direction of the water treatment room, Alex presumed -- and Alex stole another few seconds to watch Sandy's long, purposeful strides taking him away from Alex and back to his crew. Sandy's duty. Alex tried to squelch the little stab of jealousy that flared up.

What would it be like to have Sandy look at him that way?

***

The Busted Flush was a solid two notches below *Durty Nelly's*. Where *Nelly's* was clean and first class all the way, the *Flush* was clearly a working man's bar. Instead of floors spotless enough to eat off of and live entertainment, Alex's shoes squeaked from the sticky residue while zoned-out miners and meat farmers watched a three-d simulation on a raised dais in the corner that would only look real after several of the house's cut rate drinks.

Alex followed the employee who'd met him at the door to the manager's office in the back. Not the most promising signs, to be sure, still… he needed a job. Sandy's good will wouldn't last forever and Alex had better have some kind of reliable income going when it finally gave out. The glassy look in several of the patrons' eyes was equally daunting, since it meant that drugs were present to a degree they weren't at *Nelly's*.

"Here you go." The doorman would never have made it to an actual interview at *Nelly's* with his low personal grooming standards and ill-fitting clothes. The man's pants hung low enough off his well padded butt to give Alex a peek at assets he would rather not be forced to acknowledge, as well as smelling like he and decent hygiene were no longer on even a nodding acquaintance.

"Thanks." Alex smiled weakly, grateful that at least the man didn't appear to be the leering type. On the contrary, he barely acknowledge Alex's existence. "How do you like working here?"

"It's a job." Not bothering to make eye contact, the man swung a cheap synthetic door aside and gestured for Alex to enter. "Good luck."

Alex knew things were going south when he found himself hoping he didn't get the job, just so he wouldn't have to work with the greasy doorman. The greeter was the customer's first contact with the establishment and any smart business owner knew that first impressions counted.

"Mister Valentine, won't you come in?"

The distinctive accent sent a chill skittering down Alex's spine as he froze in place, one foot inside the door.

"Come, come. So nice to see you again." Vasily Brasov sat behind the battered desk, the new, expensive-looking chair he occupied an incongruous mate for it. "Don't be shy. We are all old friends here. I hope you'll let bygones be bygones, Mister Valentine?"

Alex tried to back quietly out of the office, only to find that the unkempt greeter blocked his retreat.

"Where are you going? Don't tell me you've decided you don't want the job, after all?" Brasov stood. "That's all right. I think you'll forgive us when you see what else we have to offer. A much better position with perquisites that… well, let's just say I don't think you'll even dream of considering turning it down. Am I right, Jim?"

Brasov turned his head and it was only then that Alex spotted, tucked away in a corner, far from the room's only light, the man seated in a nondescript, high-backed leather chair. The man stood and moved easily toward Alex, trapped as he was by the doorman's big body.

The chill that washed over Alex confirmed the identity in a way that the light finally falling on his well-bred face couldn't.

It was him.

"Hi, Alex. It took a while to find you, but I couldn't lose you. You mean too much to me. We mean so much to each other. I had to find you. You look well -- a little heavy perhaps, but we can fix that."

In a brutal, visceral flash, it all came crashing down on Alex.

The memories.

The beatings.

This one liked pain -- not his own, of course, Alex's -- so there'd been no salvation of unconsciousness for Alex when this man visited *Earthly Delights*.

Drugs there had certainly been, though. Plenty. To keep him aware. Erect. And, most of all, compliant.

Resistance was futile and old behaviors came back with the sickening familiarity of long habit. Alex averted his gaze, ducking his head respectfully. "Master James."

He wanted to die.

Alex hoped that this time it finally killed him.

Chapter 18

"That's it. I'm done."

Sandy threw down the phase wrench he'd been wielding like a cudgel for the past several hours, trying to beat the ship's water treatment system into submission. He still hadn't figured out the original source of the problem, being too caught up in trying to stem the flow of water, but he'd managed to get things marginally under control. Enough to stop and catch his breath, anyway; flex his hands and rub the aching joints. He'd had to do some major rerouting as a stop-gap measure. Who knew how long tracking the problem back to its source would take him?

Xuwicha and Naslund gave him measuring looks and Sandy wasn't surprised when Nas let Kai speak for both of them. "We're not done, though. How long do you think this patch job will hold?"

Bent over giving his bad knee a surreptitious rub, Sandy straightened, glancing over at the monstrosity of a jerry-rigged job he'd decided to call good for the time-being. "Don't know. A day or two, at least; maybe longer if we don't have to run it under load. Do we know when our next run is scheduled for?"

"The deal with the Martian miners guild doesn't kick in until next month. We were hoping to pick up something short term between now and then." As wet and grubby as Sandy, Kai's face nonetheless reflected nothing. No hint of emotion marred his flawless mask of calm -- probably what had made him so good at Intel for so long. Or maybe he'd mastered the ability to reflect all the fire and emotion of a mid-level bureaucrat as a result of the job, Sandy'd never figured out which.

"For now, I'd recommend against it. Too many things still need fixing and I don't think I need to point out that if something's going to fail, I want it to fail while we're here in port, not a million kilometers from a stable source of oxygen."

"Good point." Naslund was putting tools away, meticulously wiping down each one before stowing it back in the cabinet. One of the reasons Sandy never minded having Nas on his team: the man respected his tools. "You going to tell Sarhaan we're knocking off for the night?"

"Yeah. I don't know about you, but I've had one helluva week and I'm ready for things to slow down a little. I'm gettin' too old for this shit." Sandy retrieved the wrench and handed it to Nas to put away. "I think I'm ready for a vacation."

Kai just laughed at him. "Listen to you -- you even sound like a civilian. Vacation. What? You start getting it regular and suddenly you're ready to retire?"

"We're not all married to the job, Xuwicha. You could stand to de-stress a little bit yourself." Sandy pressed the call button on the nearby comm unit.

"Bridge -- Adams."

"Hey, Cal. I'm looking for Sarhaan. Is he there?"

"Yeah, sure thing. Just a second."

While he waited for Sarhaan to pick up, Xuwicha caught Sandy's eye as he grabbed his package and mouthed 'de-stress,' before heading for the door. Sandy grinned and nodded as Naslund trailed Kai out the door.

"D'abu, what's the status?"

Folding his arms across his chest, Sandy shoved his hands under his armpits, the warmth of his body there easing the ache in his fingers. "We're okay for now. It's going to take some major reworking, though. I just hope we didn't lose so much that I have to start over cycling the system again. Jesus, I'm so done with that."

"Yeah, I can imagine. So. You're finished for tonight?"

"Done and then some. Hey, do me a favor?" Work out of the way, Sandy's brain had time to process personal things again.

"What's that?"

"After I get to my quarters, don't call me for, oh say, eight or ten hours?"

"I admire the scope of your ambition, friend." Sarhaan's tone was as close to actual laughter as it was likely to get in a work situation.

Things had gotten a lot looser since they'd left Earth and Sandy could say what he thought without the need to filter it. "Fuck you. I'm outta here."

"Okay, I'll-- Whoa, hold on a second. Caleb wants to say something."

Cal's voice, came on. "Sandy, when you see Alex, would you have him comm me?"

"Sure, but why don't you just comm him yourself? He should be back by now. Did you try my quarters?"

"Yeah, I did. He's not there. Ship's log shows him leaving, but nothing after that."

"Really?" Sandy paused, running all the information through his head, not liking most of the scenarios he came up with. "Listen, would you do me a favor? Check with *The Busted Flush*. See if he's still there. If he got the job, he might be working. I'll check back with you after I put some dry clothes on."

"You got it, Sandy."

Twenty minutes later, on the ship's bridge, Sandy didn't like the information he was getting. "He's not there. The manager at *The Flush* says he never showed up."

Sandy stared back at Cal, vaguely conscious of the other faces gathered around the ship's main computer terminal on the bridge. He stuffed the fear down deep while he tried to process what Cal was telling him. "That was hours ago. If he's not there, then where is he?"

Cal's gaze flicked from Sandy to Sarhaan and Sandy knew some kind of wordless communication was going on, but he couldn't spare any mental energy to try to decipher it. Cal gave a defensive little shrug. "I don't know."

"But you tried tracking his identi-chip, right?" As the fear built, so did the frustration in Sandy's voice.

"He doesn't have one, Sandy." Sarhaan moved to stand behind Cal, one hand resting familiarly on Cal's shoulder.

"How can he not have one? Everyone has one?"

"I've been thinking about that." Cal might have come from a sheltered background, but after nearly a year with the team, he and his first-rate brain fit right in. "I think he probably has one, just like everybody else, but it was wiped when he went into that place. Think about it: it's the easiest, cleanest way to hide someone whose presence -- if discovered -- might be politically embarrassing."

"Fuck. They don't miss a trick, do they?"

"Listen, Sandy -- and Sarhaan, you haven't heard this yet, either -- I found something pretty interesting on yesterday's inbound transfer file. Remember James Van Aukken? He landed on Doradus yesterday."

Over Cal's head, Sandy caught Sarhaan's eye. "Thurmond's old business partner."

"He was up to his neck in the drugs and prostitute murders with Thurmond. How did he manage to skip hard time on Mars, like his pal?" Sarhaan gave Cal's shoulder a little shake. "Why didn't we hear about this sooner? I thought you monitored those daily."

Cal leaned back in his chair, the better to face both Sandy and Sarhaan. "The name on the file isn't Van Aukken; he obviously paid someone to hide his identity. Judging from the low rent quality of the file, it was probably the same people who helped Brasov. Good enough to get him by most screeners -- anyone who didn't know what they were looking for."

"And you do." Sandy wasn't asking a question. Cal knew his stuff.

"I should have given it higher priority. I thought something looked a little off about it, but I didn't chase it down until about an hour ago."

Cal's serious expression did nothing to reassure Sandy. He'd had a nagging sense of worry as soon as he'd realized the lateness of the hour and the fact that no one had heard from Alex. Nothing he'd found out since had done a damn thing to allay that concern. Quite the opposite, in fact.

"You did catch it, though." Sandy gazed around the bridge, only belatedly realizing that everyone present had been listening in -- Vilnius and Sutton from a few meters away. "I don't know about you all, but this is a little too much coincidence for me. First Brasov, then Van Aukken turning up. Both had ties to *Earthly Delights* and suddenly Alex goes missing? I'm going to find Alex and if either one of those sleazebags had anything to do with it..." Sandy looked at Sarhaan, not bothering to finish the sentence. He and Sarhaan had been teammates a long time and the actual words weren't necessary.

"You want some back-up?"

A quick nod sealed the deal almost as soon as the words cleared Sarhaan's lips and Sandy was already heading for the lift. Luckily the armory was on the way to the airlocks into Doradus.

Now that they were in motion, the calm of battle settled over Sandy. He and Sarhaan had run this drill a thousand times in the past and only the details of the op changed; when Xuwicha greeted them at the first airlock, Sandy wasn't even surprised. "I thought you were off on stress-relief duty."

"There's more than one way to fuck some ass. This'll do." Kai's face was its usual impassive mask as they climbed onto the tram -- the only form of transportation allowed on the station other than walking. "Loftin's going to meet us there."

"Where is 'there'? And why is the head of station security meeting us?"

Sarhaan and Seth Loftin weren't on the best of terms, so something was up that the sheriff had been alerted. That he was joining them was unprecedented. If Sandy hadn't been watching for it, he might have missed the quirk of the lips that Kai called a smile.

"Apparently the good sheriff's date for the evening fell through. Turns out he's not only available, he's a might peeved that disreputable riffraff are abusing his station's hospitality. And 'there' is a house not far from *The Busted Flush*. Brasov rents it and station security shows Van Aukken is there as we speak. Plus infrared sensors picked up an unidentified body there."

"A body?" It was a measure of Sandy's agitation that he grabbed Kai by the arm. Kai didn't like to be touched and under ordinary circumstances it never happened.

"It's hard to tell with IR. Either way, I don't think it would hurt to hurry."

***

"Poor Alex -- so neglected. I blame myself, of course."

The momentary whistle of the switch through the thick air of the station was Alex's cue that another line of blistering fire was a split-second from bursting out on his skin. He hoped briefly that it would land on his ass; at least that had some padding. He was unlucky, though, and the pain blazed across his thighs.

Bound to an X-shaped apparatus made from two pieces of fake wood, Alex's shoulders ached. Not as much as his backside, but it added to his misery.

"Look at your skin. So lovely and white -- no one marks quite like you do. Poor beautiful thing. Abandoned. Utterly forsaken. With no one who cares enough to even lash you. Except me."

The switch came down again, on Alex's back this time, and he caught his breath at the pain. If he could go away, to that place in his head, where no one could reach him…

"Alex, you're not paying attention." That voice. If he could close his ears, so that he didn't have to listen, he could think about other things. "What shall we do to keep you focused on the task at hand?"

A hand closed around his erect dick. He didn't want to be hard. He didn't want it to feel good. But he was, and it did.

He hated himself.

The hand squeezed his dick. Slowly pumping the length of the shaft from root to head.

"Oh, my lovely Alex. Tell me you've been faithful. Tell me you haven't let anyone else put their hands on what belongs to me, because I would have to punish you for that."

Alex turned his head.

He couldn't go along. He couldn't even pretend to play the game any more. What would Sandy do in a situation like this? Sandy wouldn't have gotten himself into a situation like this in the first place. Sandy wasn't stupid like he was. Sandy would have figured out that things looked wrong and never gone in in the first place.

"Alex, have you been with anyone else? Has anyone put their disgusting hands on you? Put their undeserving prick up your ass, perhaps?"

Go fuck yourself, you disgusting piece of slime. The words sounded brave in Alex's head, but a voice remarkably like his own instead said, "No, Master James."

"But can I trust you to tell me the truth still, Alex? We've been apart for much too long, I think, and your discipline is entirely gone. We'll have to start over from the beginning, I'm afraid. How I've missed you, my love."

The switch whistled again, three times in quick succession, and Alex twisted under the agony of the lashes. It was soaked in salt water for extra sensation, he could tell. It wasn't the worst, though. Things could always get worse. At least it wasn't the cane.

"Are you telling me the truth, Alex?"

I hope you fucking die in the most horrible way imaginable. I hope Sandy—

"You didn't answer me. Perhaps the problem is that you can't feel the kiss of this tiny switch through all of your unfortunate… winter weight. Yes? I think we might need our favorite cane again, to put us in the right frame of mind. What do you think, Alex?"

The cane.

He knew the remembered pain would be nothing compared to the real thing again. He hadn't been whipped in months. He cringed inside, tried to draw himself up into a tiny ball of consciousness and take that ball away to another time and place. He'd trust it to Sandy's hands to care for. Big hands that still knew how to be gentle…

A bang came out of nowhere. He was bound at the neck, too, and could only turn his head a little.

He couldn't see.

Footsteps running on the cold artificial floor.

Shouting.

Grunting.

A soft sigh.

And then… nothing.

"Alex? Baby, are you all right?"

There was a hand on his face, a thumb lifting his eyelid. He squeezed his eyes closed. Tried not to look.

"Alex, it's Sandy. Honey, talk to me. Please. Can you hear me?"

Was it a trick? He didn't want it to be. He wanted it to be Sandy, his very own white knight riding to his rescue, to sweep him off his feet and away to somewhere safe.

He took a chance and opened one eye.

"Alex, honey, it's Sandy. You're okay. You're safe."

It looked like Sandy. He wasn't sure. What if it was a trick, something to break him down?

"Sweetheart, it's okay. I'm here. Kai's here. You're safe."

A soft kiss pressed to his lips. Sandy's scent. His arms were cut loose now, his legs next. He was supported on either side as he was helped down.

"Here, baby. Can you stand? How bad does it hurt? Can't we give him something? Kai, what've you got?"

Nearby, voices argued quietly.

"Alex, can you go to sleep? We're taking you back to the ship. It's okay, baby. I'm here. Sandy's here. It's gonna be okay. Everything's gonna be all right."

***

Alex woke up screaming.

Tied down, like in a coffin, unable to move.

He fought.

He jerked his arms hard, kicked with his feet, but the restraints held.

"Alex. Ssh-ssh-shush. Hold still, honey. Vilnius! Get your ass over here! He's waking up. Jesus! What're you letting him wake up that fast for?"

Alex kept fighting, but not as hard now. Where was he? He'd never liked confined spaces, had always been a little claustrophobic. This was awful. His hands and his feet were--

"Alex? We're helping you. You're in re-gen and you have to hold still." Not Sandy. Alex thought he knew the voice from somewhere. A youngish face was peering down at him now, a mop of carroty red hair and more freckles than Alex had seen in one place before.

"Who are you?" Alex's voice was raspy.

"Jimi Vilnius. We met at *Durty Nelly's*, remember? Listen, you've got to stay still. You've got tubes running in and out of you. You were all messed up."

"Where am I?" He craned his neck, trying see what the set up was.

"You're on the *Vigilant* and we're fixing you up. I was bringing you out of it, but I must've miscalculated."

"The *Vigilant*? Is Sandy here? Forget it, don't bother him. And where's--"

"I'm right here, baby. Who did you think was yelling for Vilnius to get his incompetent ass over here and straighten things out?" Eyes bloodshot, the skin around them had more lines than ever; Sandy looked exhausted. Smiling, but more tired than Alex had ever seen him. "Don't worry about Van Aukken, honey. He won't bother you again. He won't bother anyone again."

Studying Sandy's face, it was a relief when Alex finally had a hand free to touch with. He laid his hand along the side of Sandy's face and held it there, the mere act of touching making him feel a thousand times better.

Sandy's word was gospel and if Sandy said Van Aukken wasn't a problem, Alex knew it must somehow be true.

"Are they still working you like a dog? Somebody needs to tell Sarhaan that you deserve a life, too." Sandy's skin was icy under his hand. "Your face is cold."

"Nah, your hand is hot. They have to raise your temperature for the re-gen to work. You probably feel like you have a fever."

Alex thought about it for a moment. "Yeah, I do. When can I get out of here?"

Behind Sandy, Jimi Vilnius laughed. "And I thought you were a bad patient, Sandy. You two were made for each other."

"You think so?"

***

"Sandy, who's this?"

Alex held up the picture of Sandy, looking impossibly young, with his arm draped around a woman. Equally young, she had copper-colored skin like Sandy and wavy black hair that reached down to her waist. They both smiled into the camera.

"That's Sai"

"Look at how much hair you had; you're beautiful." Alex couldn't get over the differences, glancing up at Sandy now, then back to the much younger man in the picture. "Sa-i? Who is she, your sister?"

Stretched out next to Alex in bed, Sandy took the bottle of lube he'd forgotten he was still holding. In the process of putting it away in the headboard, Alex had found a picture stashed in amongst Sandy's other personal effects.

"She's pretty, isn't she? No. She was my wife." Alex's mouth fell open. He turned his head to stare at Sandy, but Sandy's gaze remained fixed on the picture. "Long time ago. A long time ago." Touching the picture with one finger, Sandy traced the outline of the woman's face.

"You… you were married?"

"Yeah. And to a woman, too. Imagine that."

"So…" Alex was stunned. So many questions were bouncing around in his head, it was impossible to pick which one to ask first. "So, you're bi?"

Finally turning to face Alex, a smile so brief Alex might have imagined it flitted across Sandy's mouth. "I thought so at the time. I thought I could choose."

"Choose?"

"I'd known Sai all my life. Our families were part of the same community. Mostly Samoan, some other nationalities mixed in, but that only made us stick more to our own. There was always some weirdness about my dad that my mother would never talk about. It only made her more insistent that I marry a nice girl from a family she knew."

"But, a girl… I mean, a woman?"

This changed everything. Like an explosion in a feather factory, Alex was trying to stuff everything back inside, but nothing fit.

"She was sweet. A really nice girl. So nice. You couldn't imagine a better, nicer person. I knew her family. Her brothers and I played *tuila'epa* together. I liked her a lot. I thought it would be enough."

Reaching out, Alex touched Sandy's shoulder. Bulging with more muscles than Alex had in his whole arm, it was part of Sandy. How…?

"You know what life was like back on earth if you were gay." Sandy glanced up at Alex's reflexive snort, instantly apologetic. "Of course you do. That was dumb."

"Don't worry about it. Go on."

"I thought -- I was young and stupid. Just stupid. I thought: if you can be either this one thing that will make your life a thousand times more difficult, or this other thing that everyone's fine with, why would you ever choose the hard thing? It seemed so logical." Sandy shrugged. "Why would you choose to be this persecuted, despised, hated thing?"

Alex looked at Sandy with new eyes. "So, the two of you had sex? What was that like? Wasn't that just… so odd?"

"We got married right when I joined the Marines. I was gone a lot. I thought everything was my fault. Turns out I was right about that part. I -- you know what I like in bed. I thought if I could get Sai to--"

"Oh, no." Alex couldn't bear to look, burying his head in the pillow. "How did that go?"

"Not so good." Sandy rolled to his back, his elbow jostling Alex's pillow as he folded his hands beneath his head. "Our people are pretty accepting about a lot of stuff, but that just wasn't what Sai expected from her husband. We tried to stick it out for a while for the sake of the families, but it didn't work."

Alex unburied his head. "Oh, sweetie. I'll bet you were a fabulous husband."

"I tried."

"But it wasn't your fault. You see that now, don't you?"

"I should have tried harder. I should have been able to fix it. Make it right."

"Honey, there are some things you can't fix. You were with the wrong person. You just needed to find the right boy to fuck you sideways and keep you happy. That's all."

"That's all, huh?" Finally, Sandy smiled.

"Yeah. So you got divorced. That's not so bad. At least she didn't kill herself after spending one night with you."

Uh-oh. The silence that followed told Alex he'd picked the wrong subject to try to distract Sandy with.

"Alex? Are you going to tell me what you're talking about?"

Scrubbing a hand through his hair, Alex covered his eyes. He shrugged. "It was back at *Earthly Delights*. This other boy and I -- Liam, he worked there, too -- we met and got to be sort of friends. We weren't allowed to socialize much, so we had to sneak around, pretty much."

"And what happened?" Up, leaning on an elbow now, Sandy placed a steadying hand on Alex's back.

"You know. Nothing much. It was my fault. He was a good kid. Nothing that happened was his fault. You know?"

"That's okay, Alex. You don't have to tell me if you don't want to."

"No, it's okay. I can talk about it. So…" Alex glanced up and was nearly undone by the compassion in Sandy's eyes. If he kept staring into Sandy's eyes he'd break down completely, so Alex looked away. "So, I convinced Liam to let me spend the night one night. I told him no one would find out; we'd get away with it."

"And?"

"He killed himself the next day. Maybe he had help. I don't know."

"Oh, God. God, Alex. Oh, come here, honey." Sandy gathered Alex in, holding him close with one arm around his waist, the other stroking in long, soothing sweeps up and down his back.

"Don't worry about it. It was my fault. I should have known better. I thought we could get away with it. I thought I could outsmart them."

"Alex. I can't even imagine."

"Yeah. Things got really hard after that."

Chapter 19

Something about Alex's body language bothered Sandy. Alex was out in the corridor, talking to Vilnius and Sandy couldn't quite pin down what it was that bothered him. Was it the defensive hunch of his shoulders? The restless hands, maybe -- first fiddling with edges of the black vest he wore, then plunging hastily into his pants pockets? Or how about the erratic path of his glance as it bounced from Jimi's face to various points around the room?

"—but you think it'll be okay?"

Jimi nodded. "Yeah, sure. Sandy and Kai took out Brasov and all his guys. Really messed 'em—Oh, hey Sandy. We were just talking about you."

"Yeah? Who was asking and who was telling?" Although he wasn't sure of the subject matter under discussion, Sandy had a sneaking feeling he wasn't going to like it when he found out.

The way Alex's face went instantly blank would have been the capper, even if Sandy wasn't already suspicious. "Nothing. I was just asking Jimi where he got his… shoes."

The look on Vilnius' face registering surprise and the hesitation before the last word sealed it. Sandy schooled his own features. Alex had been through enough and the last thing he needed was anyone coming down on him.

"His shoes?"

"Yeah, he's got some crazy thing for military boots. I told him he should check out Cal's, 'cause that guy knows how to dress—"

"Jimi, could I talk to Alex for a minute, please?" Adding, "Alone?" when Vilnius didn't take the hint.

"Yeah, sure." Vilnius had the decency to look torn. He looked back to Alex. "So, if you need help with that… thing… just let me know."

"I will. Thanks." Alex stood silent, watching Vilnius' rapid retreat.

"Are you seriously asking me to believe that you went to Jimi for fashion advice?"

Still, Alex didn't speak. He just stood there, thoughts and impulses registering in his clear blue eyes, only to remain bottled up. A half-shrug; a helpless shake of the head, and Alex ducked his head and said nothing.

It was a good thing Sandy wasn't afraid of hard work, because being with Alex would never be anything but a whole lot of that. Sandy could curse his caretaker nature all he wanted, but being aware of his need to fix things didn't seem to do a damn thing to change it. Sandy brushed the hair out of Alex's eyes, rubbing his thumb over the beginnings of the beard showing through Alex's pale skin.

Those eyes, so young-seeming and yet so full of the world's pain. Somehow, they had reached down inside Sandy and connected in a way no one else ever had. Sandy didn't know how, or even why. He just knew that he'd give his last breath to keep Alex safe.

"C'mere, honey." Sandy opened his arms and,

after a second's hesitation, Alex stepped into them -- tucking his head, as he so often did, under Sandy's chin. Sandy was gradually coming to realize that physical touch was the most powerful weapon he had when it came to fighting Alex's self-imposed isolation and holding Alex in his arms was the next best thing to a truth serum. "What was Jimi going to help you with?"

"I heard about a new club opening up."

Sandy steeled himself against Alex's sad little sigh. "Yeah?"

"I thought they might be hiring bartenders."

"Ah. Where is it?"

Alex was relaxing into Sandy's body, melting against him so that their bodies touched from shoulder to thigh and all points in between. Meanwhile, Alex's hands had slipped under Sandy's shirt and had begun moving in slow, easy circles across Sandy's back. "A couple of blocks from *Nelly's*. You know where the *Golden Horseshoe* is?"

"Yeah. Two more blocks and you're at The Pike. Alex, that's crazy. What were you thinking?"

Just like it always did when Alex was this close, Sandy's dick wanted in on the conversation. Sandy leaned back against the bulkhead, widening his stance to take Alex's weight. When Alex tilted his head back, opened his mouth against Sandy's throat and licked, Sandy's whole body surged.

"I need a job, Sandy." Alex took nibbling little bites of Sandy's neck, while his hands flattened against Sandy's back a second before Alex's hips flexed against Sandy's. "Your teammates are good guys and all, but I need something to do that brings in some credits. Otherwise, I'm just your…"

Sandy never gave his hands the command. Rather, they seemed to take their input directly from an image in Sandy's brain, lifting Alex against him and grinding their dicks together. Alex, his hands now resting on Sandy's shoulders, looked down at him with eyes that threatened to break Sandy's heart; eyes that pleaded for love, even as they realized the futility of their plea.

"Alex. Oh, baby." Lifting his chin, Sandy closed the distance between them, kissing Alex with everything he had. Sandy poured himself into the kiss, trying to show Alex how much Alex meant to him. Pressing their bodies close, Sandy licked into Alex's mouth, a surge of heat filling him when Alex's tongue met him half-way. Pulling back a bit, Sandy nipped at Alex's full lower lip, slid sideways to rub his nose against the sandpaper roughness of Alex's jaw. "Baby, you're not 'just' anything. There's so much to you. There's no one else like you -- not even close."

Alex's rueful smile finished the job that his eyes had started. "Any idea what that pays?"

***

A week and a half later, Sandy was still worried. He'd thought he'd gotten Alex to agree not to try for any more service jobs, especially anything so close to The Pike, with its atmosphere of laissez faire commerce in the pursuit of entertainment. Van Aukken and Brasov might be out of the picture, but Doradus was still the back of beyond and it was just a matter of time before someone else moved in on the territory they'd recently vacated.

They hadn't made any headway, though, in finding something else for Alex to do. Sandy understood that Alex, more than most people, needed something outside of himself to demonstrate his worth, if only in his own eyes. Sandy only had to watch Cal gesture at the computer he was seated in front of and turn in his seat to laugh up at Sarhaan, standing behind him observing, to know that Cal wouldn't have had the same problem adjusting that Alex had.

Their backgrounds were completely different.

For all that he'd had to leave his home -- the planet, even -- to find his place in the world, Caleb's privileged upbringing had given him a confidence and sense of self-worth that Alex had never had. It was only a reflection of how easily Cal now fit in with the life and friends of his ex-soldier lover, but Sandy still found himself envying the ease with which Cal ran his hands up Sarhaan's thighs, teasing and flirting and daring Sarhaan to do something about it.

When Sandy noisily cleared his throat, both Sarhaan and Cal looked Sandy's way, Cal still laughing. "Hey, Sandy. Looking for Alex?"

Sarhaan took advantage of Cal's momentary change of focus to slip behind him, dragging him up and pinning Cal's arms, then proceeding to nibble on Cal's neck like it was just the appetizer.

Sandy was too dumbstruck to respond to Cal's question.

How long had Sandy and Sarhaan worked together? Years. Yet, in all that time, Sandy couldn't ever recall seeing Sarhaan so lighthearted. So downright playful.

"He and Kai took a break and went down to the

Café du Monde for coffee. If you leave now you might catch them." Sarhaan probably thought he was being subtle.

"Okay, I can take a hint." Sandy set down the box of provisions he'd been carrying and headed for the door.

"Take your time, buddy." Sarhaan's advice was underscored by Cal's throaty laugh as Sandy closed the door behind him.

When he got to the café, Sandy wasn't sure exactly what he'd been expecting, but whatever it was, it wasn't Alex and Kai with their heads bent attentively over a shared mini-comp.

Kai pointed at something on the screen, looking to Alex for his reaction, "But I think if we keep the overhead down by not carrying a lot of human cargo—"

"—and if you can seal that deal with the Martian mining guild—"

"Right. Then we'll be making money both ways."

"Exactly. So— Oh, Sandy. Hi." It seemed to be Sandy's morning for shock and transformations, because the change in Alex was nothing short of astonishing. The alert, energetic Alex was gone and in his place was awkward, almost diffident, Alex.

"Hi, baby." God, what if after all they'd been through, what if he was bad for Alex? Wouldn't that just be a kick in the head? "Kai. So what's the business plan y'all sound like you're hatching out here?"

Kai leaned back in his chair, glancing from Alex up to Sandy's face. "I was going to give you crap about it, but now I don't think you knew, either."

Sandy trusted Kai. He trusted Alex. So why did he suddenly have a knot in his gut that said he was a chump?

"Knew what?"

"That young Alex, here, has a major brain for business."

"I don't, really, Sandy. He's exaggerating." What was with the nervousness and why did Alex suddenly look like he was afraid of being hit?

"Don't sell yourself short, Alex. You get this stuff the way most people only do when they've either studied it intensely or been involved in it for years." Kai was back upright in his chair, tapping the mini-comp and gesturing at Alex. "You're good at this."

"Not really. It's no big deal." Alex downplayed it.

Kai was determined. "It is a big deal, Alex."

Sandy pulled up a chair, looking from Alex to Kai and back again, a smile gradually breaking over his face. Hallelujah. "Yeah? My fella's got a body born for sin and a head made for business?"

Looking up from behind the fall of hair that had slid over his brow, Alex still looked doubtful. "You don't mind?"

"Mind? Are you kidding?" Reaching out one hand, Sandy stroked a finger down Alex's arm. "Guys who know their way around a business plan get me hot."

"Do you two need to take this private?" Kai twisted in his chair, pointedly looking away, down the street.

"I don't know how good I am at it, but I like it." Alex glanced over at Kai, who now had his back turned to the table. "Would you mind if I learned more about it? Maybe got involved in the business?"

Sandy almost leaned in close to whisper in Alex's ear, but thought better of it, deciding Xuwicha could stand a little payback. "That depends: can you drive a hard bargain?" He smiled at Alex, letting the heat show in his eyes. "I mean really hard."

Grinning as Kai stood and left the table, muttering in disgust, Sandy finally gave in and stole a kiss from a flustered Alex. "Sandy!" He wished he was a better person, but Sandy adored the scandalized tone Alex got at his public displays of affection. "People are watching!"

Later, in their quarters on board the *Vigilant*, Sandy finally got to show Alex how he really felt. Both of them naked, his legs hooked over Alex's shoulders and his beautiful Alex fucking him hard, Sandy was a happy man.

***

Alex was absolutely crazy about Chinese food.

They'd found a place in the business district that served up old style traditional Szechwan cooking, just like Xuwicha's grandmother might have made. Except that Kai's grandmother had been a member of the Te-Wu and hadn't been able to cook to save her life. Literally.

Still, Alex was mad for the place and insisted on dragging Sandy, and anyone else he could talk into it, into eating there at least once a week. And now that the crew was getting ready to leave on their first long distance haul, leaving Alex and Kai behind to mind the store, Alex wanted a last meal with everyone present.

It would be Alex and Sandy's first separation since getting together and Sandy wasn't sure who was the more apprehensive.

For now, though, Alex was downing lemon chicken and the restaurant's spiciest pork dish, all the while swapping stories with the crew and nearly putting Sandy's eye out as he gestured wildly, *kuàizi* still in hand.

"Okay, so here's this Governor General, in a dress and full Kabuki make-up," Alex was laughing so hard at his own story, he had to stop for a moment to catch his breath. "Saying, 'I can explain the Raggedy Andy doll and the shaving cream, but I have no idea how the sheep got in here.'"

Sandy could watch Alex all night, letting his gaze roam over the high cheekbones; the nose that looked either elegant or commonplace, depending on the angle; lips, pink and full and utterly perfect; and the eyes.

Always he came back to those eyes.

When Alex was laughing, like now, all you could see was the humor, the animation, the vibrant life in them. When he was quiet, though -- when Alex thought no one was watching -- the pain and desolation Sandy saw in them took his breath away and left an aching pain in his chest.

It was Sarhaan's turn to entertain the group now and Alex leaned back into Sandy's side, taking full advantage of the booth's seating arrangement to press as much of his body as he could against Sandy. "Hey, you. You're awfully quiet. Was I too loud? Did I embarrass you?"

"No, you weren't too loud. And you could never embarrass me -- I love you and I'm always proud of you."

The laughter drained out of Alex's eyes and he stared at Sandy, a questioning look in his eyes; hand holding the water glass he'd been about to drink from suspended in mid-air.

"I'm in love with you, Alex." Wanting there to be no misunderstanding, Sandy'd decided to say the words. He'd known for a long time, but he wanted to give Alex the certainty, since it was about the only thing he had to offer. Life out here on the frontier was uncertain. Anything could happen and Sandy wanted Alex to know, with absolute assurance, what was in his heart.

"How…?" Alex wouldn't finish his sentence.

For the rest of the meal, and all the way back to the ship, he barely spoke a dozen words, just hung onto Sandy like a drowning man, looking deep in thought.

Back in their quarters on the *Vigilant*, it was late. Sandy pulled off his shirt and began emptying his pockets onto the bedside table.

"Sandy?"

"Yeah, what?"

From a couple meters away, Alex studied Sandy intently. He took a step closer. "Did you mean what you said, before? That you…"

"Love you? Absolutely."

"I…" Taking another step closer, Alex raised a hand and Sandy instinctively opened his arms for Alex to walk into. When Alex's hands came to rest on Sandy's bare chest, Sandy looped his arms behind Alex's back, holding his lover steady. "I don't understand how that could possibly be. But you've never lied to me."

"Believe it, because it's true."

"I want to believe it. I want to so much." So close now he was whispering against Sandy's lips, Alex slipped his arms behind Sandy's neck and they kissed. Once, twice, their mouths met and blended as Sandy tried to put everything he was feeling into his kiss for Alex to recognize.

He couldn't stay away for long, but Sandy took short breaks as he tried to simultaneously catch his breath and remove Alex's clothes. Then they were down on the bed, kissing like nothing could ever come between them, touching like they only had moments and hours to memorize the feel of each others' skin, instead of days and weeks and years.

Rolling on top of Sandy, Alex was bolder than he'd ever been, pushing back on Sandy's shoulders to indicate Sandy should stay put; kissing his way down Sandy's chest to his stomach, taking Sandy's dick in his mouth. With Alex crouched over him, sucking and licking, a groan fought its way out. Sandy tried to watch Alex's face to make sure Alex was into it and not just taking care of him, but it was too good, too intense.

His feelings for Alex were big and complicated, entwined with thoughts of the past and dreams of the future.

"Sandy, can we fuck? I'd really like to fuck you."

Looking up at his face from where Alex sat between his legs, Alex's puffy lips and messy hair made him even more irresistible than usual. It was the look in Alex's eyes, though, that made Sandy's breath catch in his throat. "I thought you'd never ask."

Alex knew by now where Sandy kept the lube and had them both slicked up before Sandy had time to urge Alex to hurry up. Slipping a finger inside Sandy, Alex stroked knowingly across Sandy's sweet spot, Sandy sighing and reveling in the feeling of Alex doing this because he wanted it, too.

By the time Alex replaced his finger with his cock, Sandy was groaning and muttering, urging an oblivious Alex on, as Alex lost himself in sensation. They were both moaning and grunting by the time Alex found his rhythm, holding onto Sandy's thighs as he stroked mindlessly in and out.

With anyone else, Sandy might have been bothered by the fact that Alex seemed preoccupied with his own pleasure. Ordinarily Sandy liked to be at least a factor in the pleasure equation, but there was no doubt Alex was out for himself this time. The pleasure Sandy got from seeing Alex this way almost trumped the pleasure he got from just how bloody good it all felt.

Almost.

Then Alex found a new angle, one that had him nailing Sandy's prostate with every inward stroke of his dick and Sandy stopped thinking about anything else. He just rode it, letting the waves of pleasure build up in him until they crested and broke.

Epilogue

Eight weeks later.

Alex leaped off the tram, not waiting for it to come to a full and complete stop. It was an automated train, so there was no human attendant to give him grief -- not that it would have made a bit of difference to him if there had been.

The *Vigilant* was home and Sandy was back!

Ever since she'd hailed the traffic control warden that she was approaching Doradus station, Alex had been watching the clock and counting the minutes. Longer than that, even. Since the day she'd left him standing on the deck of the docking station, biting his lip, determined not to disgrace himself by crying, Alex had been waiting for this moment.

He and Sandy had been in almost daily contact by video link, but that wasn't nearly enough. Alex missed Sandy. Missed Sandy so much he'd even stopped touching himself, because nothing seemed to make any difference.

Skidding to a stop in front of the bank of screens detailing which ship was docked at which berth, Alex breathlessly scanned them until he found the *Vigilant*, then ran the rest of the way to the south dock's waiting room.

"I told you they wouldn't be through the

airlocks yet." Kai ambled into the room a few moments later, his usual air of preternatural calm only slightly disturbed.

"Oh, shut up." Alex's mind was racing, too preoccupied with thoughts of Sandy to come up with anything more original.

Hands in his pockets, Kai was a hundred times more relaxed than Alex was, but Alex didn't care. The lights above the airlock door signaled that personnel were moving through the system, with only two more doors left to clear. That meant one more door cleared and Alex would be able to see who it was through the narrow window.

"After all that, that's what you decided to wear?" When Alex turned his head, Kai was looking him up and down, a perplexed look on his lean face.

"What's wrong with this? I look good in this."

"No, you look fine. You look great. I just thought…"

Frantically scanning his clothes, Alex looked for anything wrong. No stains. Nothing torn. His fly was zipped. Did they make his butt look fat? "What?"

Kai's snicker was his first clue. Alex looked up to find the other man openly laughing at him, his shoulders shaking with mirth.

"You dick." Alex knew slugging Kai in the arm would only hurt his own hand, but he did it anyway. After eight weeks of working with each other constantly, Kai now treated him like a pest of a younger brother, needling him relentlessly. It was a measure of Alex's distraction that he hadn't caught on sooner.

"I know it's wrong, but I'm weak."

"Oh, go fuck yourself."

"Wouldn't life be a lot simpler if we could all just master that particular skill?"

Alex wasn't paying attention to Kai's smirk any more because the second set of doors was sliding open and Sandy was the first one through. Alex's breath caught at his first glimpse of his lover. Sandy was wearing some kind of high-necked jacket, buttoned all the way from his chin to his waist. Below it was something colorful that Alex couldn't quite make out, then Sandy was standing close to the window, pressing one huge hand against it while he smiled and mouthed something to Alex.

I love you, Alex.

Pressing his own hand against the glass, Alex took a quick swipe at his eyes with the other, a whispered "I love you, too" coming unbidden to his lips.

"Thank Christ no one here's diabetic. It's getting pretty thick."

Alex turned briefly to flip Kai off before returning his gaze to the window, staying that way until the door slid back and Sandy was sweeping him up into a powerful embrace. Alex's arms were around Sandy's neck in a death grip and they were kissing, Sandy squeezing a handful of his ass in one big hand.

"I missed you."

"I missed you, too."

"God, you feel good."

"You look great."

Breaking away long enough to steer Alex back to the tram, Sandy tugged self-consciously at the collar of his jacket. "I wanted to get cleaned up for you. It's called a lava lava. It's Samoan. Very traditional."

Looking away from Sandy's face, Alex followed the sweeping arc of Sandy's gesture. The bottom half of Sandy's outfit was a long wrap-around skirt of some kind; colorful, it followed the contours of Sandy's powerful body. The boots he wore on his enormous feet should have looked incongruous, but they only completed the picture as far as Alex was concerned.

"Come sit with me."

Following Sandy onto the last seat of the last section of the tram, Alex couldn't resist running his hand along one muscular thigh, slipping his fingers underneath the fold of the skirt. Encountering bare skin beneath, Alex jerked his hand away, shocked.

It wasn't until Sandy turned to sit that Alex spotted his smile. Drawing Alex astride his lap, Sandy moved Alex's hand back to the skirt's side-opening.

"It's a long ride into town." The tram kicked into gear and Alex began to explore beneath the loose folds of the lava lava, encountering only centimeter after centimeter of warm, smooth skin. "Not all of the old ways are bad."

The heat that had been present, building inside Alex since the *Vigilant* had docked, since he'd laid eyes on Sandy, touched and smelled and tasted him, threatened to send Alex up in flames.

"Welcome home, Sandy." Smiling, Alex's hand moved unerringly to Sandy's dick, grasping its familiar weight, giving it a preliminary tug.

"It's good to be back." A hitch in his breathing, Sandy smiled back. "What've you got planned for tonight?"

"I've got a few ideas."

Taking a firm hold of Alex's ass with both hands, Sandy leaned in for a kiss. "Yeah? So let's hear 'em."

Stephanie Vaughan

Printed in the United States
123672LV00001B/19/A

9 781603 701150